Nelson's Daughter

Also by Miranda Hearn

A Life Everlasting

Miranda Hearn

Nelson's Daughter

SCEPTRE

Copyright © 2005 by Miranda Hearn

First published in Great Britain in 2005 by Hodder and Stoughton
A division of Hodder Headline

The right of Miranda Hearn to be identified as the Author
of the Work has been asserted by her in accordance with the
Copyright, Designs and Patents Act 1988

A Sceptre Book

1 3 5 7 9 10 8 6 4 2

A CIP catalogue record for this title is available from the British Library

ISBN 0 340 82756 4

Typeset in Sabon by
Hewer Text Ltd, Edinburgh
Printed and bound by
Clays Ltd, St Ives plc

Hodder Headline's policy is to use papers that are natural, renewable
and recyclable products and made from wood grown in sustainable forests.
The logging and manufacturing processes are expected to conform to the
environmental regulations of the country of origin

Hodder and Stoughton Ltd
A division of Hodder Headline
338 Euston Road
London NW1 3BH

For my brothers

On the quay, a sailor steps back and catches her elbow with his arm. *'Pardon, M'sieur,'* he says. She looks down at her shoes. Black leather, with flat heels and silver buckles. She looks up again and smiles, but the sailor has gone. It's early, and the sky is wide and pale, and the sun looks like the moon. There are clouds like clouds of ash, fat with the cold and almost white. Gulls hang balanced on the morning air.

The consul puts an arm on her shoulder. 'All right?' he says. She can hear a loose plank on the gangway as the people in front of them board the Dover packet: *thunk* and then *thunk*. The wharf is crowded with passengers, with porters and children, carriages and dogs. Packages, bags, a side of beef. It is January 1815. In front of her are the harbour and the old fort; behind her the town and months of exile, the smell of small cold rooms and wine.

'Up we go.' The consul takes her arm, and leads her towards the boat. She can hear the slip of the sea against its wooden sides. Wish-wash, slip-slap. She knows that she is going, but still it seems improbable, as do the things we wish for most. The woman who brought her to this place is dead, buried in the graveyard of the Church of St Pierre; she lived all her life in hatred of the French, and now she lies among them, with a wooden sign to mark her grave. Fifty men followed her coffin, but there are few who mourn her death. She is gone, and it is over. The girl wipes a sleeve across her face; there is salt on her lips, but not from tears. As far as she can tell, no one has come running after her; no one is scouring the quay for a sight of her. Nevertheless, they have been cautious, and keep

1

themselves hidden in the crowds. The harbour is small, but to her it seems a vast place, as if someone has thrown Worthing and the Port of London together, and made its people speak French.

Then something strange happens, though not unexpected. That's the point: they had expected something like it. Francine Caillois appears only yards from them, a frown, as usual, on her face. She looks like someone with a message, someone who knows there is no time to lose, who will stop the boat with her own hands if she has to. She has walked two miles to be here, unless someone gave her a lift. The girl almost says her name. It feels like madness to be avoiding, at such great lengths, someone like Madame Caillois. Has she been here every day, searching the crowds, not choosing to believe what she's been told? Their eyes meet, but Francine doesn't recognise her. She moves on, pulling her shawl over her chin.

The girl turns, and kisses the cheek of the consul's wife. The older woman smiles. 'Handsome,' she says, straightening the hat on the girl's head.

She pulls a face.

'Really. It suits you.'

The coat she wears is sapphire blue. It is too big for her, but it's warm and hides what shape she has. Underneath it she has on a waistcoat of striped silk and buff-coloured nankeen trousers that end above her ankles. A starched shirt frill runs down her chest, and her chin rests on a high white neckcloth. She is too tired even to feel ridiculous. 'Thank you,' she says.

'It's true!'

'For everything, I mean.'

There are shouts behind them, and the farewell is brief. The consul kisses his wife. 'Go home before you freeze,' he tells her. 'Expect me back when you see me.'

As the boat navigates the narrow entrance of the harbour,

the consul goes below to the passenger cabin. The girl stands for a while on deck with the wind in her face, a small, isolated figure in a blue overcoat. The larger sails are being set, catching the breeze as they rise against the sky. Then, because it's cold, she goes below.

Part One

ONE

Downstairs, a door banged. Someone coming in, or going out. Then the silence again of an old house on an empty plain. The shutters were closed and the room was dim. Beyond the window she heard the cry of a collared dove, the distant knock of a log being split. 'Wake up,' she said.

The farmhouse was two miles from Calais, in the Commune de St Pierre. The rooms were large, and its roof was steeply pitched. All day long they could hear the cackling of geese from a neighbouring farm, and at night they heard wolves. She opened a window and then the shutter, which slammed against the outside wall. The day beyond the room was like another region, filled with a wide, flat light. A crow flew slowly from one side of the sky towards the other, as if it would take for ever. She turned back to the room. The shape on the bed had not moved. She took two steps and prodded it with her finger. 'Wake up,' she said again. Nothing.

She stood motionless, her eyes on the chair, the untouched tray, a mirror. A pair of shoes lay on the floor, as if they had come together to pray.

The mountain of bedclothes spoke: 'Horatia, go away.'

'Are you going to get up?'

'Go away.'

The boards creaked under her feet. At the door she paused and turned. 'It's nearly ten,' she said.

'Out!'

7

Horatia pulled the door closed behind her, and the latch clicked. She made her way down the stairs, trailing a hand against the wall. It was September 1814; she was thirteen years old, and the future was nothing but the next thing, then the next one. This step, then the next.

When she entered the kitchen, Fatima turned to look at her with eyebrows raised. Horatia shrugged and made a face. 'Never mind,' said Fatima. 'I'll go up in a minute.'

'She never opens a window. It smells up there.'

Fatima was Lady Hamilton's Egyptian maid. She was a tall woman, with a long straight back and large black eyes. She had been brought from Alexandria by Nelson after the battle of the Nile, as a gift to Emma.

'She told me to wake her up.'

'In French, *chère*. Berthe is here.'

'Sorry, Berthe.'

The French girl grinned. 'I made some coffee,' she said.

The kitchen door was open, and Horatia could see the baked dust of the yard. Beside a small barn, an old harrow lay grown over with nettles and red stalks of dock. Brambles climbed up one side of the well, and on the roof of the barn a weathercock had rusted facing east.

Berthe turned back to the stove, and poured hot milk into a bowl of coffee. Fatima was already sitting. 'Come here,' she said. 'Here, so I can see you.' She lifted a hand, and held the girl's chin. 'Peaky. You and me, we can go for a walk later on. Put some colour in them cheeks.'

'Put some in yours.'

'Ha.'

Horatia pulled out a chair and sat. Without Fatima, she thought, their lives might fly off in pieces. Rise and scatter, and end somewhere in a pond or in the sea.

'Berthe got little chops for dinner,' said Fatima. 'I can show her how to make Irish stew.' Berthe cleaned the house and cooked their meals. She was seventeen, with a wide round chin and ruby lips; her eyes were green, and she had lost a front tooth. Her father was a mason in the village.

'*Irish* stew? You don't know how to.'

'How much you bet me I don't? I know how to make it. We made that on the boat at Dresden.'

Horatia squinted at her.

'Yes, we did. It was the river Elbe, and milady would eat nothing else. It were a gondola with a canopy, and Mrs Cadogan peeled the potatoes in the back before we was even sailing. I remember it like yesterday. Lord Nelson was told he must go home and cannot have his ship, so we have to go over land, and up one river, which were the Elbe. Some of the provisions had not arrived, and I yelled many French words from one boat to another, what many people had never heard before.'

'Elba's not a river,' said Berthe. 'Whatever it is, it's not a river.'

Fatima rolled her eyes. 'The river Elbe,' she said. 'In Germany.'

Berthe shook her head. She was still at the stove, scrubbing off a burn. The Emperor Bonaparte had been exiled to Elba in April, and it wasn't in Germany and it wasn't a river.

'Sir William have to come home, too, after many years. That were a shame for him, but he was quite old.' Fatima paused again, looking at the wedge of light in the doorway. Sir William Hamilton, ambassador to the Court of Naples, had died ten years ago, more. His face, in her mind, was long and intelligent, the face of a pale and sober ghost. 'Lord Nelson was not well,' she said. 'He were fagged after battles and war, but he was given many cheers and celebrations.'

Horatia sat without moving. She had not touched her coffee, or the bread that Berthe had placed beside her bowl. Trieste, Laibach, Klagenfurt, Graz. She saw her father, decked out in medals and ribbons, the glint of crystal as he was

9

toasted at all the courts of Germany and at every port and town. Toast after toast and bumper after bumper, drunk to the hero of the Nile. She saw the night sky thrown up in glittering bursts, and heard the martial sound of bands. Vienna, Prague, Dresden. Champagne, dinners, concert parties.

'Eat,' said Fatima.

'Was I there?'

'In Germany? No, *chère*. You were still on the way.' She lifted a hand and scratched the side of her nose. She was thinking. 'Actually, you was already born, but not there. You were in London.' For a moment she was still, halted by the image of her mistress throwing up on board the *Foudroyant* on the crossing to Leghorn, the one and only time she had been sick at sea. Then, in Germany, wanting only Irish stew. And, also in Germany, indigestion. 'When we come to Hamburg, milord hoped there may be a frigate waiting to take us home. There was no boat, though, not for us. He wrote to the Admiralty, but nothing happen there, and in the end we have to take the Yarmouth packet.'

Berthe placed a bloodied package on the other end of the table. 'Meat and what else?' she said.

'Irish stew, what do you think?'

Horatia stirred her coffee and drank. Dresden, Magdeburg, Hamburg. Great Yarmouth under a steady rain. As Nelson stepped off the boat, the men of the town came running down to the quay, their shoulders damp and their boots loud on the cobbles. They took the horses from their traces and dragged the carriage themselves. All the boats in the harbour were flying colours, and a band played in the square; church bells rang out in victory peals. They moved up into the town through waiting crowds, her godmother, Lady Hamilton, in a muslin gown embroidered with his name. She stood with him on the balcony of the inn and waved at the cheering throng. All this Horatia saw and remembered, and it had happened, but not to her. She remembered these and a thousand other things she had not seen, as if she had slipped back, a ghost of her living self, to be there and belong.

'Potatoes,' said Fatima.

2

The garden was longer than it was wide; it contained a few fruit trees and a low vine between two clay walls. Ladders had been left propped against the trees, and there was a scruffy outhouse with a door swollen shut. The odd gardening tool, left in the long grass, had turned a rusty brown. At the far end, beyond a small gate, there was a deep but narrow stream. There was a dog, too: Janot. An old hunting dog, left behind at the end of his useful life for anyone to look after. He lay under a pear tree, and looked up out of brown eyes at whoever went in or out of the house. His coat was brown and white, as if the colour had been thrown at him.

Horatia wandered to the far end to watch the deep green running water of the stream, then turned back and walked along the wall to the side of the house and into the yard. At the gate she stood and looked out over the road. They had been in France for nearly three months, first at Dessein's hotel in Calais and now here. It was a place where they did not belong, and where there was nothing to do. She was waiting, but she had no idea for what, or how long it might take. For a letter, a man on a horse, a miracle. Waiting for the world to turn and put everything back in its proper place, for events to run against themselves to where it had all gone wrong. Waiting for something or someone to explain how the woman famous everywhere for her beauty and her heart had become the heap on the bed upstairs, and how long they would stay here, and where, after this, they would go.

Janot wandered over and stood next to her in the gateway. She rested her hand on his smooth head, and together they watched the empty road, a brown and dusty line that

11

disappeared in both directions, left and right. There was an urge in her legs to walk and never stop, to cover mile after mile and not turn round, while a separate instinct held her firmly to the spot on which she stood. Sometimes she wondered why they didn't all die, overwhelmed by some fantastic accident. Herself, Emma, Fatima. Why fate, out of plain scorn, didn't cut them off like a complicated knot. Come here, stand still, snip. By day, brief and unexpected landscapes came into her head as she sat on her own, or went from one room to another. She saw places she had never visited, and others that had been her homes, and they came with such equal force that she could not always tell one from the other. She saw faces, and could not say whether they belonged to people she had known or only heard about. George and Horace, Mr Perry. The Queen of Naples, scribbling her prayers on pieces of paper and eating them. Cribb and Mary Gibson, Frank. They all flew up, like birds at the sound of a gun, and vanished again in the air.

At night she would lie in bed and listen to the darkness. She imagined that she could see the countryside around her covered with the tents of soldiers – recruits camped on the common or in the fields, their faces raw and their backsides damp. She saw them, dark and still, and heard the low *thup* of canvas in the breeze. Peace with France was only five months old, and she was dimly sure that the ghosts of war still wandered from here to the coast. She imagined the sound, in the deepest part of the night, of tethered horses, standing awake, and the hard hollow champ of their teeth. And she did not know, when she woke in her bed, where she was or who she had been up to now. She tried to remember which side of her the window was and where she might soon see a narrow plank of dawn between the shutters. She listened for the first birds, and the cockerels, then heard the clock of St Pierre strike one, or two. A thin sound in the dark, and strangely flat. She tested the present against her memory of other places, turning them over one by one. Merton, Richmond, Piccadilly. Bond

Street, Temple Place. All the houses she and Emma had lived in between her father's death and now; the different beds and ceilings. It seemed to her that she had been wandering, and sometimes fugitive, for more than half her life. One place then another, another and then here. When she dreamed of going home, she did not know, any more, what she meant.

Berthe had come out to pick herbs. Stalks of rosemary, garlic bulbs and mint. It was going to be a French Irish stew.

When she went in again, Emma was sitting at the table in the dining room, drinking coffee. She was wearing an old morning dress with a short bodice and a low neck. She was forty-nine, and grey. Horatia could smell the coffee, and something sweeter, like age or sleep. 'You're up,' she said.

'Let me finish this,' said Emma, 'and we'll have a lesson.'

In Calais, Horatia had gone every day to a school run by an Englishwoman, in a tall narrow house that seemed to have its shoulders tucked into its neck. She went at eight and came home at one. There was nowhere suitable for her in St Pierre, however, so Emma had been teaching her in the mornings: ancient history, German, French and Spanish. At least in the mornings she was usually capable of talking sense.

'You're in a dream today. What are you thinking about?'

In the kitchen, Berthe was slicing potatoes. They could hear the knife on the chopping board.

'Nothing,' said Horatia. 'About when you came back from Italy.'

'Good Lord, what put that into your head?'

'Fatima was telling us.'

'I just remembered something else,' said Fatima, from the kitchen. 'That storm, when we came to London.'

A weary life swam in Emma's eyes. 'A storm?' she said. She frowned, as if the past had a hard bright surface. 'I remember. It poured.'

'It was a tempest.' Fatima was moving around as she spoke,

her slippers flapping on the kitchen floor. 'There was thunderclouds and rain, and the wind had torn up trees in the parks, and the streets were wet and windy and dark.'

'You're right,' said Emma. 'It was bucketing down, but they still came out to look at us and cheer. People, crowds.'

Horatia watched her as she talked. Eyes, mouth, hair. She saw her in a fur collar and a headdress with feathers and plumes, standing in the porch of a London hotel. Her oval face, her cherry lips and Grecian nose; her light blue, almost violet eyes. The rain and the cheers and the leaves and the people. It had gone, now, all that and everything. Emma was old, and her face was ordinary. Sometimes she did not get out of bed for days on end. She drank cheap wine, and forgot hour by hour what was said and what was done; she could remember only distant things, and briefly, and in the early part of the day. She could, and then she couldn't. It was as if someone had come and split her mind in two, made one half dark and the other bright.

Now Fatima came and stood in the doorway between the two rooms. 'I thought that this was what London may be like all the time,' she said, 'pissing down with rain like a cow. Thank God it was not.'

'The King was an absolute pig,' said Emma.

'Why?' Horatia pulled out a chair and sat.

'To your father. He and Sir William went to a levee at St James's Palace. The King asked him if his health was any better, then turned his back on him and talked to some old general for half an hour. Unbelievable. This is Vice Admiral Lord Nelson, hero of the Nile, you doddering old man – are you mad?'

Horatia grinned.

'He was mad,' said Fatima.

'As a matter of fact, he was. All the same.'

Fatima winked at Horatia. It was also true, though never said, that Nelson had turned up at St James's looking like the night sky, wearing not only all his usual medals but also a full blaze of foreign orders, with a spray of Turkish diamonds in his hat.

'They appeared from nowhere,' cried Emma, 'crowds and crowds of people, cheering and waving and trying to touch his coat. You've no idea. The papers all praised his courage and reported his every move. Mine, too!' She frowned, remembering something else, something much less agreeable, then smiled, forgetting it again. 'The City of London gave him a sword with a crocodile on it and said that the shores which had beheld the destruction of the Persians by the Greeks now resounded with the echo of British thunder. The women all wanted to kiss his hand, and they did! In the streets, anywhere. Baron Nelson of the Nile! You should have seen him at Covent Garden: he had to take bow after bow before the curtain could go up. The cast sang "Rule, Britannia", and he had to stand up again between acts while the audience cheered. We met the Prime Minister and the Prince of Wales, and the Prince said he'd heard all about me and wanted to hear me sing. He was madly in love with me! Really, he was.'

'Where was I?' said Horatia.

Emma scratched the palm of her hand. 'With Mrs Gibson. You were tiny. Fatima, will you get me a glass of wine, please?'

'Yes, milady.' She took the empty coffee cup, and avoided Horatia's eyes as she left the room.

'Do you remember Mrs Gibson?'

Horatia nodded. 'And Mary, and Little Titchfield Street.' She made herself completely still, and fixed her eyes on the surface of the table as Fatima returned and placed a glass of dark red wine in front of Emma. The smell of it made the sides of her throat ache. 'I remember coming to Piccadilly,' she said, 'to see you.'

'No, you can't. Not possibly.'

'I do.'

'Horatia, now you're talking nonsense. You were a baby.'

15

Emma lifted the glass to her lips. 'Your head's full of stories. What you remember and what you think you remember are two different things.'

Fatima went upstairs to do Emma's room. A single board creaked above their heads as she made the bed.

3

Horatia's mind drifted over corners of her childhood, all of them low and close to the ground. A shelf in the pantry at Little Titchfield Street, a cupboard in the kitchen full of pans and bread tins, jelly moulds and sieves. A rolling-pin, a cheese-grater. It was a mystery to her, now, how so much could have come out of one small place.

'Listen, darling. Listen.' One drink, and she was sliding.

'What?'

There was a twitch under Emma's eye, as if a small moth had landed on her cheek. 'I don't know, it's gone. I wish you'd listen.'

Horatia lifted her eyes. The effort of vigilance, every day, was as exhausting as it was useless. Each time Emma drank from her glass, she felt a small shrill whisper run beneath her skin: *Don't, please don't.*

'Tacitus!' shouted Emma. 'That's what I was saying. I'll start, and you can go on. Berthe! We're reading Tacitus. The history of Greece!'

'Rome,' said Horatia.

'Darling, I know that. Rome. Just wait a minute. Berthe!'

Berthe brought more wine, and left the room again. 'Now,' said Emma, reading, 'Titus Vinius. "I am entering on the history of a period rich in disasters, frightful in its wars, torn by civil strife, and even in peaceful . . . even in *peace* full of horrors." This is awful.'

'Give it to me,' said Horatia gently. 'I'll read.'

'Yes, you read. I'll listen. Skip forward a bit if you like.'

Horatia turned a few pages and puffed out her cheeks. ' "Syria and its four legions were under the command of Licinius Mucianus, a man whose good and bad fortune were equally famous . . ." ' These lessons were the only sane hours of the day. This bit of knowledge, and then this bit; wars and lies and conjugations. On a good day, they would do an hour of history, an hour of French or Spanish. On a good day, Emma did not start drinking until noon. ' ". . . His resources soon failed, and his position became precarious, and he withdrew into a retired part of Asia, and was as like an exile—" '

'Do you know what, darling? I'm sorry to interrupt, but I've just had a thought. I'm going to write to Fulke Greville again.'

Horatia sighed, and put the book down. Fulke Greville was the brother of Sir William's nephew, Charles. As far as she knew, she had never met either of them. They were seldom spoken of, except to do with money. Charles Greville had inherited Sir William's estate, but he, too, was dead now, and his brother had taken over the administration of the funds. It was Fulke Greville who, at least until recently, had been sending Emma the quarterly payments from her annuity. But there was no point in writing to him: the last letter from Greville had said clearly that the whole of Emma's allowance had now been pledged to creditors, and that she could hope to see no more of it until the mess she had left behind was sorted out.

'We'll do it now. I'll tell him how well we're getting on, and how cheap everything is.'

Everything was cheap. Turkeys were two shillings each, milk was two pence, and meat five pence a pound. Chickens thirteen pence, and a pair of ducks the same. A turbot, fresh from the sea, was half a crown, and good wine was fifteen pence, though they could get a bottle of *vin ordinaire* for six. It still had to be paid for, though, even if it was cheap.

'He can send us a hundred pounds. He's got the money, he can afford it.' She leaned close over the page in front of her and scowled at it, as if something small but intriguing were creeping over it.

' "He was a compound of dissipation and energy, of arrogance and courtesy, of good and bad qualities—" '

'Horatia, stop it. I'm just writing one letter. I'm telling him how well you're getting on. Listen: "She speaks French like a French girl, Italian, German, English, etc." '

Horatia stood and walked to the window. The day was over now. Outside, the sun was moving up in the sky, but in this room the day had ended.

'Did you hear what I said?'

She folded her arms. 'He'll be pleased to hear that I can speak English.' It came out before she could stop it.

Emma looked up from the page. 'What?'

'Nothing.'

'Don't be sarcastic.' Emma laid down her pen.

'I didn't say anything.'

'If you want to talk like that, you can go upstairs. Or outside.'

Horatia watched the anger grow in her face. It was like watching advancing rain, or the development of a bruise. This was all it took – a few words, and cheap wine. It was always there, waiting.

'God almighty!' said Emma.

'You wrote to him yesterday. What's the point?'

Emma spread her arms, and the page on which she had been writing floated to the floor. 'I spend the whole morning teaching you so that you'll grow up with something to show for yourself, and all you do is moan. One of these days you're going to wish you'd learned something, you're going to be sorry that I'm dead and that you never listened while you had the chance. You're going to open your mouth and find that nothing comes out of it because there's nothing in your head.'

'I'm sorry.'

'No, you're not.'

Horatia waited. Something bitter in her mouth, behind her teeth, was the taste of her own growing rage. As Emma changed moment by moment into an ugly stranger, it crept up her ribs with a sour muttering. She bit her tongue and kept herself still.

Emma shook a finger, as if prodding the air to find the point where it would break. 'I don't know what to do with you,' she said. 'If I can make the effort, so can you. It's not that difficult to sit down for an hour and read a book. You don't have to be rude every time I try to do something to make our lives a bit better. You're my responsibility, Horatia. I promised your father I would bring you up to be the sort of girl he could be proud of. He made me your guardian because he knew that you would get a proper education. Do I complain? Am I rude? No. I take my commitments very seriously, and I don't expect sarcasm in return. It beggars belief, it really does.' Her hand, motionless in the air in front of her face while she spoke, came down on the table.

Horatia felt something inside her fold. Shut up, shut up, she thought. I wish I was a hundred miles from here. As if she had uttered these thoughts aloud, Emma suddenly picked up the nearest object and flung it out into the room. Inkwell: spatters, splash marks, permanent stains.

Horatia turned and strode towards the door.

'Where are you going?'

'Outside.'

'Good. Stay there.'

TWO

For months, letters had been going backwards and forwards between Emma and Nelson who, for fear of the Navy censors, had pretended to be a couple called Thompson. The man was a seaman in Nelson's command, and the woman was one of Emma's servants. There was a baby on the way. Because of an uncle who stood between them, they were not yet married, though for the sake of appearance, they used the same name. Because of the war and the threat of invasion, the father had no way of knowing how long he would be at sea. The mother was frail, and would not be able to look after the child when it came. Neither could write, and the letters were composed and sent on their behalf. Nelson and Lady Hamilton would be the child's godparents, and shoulder the responsibility for its care. As a pretence, it was ridiculous. Nelson kept forgetting who he was, and how to spell his *nom de plume*. Poor man, he wrote, he's dying for some news. He wishes there was peace, and he could come and marry you. He can't bear being here while you are there. I wish our fates had been different. Sometimes I worry that you won't be as true to me as I am to you. My love, my darling angel.

He was in the Channel. It was January 1801. Newly promoted to vice admiral, he had been made second-in-command of the Channel Fleet and ordered to join his flagship, the *San Josef*, in Plymouth. He had captured the vessel, a Spanish first rate of a hundred guns, off the coast of Portugal in the battle of St Vincent four years before. He had boarded it from the *San Nicolas*, already boarded and taken, using one as a stepping-stone to the other. He had hauled out of line against orders to do so, and it was the moment at which he had become, for the first time, a hero. Though not exactly. He had become a hero when his own accounts of the battle had reached London and were published in *The Times* and the *Sun*.

Now, off Portsmouth, he was suffering from anxiety that was sometimes so bad it gave him cold sweats and pains in his heart. His wife had sent everything wrong, and he had to break into his chests because only one key could be found. There were no plates and only half his clothes, and nails had been driven through a mahogany table. He wrote to her in a rage from the *San Josef*, telling her that he would do it himself in future, in ten minutes, and for a tenth of the expense. She had gone to Brighton and, though he managed not to say so in his letter, he hoped that she would stay there, out of the way. In his heart, he hoped she would vanish altogether. Where is she? Don't know, disappeared, what a relief. To Emma, he wrote: She's such a fool, thank God you're not one bit like her. You're you, and nothing can alter my love for you, no time, no separation, nothing.

Mostly, though, his letters were wild with jealousy. Nobody knew where it had come from, but there it was. He had got it into his head that the Prince of Wales wanted Emma for his mistress, and was almost hysterical. Don't let him into the house, he wrote. Don't let him touch you. He'll whisper in your ear, he'll play with your foot under the table. I've seen the way he looks at you. He might have been hanged for high treason for some of the things he wrote to her. God blast him to hell, I wish I was dead – I wish *he* was. I can't eat or sleep for thinking of you, and Mr Thompson is just about as miserable as I am. He wishes that your uncle would drop dead, so that he could marry you tomorrow.

Emma and Sir William were living in London, at 23

Piccadilly. The house was small, and from its windows they could see Green Park, with its dark, leafless trees. Sir William had lost a fortune to looting in Naples, and there was not much left now to keep them going. He wasn't about to get another posting, not at his age, and he was having to sell part of his collection of paintings and vases to find the money for the house. Emma had sold the diamonds given to her by Queen Maria Carolina to buy furniture. It was all over the papers that she was enormous, and that she had not been received at court. Fanny Nelson had, but not Lady Hamilton.

'Bitch Fanny Tom Tit,' she said to her mother. She scratched her elbow. Her rashes were coming back. Arms and elbows, the backs of her knees. 'Black vomit shitface Tom Fanny Tit.'

Mary Cadogan was a small woman, with a blunt nose and a narrow mouth. Her chin was small and round, and her eyes were half lost in folds of age and the endurance of a sorely tried constitution. She wore black dresses and white caps, and in Naples had often been taken for the Hamiltons' house-keeper. This had never caused her offence; she was, to all intents and purposes, their housekeeper. In Naples, and now in London. She was level, quiet, competent, and did everything from the supervision of the servants to the ordering of meat and tea. She arranged, she tended, she wrote things down in books and settled the accounts. Just now she was mending a seam in one of Emma's dresses. The fabric, a thick and rustling silk, lay over her knees in careful folds. She opened her mouth to remind her daughter that Fanny was Nelson's lawful wife and Emma was not, but shut it again. Lady Emma Hamilton, she thought suddenly, and she shook her old head, thinking: How did that happen? 'Don't scratch,' she said.

It was because of Charles Greville that they had gone to Italy. When she was sixteen, Emma had been Greville's mis-tress. She was wild then, and reprobate. Greville had taken her in and given her a home, Mrs Cadogan, too, at a time when things had been very bad. They had lived quietly under his roof, but after three years Greville could no longer afford to keep them. He had run out of money, and it was clear that he would have to marry or remain a pauper. So he had given Emma to his uncle in return for becoming his recognised heir. Take her to Italy, he said. Put her in one of your villas. She's well-behaved these days, and much better that you should have her than anyone else. They had gone to Naples, and five years later Emma and Sir William were married. She was twenty-six; he was sixty.

It all seemed a long time ago, thought Mary Cadogan. A long time ago, and another world. In Italy, Emma had been at the centre of everything. She had existed in a place of old gods and beautiful shores, of sunlight and volcanic slopes, of palaces and gambling, singers and long nights. She had been young and very beautiful. The Queen had adored her, and relied on her for companionship and advice, for political gossip and information. Maria Carolina was a woman for ever devoted – after the murder of her sister, Marie Antoinette – to the politics of revenge and hatred of the French. She wanted her own back, and Emma, who also hated the French, had been hungry for an important public role. The letters that went between the two women every day were thick with endearments, to the point where anyone reading them might have thought they were two people in love.

Mrs Cadogan had slipped without awe into this life of intrigue and beauty, managing equally in times of ease and crisis. She had watched with pride – and some amazement – the advances her daughter made. There were singing lessons, French and Italian, dancing; all the social skills of a foreign court. Hours, every day, from morning until night. Emma had learned to entertain, to sit at the head of the table with sixty guests, to throw a ball for four hundred. She was diligent, bright and willing. She had transformed herself. Saved from a precipice, she had shown her gratitude by loving Sir William with all her heart, and by earning the respect and admiration of the Neapolitan court. And Mrs Cadogan had taken pride in the very fact that this was where they were, this was where they had arrived. In the middle of all that glitter, the ballrooms and the brilliance, she had sometimes thought back to the places they had left behind: the black and windy streets of the village in Wales where she grew up, and her own mother, loading her market cart with fruit and carrots and sacks of coal. Her father, standing over a flock of sheep on Saltney Marshes with an ancient shotgun under his arm; her husband, Henry, a smith in the flat Wirral peninsula of Cheshire, leaning into a shower of sparks.

She lifted her eyes from the work on her lap. Henry had died less than two months after Emma was born. Mrs Cadogan could see his clothes – his boots, his breeches and leather apron – but could not bring to mind his face. What would he have said, to see them now? It was all a far cry from the mining villages of Wales and the Wirral, and Emma might well believe, when she reflected on where she came from and how far she had come, that nothing could be denied to her here at home. She had only been back in England for two months; she had not yet taken the measure of the social climate here. She had not yet understood, and perhaps she never would, the finer distinctions of protocol between London and Naples. Mrs Cadogan resumed her sewing. 'At least,' she said, 'they only think you're fat.'

'That's true.'

In fact, Emma was only days away from giving birth. She pulled back a sleeve to scratch her arm. Underneath everything, under the ceremony and adulation, the songs and the cheers, there was a ghastly vein in London of derision. The papers never left her alone. It was not enough to call her *embonpoint*. They printed verses about her, and asked if she was the only curiosity that Sir William had managed to hang on to after nearly forty years of ransacking Herculaneum and

25

Pompeii. There were caricatures, most of them lewd. Anyone who could read a newspaper – and even those who could not – knew that she and Nelson were lovers, though it had to be denied, and it was and it would be. In the eyes of the world, their friendship would always be pure, and damn to hell and back the *Herald* and the *Post*. Still, as her mother had pointed out, at least they only said she was fat, whatever they might imply. If they knew any more than they suspected, there would be an explosion and scandal, and he would leave her and she would die.

Her task, now, was to win the affection of Nelson's family away from Fanny. His father, his sisters, his brother. To win their love, their loyalty and devotion. They were provincial people, and holy; she would convince them all of the purity and innocence of her relationship with Horatio, and persuade them that she was a devoted friend to whom they were all, one way or another, indebted. In the meantime, they must be the last ever to suspect that she was about to have his child.

Who did know? Her mother and Fatima. No one else, no one on earth, and Fatima had been made to swear on her life and on all she held precious that she would keep the secret. If one word of the truth ever escaped her lips, the scandal would destroy not only her mistress but also the nation's most glorious hero. On her shoulders would lie a burden of guilt so great that the whole world would turn its back on her. If she told a soul, she would go to hell and God would hate her. She would be out on her ear with only the clothes on her back, no money and no written character, nothing. Alone to wander the streets of London, and not Piccadilly, either, but the mean and unforgiving lanes of Wapping or Southwark, the rookeries of St Giles. She would end up in the workhouse and no one would come to look for her, and then she would die and go to hell and burn for ever, and there would be no end to her suffering and her torment.

In all her life, Fatima had never broken her word. She knew, however, that hell was filled with those who had carelessly uttered words that displeased God. She knew that the workhouse was filled with lice and diseases, with whores and thieves and children weeping at the cold. And she knew she was a thousand miles from home.

As for Mrs Cadogan, she would do whatever she must. She felt, not for the first time, a sort of crumpled fear in her chest as she contemplated the lengths to which it was necessary to go to protect one's reputation, to make sure you had a roof over your head and food to eat. Emma had been pregnant when Greville took them in twenty years ago, though not by him. That child, too, had been born in secret. No one had ever known about her, only Greville, and then Sir William. Not Nelson: especially not him, never. The girl had been brought up with a family in Manchester. Emma had closed up her heart against her, and if she ever spoke of her, it was as a cousin, a friend, a distant relative. She was living abroad somewhere, now, a grown woman. Another Emma – Emma Carew. Mary Cadogan had closed up her own heart. What else can you do? No, this was not the first time that Fate had thrown them a monstrous choice, though really there was no choice. Not then, not now.

'Poor Ma,' said Emma.

'I'm sorry?'

'You look sad.'

'Oh, for heaven's sake. When I finish this, I'm going to ring for some tea. I can't move at the moment.'

'I'll ring. You stay where you are.'

Mary Cadogan was not a woman given to dreaming, but now, with great folds of blue silk over her knees, and her daughter struggling to her feet to ring for Fatima, she dared to imagine another reality, one where the child of a glorious father and a beautiful mother was held up for the world to see and admire. She permitted herself, in this moment left for some

27

reason unguarded, to long for such a thing. She held a small and perfect hand in her own; she felt the quiet burden of a sleeping infant in her lap. Was it too much to ask? It was, because now, as before, there was too much at stake. One day, however, this child would come to live with them. This was not a dream, but a hope. One day, when the time for speculation was over, when the fuss had all died down, even if they must hide the truth of its birth. In the meantime, Mary Cadogan would use all her resources, and all her devotion, to organise Emma's lying-in without Sir William suffering any discomfort, and without anyone having to fear the consequences of revelation.

2

The night that Lady Hamilton drove to Little Titchfield Street was bitter. When Jane Gibson opened the door, the cold caught her ankles. The air outside smelled of smoke and horses. Clumps of snow, black with dirt, still lay in the narrow street. Wrapped in the warm folds of Lady Hamilton's muff was a small child, less than a week old.

Jane Gibson had been found after discreet enquiry by Mrs Cadogan. She was young, strong, sober. Her hair was gathered into a knot of curls on the back of her head, and there was a kind and intelligent fortitude in her face. Her own daughter, Mary, was three or four years old with pretty, clever features like her mother's. A hump on the child's back made her look monkish and ancient, as if she lived somewhere between the walls of the house, somewhere dark and small. There was no Mr Gibson.

Emma found herself in a small front parlour, with a good fire and heavy curtains. The room was the colour of strong tea. A crib stood in the corner near the fire and next to a low nursing chair. There was a small dresser against one wall, and tidy piles of mending and papers. 'This is . . .' Emma smiled, then frowned, as the words flew out of her head and circled in the air above it. She had got out of bed too soon. Not only that, but she had been to a concert the night before, given by the Duke of Norfolk at his house in St James's Square. It had worn her out, but it had shut up the speculation in the papers: no woman was going to go out in full evening dress five days after she had given birth. 'It's just as I imagined it,' she said, looking wildly round her. It didn't sound much like a compliment, and she grinned to show that it was.

'And this,' she said, 'is my godchild, Horatia.'

Mrs Gibson made her sit down. Before you fall down, she thought. 'She's a pretty child,' she said.

Emma held the blanket away from the baby's face. 'She . . . there was a sister, but she didn't survive.' Why had she told her that? Too weak, too small, too long in coming out, the second child had lived for less than an hour, and had been taken away for secret burial by Fatima and Mrs Cadogan, a tiny grey thing wrapped in linen. 'Would you mind . . .?' she said.

Mrs Gibson took Horatia while Emma dug in the pocket of her coat for an envelope. 'Her father asked me to give you this.'

The envelope was almost as big as the baby. So we are talking above all, thought Jane Gibson, about discretion. We are ignoring the fact that my lady looks as if she has only just got out of bed, and as if what she is doing now is harder than she had expected. She smiled down into the small, puckered face. 'Mary,' she said to her daughter, 'come and see.' Mary looked like a mouse, hiding behind the chair. Her grey eyes were watchful, and her nose was twitching. Jane Gibson laughed. 'She's shy,' she said to Emma. 'She's been waiting for this.'

Little was said then about the child's parents – only that the mother was ill, and could not look after Horatia herself. Emma told Jane Gibson that she had agreed, at Lord Nelson's wish, to act as the child's guardian, to see that she was cared for and that she had a good home until such time in the future when other arrangements could be made. Her voice, as she spoke, sounded stiff and formal even to her own ears. She did not want to be stiff and formal, but this woman was a complete stranger to her and she could find, in her exhaustion, no other tone. Horatia would be known as Miss Thompson. Lady Hamilton would want regular reports on her health, and to see her often. Her godfather, Lord Nelson, would come to visit her whenever he could, and Mrs Gibson must be ready to receive him at short notice, although there was no need to stand on ceremony.

'One other thing . . .' As she spoke, she looked not at the baby or at Mrs Gibson, but at a badly done picture on the wall of some brown and sketchy marshes. 'Her birthday is in October.'

It was a precautionary lie: Emma herself had been in Dresden in October, dining with the British minister, dancing the tarantella, sitting for the court artist, Johann Schmidt.

Mrs Gibson felt as if her face had fractured with astonishment. 'This child,' she said. 'October.'

'This child, yes. You may find it strange, but it is her mother's wish that we say so. She has her own reasons, and I support them.'

Jane Gibson collected herself. She nodded, her head not quite straight on her shoulders. 'By all means,' she said. For the amount of money she was being paid, the child might have been born last June.

3

The news of his daughter's birth reached Nelson on board the *San Josef*. His eyes were so bad that he could hardly read the letter, but he stood up to get more light, and lifted the page to his face again. There had been twins, two girls. One lived, and one had died. Poor Emma, poor little child. He wept with sorrow, with joy and pride and sorrow and more joy, until there was no room in his chest for all that was in his heart. He sat down and wrote a letter to Emma, then another, and another. He wrote his will again, and made plans for the christening. He strode the length of the cabin, bruising his leg on a corner of the desk. He told Emma that he was on his knees, that Mr Thompson was at his elbow, begging him to tell her that his love for her and his child was greater, if possible, than ever, and that he called on God to witness that he would marry her as soon as he could. I think Thomson may go mad with joy, he said. Thompson, Thomson. He does nothing but rave about you and her. He is very proud to have me as her godfather, and wishes that I might have a lock of her hair. He has forgotten his headaches and the cold and all his misery in the thought that he will see you soon. My own dear wife, for that is what you are. I wish I was setting off with you for Italy. A walk under the chestnut trees, even though you might be shot by a bandit, would be better than having our reputations attacked in England. And by the way, don't forget to burn all my letters. I mean it, burn them.

He became, not for the first time, taken with God. Years before, in the blue rollers of the South Atlantic – suffering from extreme weakness after a fever that nearly killed him – he had been granted a vision of his future mission in life. He had seen in front of him a radiant orb, and felt an inward glow of joy and patriotic zeal. He had vowed at that point to become a hero, and to brave every danger he met. Since that day, he had been in everything he did the happy instrument of a divine will, and the hand of God had been visible in every battle he fought. Emma was now part of that same mission. You're a saint in an age of wickedness, he wrote, an example of virtue and good-ness, and in the eyes of heaven we're man and wife. Somehow, his love for her had removed itself from the laws by which other men and women were bound, and from the very precepts of his religious beliefs. He prayed for her, and for their

31

daughter, and for the soul of the child who had perished. He prayed for support in this transitory life, and for relief in death from the miseries of the world. Amen, amen, amen.

It had been settled that a fleet would go to the Baltic. Across Europe, Napoleon seemed invincible. A new army of invasion was gathering across the Channel, and the threat of an allied fleet meant that a major show of force might be needed to keep British trade moving to and from the Baltic ports. Coal, salt, sugar, tobacco, tea and manufactured goods in one direction; canvas, timber, hemp, pitch tar, copper and iron in the other. The commander-in-chief, Vice Admiral Sir Hyde Parker, had orders to go to Copenhagen and persuade the Danes, by whatever means, to withdraw from the alliance. He was to deal with Denmark first, then the Russian ports, and then Sweden.

Nelson would need a shallow draught, and was ordered to move from the *San Josef* to the *St George*. The ship was dirty. Its decks leaked, and it was truly uncomfortable, but it suited his mood. The weather was bad, and he was seasick. He was mad with happiness, though ill and tired, and looking forward to being second-in-command to an elderly, unimaginative and indecisive admiral in an unworthy and filthy ship. Don't let Sir William have that man in the house, he wrote again to Emma. Does he really not know that if he opens his door to him, your reputation will be ruined? All the world has its eyes on you, and you'll be lost just as if you were guilty. You have to show that you're above temptation, and can't be drawn into the paths of shame for the sake of pride or riches. Just tell the Prince to go to hell. Please. And kiss Horatia for me. He dashed off a letter to the Society for Promoting Christian Knowledge, asking them for nine hundred Bibles to give to the crew of the *San Josef* as a parting gesture. Then he sailed round the coast to join his commander-in-chief at Yarmouth.

At the end of February he was granted three days' leave. As soon as the signal came, he leaped into a carriage and travelled overnight to London. From Lothian's Hotel, where he changed and had breakfast, he went straight to 23 Piccadilly. Fatima let him in, and he ran upstairs to Emma's room.

Downstairs, Sir William was finishing his breakfast. Tall and lean, Sir William Hamilton still looked distinguished, still intelligent, but he was beginning to show his age. He knew perfectly well what had been going on under his roof – for one thing, his wife had grown, in the space of months, from fat to colossal – but he was seventy years old and a diplomat through and through: for the sake of peace and Emma's happiness, and because he valued his friendship with Nelson, he had decided to know nothing about it and to remain in dignified oblivion. It was a measure of his discretion, or of his desire for a quiet life, that he showed no sign of knowing that Emma was suffering from anything more than a bad cold. If he could make himself believe that nothing was going on, then so could the rest of the world. He went out. He attended meetings of the British Museum and the Royal Society; he went to his clubs and to salerooms. At his age, his comforts and pastimes were more important to him than going to bed with a beautiful wife, and Emma still made him feel loved and needed.

The hallway, the dining room and one side of the staircase were covered with pictures, busts and ancient vases. There were crates and straw everywhere. Roman faces peeped from between the balustrades, and marble arms reached for the ceilings. There were paintings stacked against every wall – Titian, Rubens, Velázquez.

'Everything's going to Christie's next month,' he said, when Nelson came down again. 'In the meantime, I have to catalogue them. I'm not even half-way through. Have something to eat, have a cup of coffee.'

'Not for me, no.'

'Then come next door. I've got to go out in a minute, but I want to hear your news.'

The study was in a similar mess. 'It could have been worse,' said Sir William. 'At least I've got something to sell. We thought the best things were at the bottom of the sea.'

Nelson lifted a bust from a chair and sat. 'Why aren't you getting a pension? You're a retired minister, you were His Majesty's ambassador for nearly forty years. You should get two thousand a year, at least.'

'I'm out of favour, Horatio.'

'In God's name, why?'

'I've been away too long.'

This was not the reason at all. Nelson knew it; they both did. Sir William had been out of favour with the King and his ministers ever since he had made Emma his second wife ten years before, after living openly with her in the Palazzo Sessa. In Naples there had been hardly a ripple but in London the marriage had caused a scandal. There were people, too, who knew enough about Charles Greville to remember his relationship with Emma, and the deal he had struck with his uncle. The King might well be aware of all the things that were said about her, and stick his nose in the air.

'You should go and see the Foreign Secretary,' said Nelson.

'I've been. I kicked my heels for hours outside his office, but he wouldn't see me.'

'Then you should write to the King. Make him see sense.'

'I know, yes. The trouble is, he's mad. He was in a coma for several days. Everybody's talking about it. Apparently he looks ghastly.'

Nelson nodded and rubbed his face. 'I'm sorry,' he said. 'Not for him, for you.'

Upstairs, Fatima was helping her mistress to dress. 'Stand still, milady,' she said. 'Breathe in.' Emma breathed in, and Fatima fastened a row of buttons down her back. Even with the loose cut of fashion, and even with Lady Hamilton's big fat proportions, it seemed extraordinary to Fatima that she had managed to disguise, right up to the end, that she had been pregnant

34

with twins. She had a bit more waist now, a bit less bosom, but it was still a struggle to get her into dresses she had not worn for several months.

What did it feel like to be so fat? Comfortable, on hard chairs. Difficult, getting in and out of bed and carriages.

She was still doing Emma's hair when Nelson knocked and came into the room again. 'Fatima,' he said, 'are you well? I raced past you just now, I didn't ask.'

'Very well, milord, thank you.'

Nelson himself looked awful. His hair was white, he had lost several teeth, and his cheeks were sunken. There was a film over both eyes that made him appear almost completely blind and, in a plain coat, without all his stars and spangles on his chest, he looked nondescript. Fatima could not help seeing him on board the *Foudroyant*, in the Bay of Naples, lifting his face when the gun announced the execution of Caracciolo; lifting his glass to the death of a traitor. The same man, there and here. She placed a hairpin between her lips and held it there while she brushed.

He threw himself into a chair, and sat there with his gaze fixed on Emma. What did it feel like, Fatima wondered, to be so adored?

'He's selling everything,' said Nelson. 'He's spent his life collecting, for God's sake. He ought to be allowed to keep his treasures.' A piece of coal slid in the fire behind him and settled again. Beyond the windows, the day was grey. 'Why isn't he getting a pension? It's mad.'

'Of course it is! After everything he did for his country, and everything I did, too. Who helped to secure entry for the fleet at Syracuse? Not the government, me!'

This, as far as Nelson knew, was true. Before the battle of the Nile, the Kingdom of the two Sicilies had been technically neutral. Napoleon had told Ferdinand that he would leave his country alone as long as it did not take sides; as a result, the King had not dared to open his ports to Nelson, or to supply him with frigates after he had lost his own in a storm. He had allowed him, eventually, to provision his ships at Syracuse, if only because Emma had made the case to the Queen. Would he have done it anyway? Possibly not.

Nelson leaned forward and brushed some dust from his knee. Then he changed the subject. 'By the way,' he said, 'I want Horatia to be inoculated.'

Emma looked at him in surprise.

'Smallpox. No, I know about it, I've been thinking about it. I met someone only last week who told me about his own child. She had it done, and was feverish for a few days, and now she'll never get it.' He glanced up at Fatima and winked. 'Mr Thompson has said he wants it done.'

Emma shrugged. 'Then we'll do it.' She placed a hand on his cheek. 'We must go,' she said. 'We'll be late.' She traced his brow. 'How are your eyes? Still bad?'

'Not good, no.' The ship's doctor had told him not to write any more letters, to bathe them every hour and to wear a green shade. She leaned forward and kissed them, one and then the other.

When they had left, Fatima started to tidy the room. She went round picking up clothes, straightening brushes, pulling the sheets off the bed. In the middle of these tasks she stood by the window and looked out over the park. London was cold. It rained every day, and the streets smelled of wet horses. Men and women went in different directions, and in the same direction, getting mixed up with each other and, more extraordinarily, not getting mixed up. In and out of shops, up and down the street. The shops on Piccadilly had shelves and shutters and boxes and glass doors; in the evening there were lamps, and light spilled on to the street. Carriages went up and down in such numbers that it sounded as if Napoleon had come in the night. Sometimes she thought he had, and she waited to hear the sound of guns from the river, and to see the Horse Guards mustering in Green Park.

A woman glanced up towards the window, and for an

absurd moment Fatima thought that it was Lady Nelson below her in the street. It wasn't, of course not. But it made her wonder: whatever was going to happen to her? She saw her, now, a still, pale figure in white who dropped away like something falling quietly from a tree. She saw her again on the night of their arrival in London in November: Lord Nelson had been away for three years, but when he greeted his wife on his return, he had looked like a man who had seen her only a month or a week before, and who wanted only to go away again as fast as his feet would carry him. And there were the two women, the wife and the mistress, face to face in Nerot's Hotel in St James's. The gale throwing itself against the windows, the dark and the cold and the rain beyond them. Lady Nelson, angular and narrow, with a look of fixed civility on her face; lace collar high and tight around her throat. Lady Hamilton, six months pregnant and hiding it beneath a high waist, her voice loud with anxiety. Big, round, loud and beautiful. Two different women, from different worlds, opposite in temperament, with opposite yet matching fears. After that, whenever they met at dinner or the theatre, one or other of them had fainted, was sick, or burst into tears. Then, when Christmas came, Nelson had been invited, with the Hamiltons, to spend it in Wiltshire with Sir William's cousin, William Beckford. Fanny Nelson had not been included in the invitation, and stayed in London. Why had she been left out? It had seemed to Fatima both strange and cruel, and she understood for the first time that Nelson was a coward in these things. He was afraid of confronting his wife with his own betrayal so he treated her badly. He could not speak to her about what had happened in his heart so he did not speak to her at all.

Below her, a crossing sweeper stood with his hands on his hips, the handle of his brush tucked into an elbow. White face, splattered coat. Carriages swept past him, throwing up more mud. Beyond every new world that Fatima found herself in, there were other, invisible worlds, where lives became unimaginable. She turned, and placed the comb she was holding back on the dressing-table.

At Little Titchfield Street Horatia lifted her fists, as if each one contained something tiny and mysterious. She banged the air with them, and her legs kicked under the coverlet. Nelson was staggered by her ears. By the crease in her neck, her hands. 'She looks like you,' he said.

'Like me?'

'Like her mother, I mean. She looks like her mother. Here, the top part of her face.'

The child found him with her eyes and seemed to study what he had said. Her arms pumped the air again, and her legs moved with them, as if someone had pulled a string.

'She's perfect. No two people ever produced anything so perfect.' His face was lit with pride as he examined the tiny fists and fingernails, the pearly cheeks and windy smiles. 'She's a true gift of love,' he said. Jane Gibson stood back and watched as the man who had secured the Mediterranean for Britain pursed his smiling lips to kiss the little face. When he straightened, he stood for a moment on tiptoe. 'A true pledge of love from her mother,' he said. Who, thought Mrs Gibson, we have heard not a word about for several weeks. At the last mention, the woman had been at death's door. Most probably she had hopped the twig by now.

Two days later, Nelson left to rejoin his commander-in-chief. They left Yarmouth on 12 March, with a powerful fleet of fifteen ships of the line, two fifty-gun ships, brigs and frigates, and sailed for Copenhagen.

4

News of the British victory reached London on 15 April, in the middle of a dinner party at 23 Piccadilly. Emma shrieked and leaped up from the table. A plate with sirloin of beef, gravy and horseradish landed with a quiet thud on the rug. A glass went over and Mrs Cadogan, shaking her head with the force of her joy, lifted the cloth from the table and sprinkled salt on the stain. The meal was forgotten as Emma danced a tarantella, first with her husband, then with the Duke of Noia, and then, when they could not keep up, with Fatima. The Duke of Queensberry, too far gone in years for violent exercise, watched with a battered smile on his face as the dance grew faster and more outrageous. Charles Greville was there, and Prince Augustus, the Duke of Sussex. There were screams and embracing, castanets and tambourines, the occasional gasp of a torn seam. After the dancing, Emma went to the piano and banged out every patriotic song she knew with her foot hard down on the pedal. The admiral's older brother, the Reverend William Nelson, put his long pale hands together in applause, and held them there, in prayer. He was a Norfolk rector, William, but ambitious: with this further victory, he dared to feel a bishop's mitre within his grasp.

In the early hours, while Fatima was getting her ready for bed, Emma took out the letter again. 'Read it,' she said. 'I'm too tired, I've had too much to drink. Bring a lamp over.'

Fatima took the letter. It was astonishing to her that, in the exhaustion of all the fighting and the negotiations, Nelson, weak as he was, could find the strength to write. The city of Copenhagen, he said, and the whole nation from the King downwards, had given him thanks and praise for his humanity in saving the town from destruction. 'He has beaten them and they're grateful?' she said.

'Just read it.'

To Fatima, it didn't sound much like a victory. The battle had been close-run and bloody. Hyde Parker had dithered. When negotiations with the Danes had come to nothing, he had been inclined to believe that the best plan was to stay where they were, off Elsinore, and from there to maintain a blockade of the Baltic. Nelson had been inclined to believe that they should go in with all guns blazing.

They had gone in with all guns blazing. Fatima read with care and slowly, with the flat and even tone of someone not very good at it. Squadron, stationary, anchoring. It had been a battle between the stationary defences of Copenhagen and a squadron moving between deep channels in front of the city. British ships had become lost in the smoke and stranded on the shoals. Others, anchoring by the stern and presenting their broadsides to the shore, had come under fierce fire from the Danish batteries. There had been deafening, half-blind duels between cannons at point-blank range. After three hours, Hyde Parker, from his position north of the city, had given the signal to discontinue action. Nelson disobeyed it. If they had stopped then, before the enemy struck their colours, they would all have been run aground and destroyed. As it was, the narrowness of the channel and the batteries on shore had left three British ships on the shoals. Some of the Danish ships surrendered, but when British boarding parties rowed towards them, they were fired on. Nelson had called for paper, pen and ink, and sent a letter ashore proposing a truce. If the Danish did not cease firing, he said, he would burn every one of their ships, and all the men in them. He would blow up all the floating batteries he had taken, without the power to save the men on board.

If it was a victory, thought Fatima, it had been won at great cost. More than two thousand sailors had been killed or wounded, and most of the British ships were badly damaged. She was not sure, either, about Nelson's humanity. He would have done it, she was sure of that: he would have set fire to the Danish batteries and let the men in them burn to death. ' "I am a warrior, but will not be a butcher," ' she read. ' "If you had seen their adoration and their respect, you would have cried for joy." '

'I do cry for joy!' said Emma, pushing herself up out of her chair. 'I'm so proud of him, Fatima. I wish I could be there. I should be by his side.'

There were things, Fatima thought, that she did not understand about war between nations. Do the vanquished adore those who vanquish them? Is it not a ruse to demand a truce when your ships are being shelled to pieces, and you have still to get beyond the guns and take the city? When three of your own ships have run aground, and three more, and they are under heavy fire? She read to the end of the page. When the armistice had been signed, the commandant of the Danish Naval Academy had received a gift from Nelson of a gold medal commemorating the battle of the Nile, as well as a short account of his own life, so that young men in his command could learn that perseverance and good behaviour will raise a person to the highest honours and rewards.

She stood up and blew out a candle. 'Time for bed, milady,' she said.

5

Nelson was miserable. He had wanted an earldom, and to go home. Instead, he was made a viscount, and commander-in-chief of the Baltic fleet. Sir Hyde Parker, for giving the signal to withdraw from action, was recalled. There were no medals for the captains who had taken part in the action, no promotions for lieutenants, no vote of thanks from the City of London, and precious little prize money from the Admiralty.

Nelson fell into a typical bout of self-pity and kept threatening, in his letters, to die. To Emma he wrote like a man who had lost his mind. For God's sake, don't tell me off. I can't come home yet, and there's nothing I can do about it. I'm ill, and if you're unkind to me, you'll kill me much sooner than any shot in Europe. He managed, nevertheless, to get up early in the morning as usual, to work a full day and keep his fleet provisioned and active.

He went hunting for the Russians at Revel, and would have blown them out of the water there had they not moved north through the broken ice to Kronstadt three days before. It was just as well that they had: the emperor Paul had been murdered, and the new Tsar was all for peace. Instead of watching a battle from the port, the people of Revel rowed out in their hundreds to look at Nelson and to get his autograph in books of public record. You see, he told Emma, a good name is better than riches. They point at me, and say, That's him, that's him. I've been invited to St Petersburg, but I need a rest or I'm going to die. Something happened last week that nearly carried me off, I think it was a stroke. I haven't had my fingernails cut, by the way, not since February. They're so long I'm afraid they'll break, but I've been waiting so that you can do them for me.

In the third week of June he was relieved of his command and allowed to come home.

Fanny wrote to congratulate him on his victory. I've tried to do everything you wanted me to, she said, and if there's anything I haven't done, I'm sorry. She was going to stay with his father Edmund, who was ill. What else do I have to do to show you that I'm truly your loving wife? He didn't answer the letter. Instead, he wrote to his agent, Alexander Davidson, to ask him to tell her to leave him alone. He would give her sixteen hundred pounds a year, but he would go abroad for ever rather than live with her again.

He had time for a short holiday with Emma and Sir William in the Thames Valley. The Fox and Hounds, the Bush at Staines. Fishing, chatting, eating, walking. His brother William joined them at Staines, and badgered Nelson to use his influence to give him a leg up in the Church. As incumbent of Hilborough, in Norfolk, he didn't think his position anywhere near worthy of the brother of a viscount, and told him so. 'Six hundred pounds or so,' he said, 'and a good house. There are several deans on their last legs: Hereford, Lichfield, Coventry, York. Any one of those, if you can.' Dead men's shoes. Nelson promised to do what he could. William was loud and pushy and too big for his boots, but he was his brother. 'Leave it with me,' he said, 'and try to talk about something else for five minutes.'

Then suddenly he was summoned to Whitehall. Bonaparte, according to reports, was planning an invasion. Ships and landing craft were building up in large numbers off the French coast at Boulogne, and an army of up to forty thousand was gathering around Flushing and in the Pas de Calais.

'Don't go,' said Emma. 'You've just got back, don't go.'

'Don't be silly, it's only the Channel. You can come to visit me.' They were walking beside the river. Boats had been pulled up onto the bank, and in the mud below them lay delicate forks left by coots and moorhens. 'Listen,' he said. 'I want to buy a farm. Outside London, but not too far. Somewhere I can come home to on leave. You'll live there, and Sir William, and Horatia. We'll have pigs and poultry . . . I don't know. A cow. Sheep to keep the grass down. We can eat plainly, and have good wine and good fires. People can come and stay. I want you to do it for me, I want you to find somewhere. You'll have to keep the house in Piccadilly – you'll have to have somewhere in London. Not for you, for him. I can put my hands on three thousand, I think. Another two for the furniture. That'll be enough. A place where we can be together, a place where we can be quiet.' He stopped walking, turned to her and took her chin in his hand. 'I love you, I never loved anyone else, and I want to be with you. If you were single, and I found you under a hedge, I would marry you in a moment.'

Fanny wrote to him again, asking him to go back to live with her, to bury everything in oblivion and forget. I can't bear this silence any more, she said. Please let us live together. The only thing I want in the world is to live with you and make you happy. I received the money for this quarter yesterday, and I don't know how to thank you. It's generous, more than I would have expected. You must believe that every one of my wishes is to please you. God bless you, my dear husband. He sent the letter back with a note saying that it had been opened by mistake. He never wanted to see her again, and he never did.

THREE

I

Janot ran on ahead. The fields were wet, but the ground was still firm. After a hundred yards, they turned off the road onto a rutted lane. Summer had ended, the winter was not yet in. Cows were out in the fields, broad-faced and white. When they saw Janot, they began to drift towards him, blowing, heads low. They made a semi-circle in the dry mud on the other side of the gate and studied the old dog through the bars. From time to time, one went plop, plop, plop without moving. Horatia and Fatima leaned on the gate and reached out to feel the soft rough lick of their tongues. They had left Emma upstairs in her room, sleeping.

They continued walking. A buzzard circled overhead. They could hear the geese half a mile away, but there was no other sign of life. Then they heard the clatter of metal on metal, and an old man appeared on the lane in front of them, stooped like a tree and strung about with traps. Monsieur Costes, the mole-catcher. Ancient, impassive, toothless. His breeches were held up with twine, and he wore a leather waistcoat and a moleskin cap. Sometimes during the summer they had seen rows of moles hung out on the hedges, grey and silky and humming with flies. As they passed him they nodded, and Fatima said hello. The mole-catcher's jaw twitched; he cleared his throat and spat.

'He thinks I'm a heathen,' said Fatima, when they had left him behind.

Horatia turned and walked, for a few steps, backwards. Then she turned again. 'You go to church,' she said.

Ever since they had arrived in St Pierre, Emma had professed the Catholic faith. She liked saying her prayers in French. She went every Sunday to mass, and took Horatia and Fatima with her. The woman who had vowed revenge on behalf of the Queen of Naples, who had sent French supporters to their execution, now had French prayers on her lips, and was up to her eyes in debt to a French wine merchant and a French butcher. But this was not about Emma. 'I'm black,' said Fatima, 'and an unbeliever.'

'You!' Horatia laughed. 'No.'

'I was not born a Christian.'

Horatia slowed to a stop. Above them, the cry of the buzzard turned in the air. Fatima looked at her face and laughed. 'What? You think I may go to hell?'

'No!'

'Anyway, I was baptised, though sometimes I forget, and pray to the other god.'

The fields were giving way to woods, and there were trees on either side of the lane. Elm, birch, chestnut, oak. Horatia stepped between a long string of dry brown cow pats. 'Where were you baptised?'

Fatima turned and shook her head. 'The same thing again,' she said.

'What?'

'Asking questions you know the answer to.'

Horatia shrugged. 'Where?'

Questions, almost always, about the past. But if it seems that you have no future, what else are you going to think about but the past? 'In Merton Church. Fatima Emma Charlotte Nelson Hamilton, a negress of about twenty years of age. We went in three carriages. Lord Nelson's papa had just died, I remember. He died on milady's birthday, and his funeral was on that day, but milord didn't go. He wasn't well – he had shitting all the time. Also his wife might be there, and they was on bad terms. Instead, we went to Merton

46

Church, and I was baptised. If you want to know why, I don't know why.'

Ahead of them, under the trees but with an open view at the edge of the wood, stood the mole-catcher's house. It was the colour of sand. Layers of plaster had fallen away from the walls in front and behind, leaving patches of white. The exposed beams were grey, and the door was hanging off its hinges. Under a lean-to at the side of the house there was a collection of ladders, benches, baskets. Old traps, a table, chains. A line had been strung between two walls, and items of washing hung from it, as if they had been dead for years.

'It was the right thing to do,' said Horatia.

'What?'

'To be baptised.'

'Oh, well, good.' There was, suddenly, anger in Fatima's voice. 'You think it was? Me, I don't know. I don't know if God can look down on us, and if he can, I don't know which one. I think, even if I was baptised in the Christian faith, maybe that god doesn't know me because I was born in Alexandria, and under another one.' She ran a hand down the front of her dress. 'And maybe that other one does not look down over England and over St Pierre. Everyone say there is only one God, and no other, and all other gods are heathen. That is all very well if you did not start with one and end up with one other. If it is the same god, and only one, then why must he say one thing to these people, and a different thing to those ones, and have different books and scriptures? I do not know if they are both the same, or if one is good and the other is not. I have seen the works of Christian men, *chère*, and they were not all good.' Her thoughts took off from under the trees, still full with leaf, and circled, in the scorching sun, the men and ships in the Bay of Naples. The stink of fire from the shore, of pine and vegetation from the hills. 'There are many bad things,' she said, 'done in the name of God.'

'But, Fatima . . .' Horatia's legs were tired. Though they had

47

not gone very far, the strength had gone out of her. Beyond the mole-catcher's house there was a pile of logs, and beside the logs, a fallen trunk. She sat on this, and Fatima sat beside her. Janot dropped in a heap on the ground in front of them.

'It's true,' said Fatima. 'It is true of this God, and of that one. Many bad things. I may pray to the God of Jesus that things may change, and we can stop going from one place to another, and milady may be well again. I pray with my heart, till my heart aches so hard to be heard, but it is not, no. Some may say God has other plans, and whatever might befall us is his will, and we must only wait to understand, but me, I have a worm of doubt in my soul. I have waited, and I do not understand.' All the anger had gone from her voice. 'I say my prayers, and I hope they go to the right god, whichever that one may be, and that one day I may go to heaven and not to the other place.' She was slung between two faiths, and between two visions of hell. The first was a place of weeping and thirst, of torment and outer darkness, of snares and of sorrows, where souls were tortured with fire and brimstone, and tossed into a bottomless pit by devils with pitchforks and horns. Lakes of sulphur and boiling cauldrons; tears and gnashing of teeth. The other was a place of mostly women, dragged by their hair and by their feet through boiling water, and thrust into layers of fire with hooked rods of iron. They were bitten and stung by ninety-nine dragons, and ate the fruit of the Zaqqum tree, which burned their bellies like molten brass. The awnings of this hell had four thick walls, and each thick wall had a distance of forty years, and though the souls in torment begged for mercy and for water, they were given neither and were in despair. And there was no doubt in Fatima's soul that both these places existed, and that one or both of them waited for her, should she ever utter a careless word.

Horatia took her hand, and placed it in her own lap. 'Fatima Emma Charlotte Nelson Hamilton,' she chanted.

Fatima smiled. The girl beside her was almost a woman and,

in fact, in the last few months she had become more woman than child. The life they had been forced to live had added years to her, and yet like a child she was looking everywhere for signs of herself, and of who she might be or become. She had been sent out of her own country, and did not know if she might return, or when; sent away with a woman who drank herself into rages or until she was unconscious, living on almost nothing, on memories. And yet beneath it all was a resilience that might have come from nowhere; something like patience, as she waited out her time. She fought her battles with Lady Hamilton, and retired to mend her wounds. She sat in corners, knowing she was not free, but that the day would come when she was. Perhaps it was because she knew only one god, and believed that he was good, and that things could never be this bad again. For a while they were silent, looking out through the edge of the wood. Then, because the log underneath her was damp, Fatima stood. 'Up,' she said. 'You all right?'

'Yes, I'm all right. Fatima . . .' Horatia stood and shook out her skirts. 'Don't you ever want children of your own?'

Fatima leaned to pick up a twig, then threw it away again. Janot, also on his feet, sniffed it, then headed towards home. 'I do,' she said. 'But I think I never will.'

'Why not?' Their lives could not go on like this for ever. Somewhere, a normal existence must be possible.

'Who will marry me? I come from Egypt, and am black.'

'Someone will.'

'I have never seen it, one black, one white.'

'You could go home. One day, you could.'

'One day, chère, I will be old.' She took Horatia's head in her hands, and kissed her cheek. 'For now,' she said, 'I have you. You are my comfort and joy.'

Horatia took her arm, and they walked side by side. She kicked out her skirts with long, high steps, and laughed. 'Who's this?' she said.

Fatima looked at her and scowled. 'Don't know.'

'Yes, you do.'

She scratched her chin and made a guess. 'Bonaparte.'

'No, Madame Pechard. Who's this?' Horatia made a beak of her hand, and waved it in front of her nose.

'A goose.'

'A goose? No.'

'I don't know. What?'

'Not what, who.'

'Give me another clue.'

She stuck out her bottom and wiggled it. She lifted her chin and raised her face, and her head and shoulders bobbed in time with her backside.

'Oh,' said Fatima. 'Francine's husband. Monsieur Caillois.'

'Yes! You get the prize.' Her face became sober again, and she sighed. 'I don't know who can help us,' she said. 'She writes letters every day, but nothing happens, nothing comes of them. What can I do? I'm thirteen, I can't do anything. My uncle Matcham would send us money, but she won't ask him. No one knows how bad it is. She can't bear for anyone to know, and I don't understand why any more. She thinks that things can go on as they are, but they can't. My aunt said I should go to live with them, but she jumps down my throat when I bring it up. Why won't she let me? She's got you and Berthe.'

'Maybe she doesn't want to lose you. You are her precious girl, and also her goddaughter, what means she must look after you. That is what your father wished.'

He had put it in his will: I leave my dearest friend Emma, Lady Hamilton, sole guardian of Horatia until she is eighteen years old. She shook her head. 'She could ask them for some money.'

Fatima nodded, but said nothing. Lady Hamilton was too proud to ask for help from Nelson's family, though in fact George Matcham had lent her a hundred pounds three years ago, which she had never returned.

50

'Sometimes,' said Horatia, 'I think that we should be able to walk back along our own lives, and go to the places that we remember, and start again from there. They're our lives, we should be able to.'

Janot barked once and vanished into a hedge. Fatima felt the wide open sadness of everything that was uncertain. The love of God, the truth of the past. 'And where would you go?' she said.

Horatia did not answer her. She screwed up her eyes and looked into the low, thin sun. 'Fatima, do you know who my mother was?'

Fatima watched the ground in front of her, the dry mud of the lane, the grass that grew up between the tracks. 'No, *chère*, I do not.'

2

That night, on her way up to her attic room, Fatima saw a light under Horatia's door. She pushed it open. The girl was lying in bed, a candle burning beside her.

'You should be asleep.'

'What time is it?'

'Late. You have a bad dream?'

There were tears in her eyes, and her body was shaken by a lingering sob. Fatima crossed the room and blew out her own candle. 'Move up,' she said. She sat on the narrow bed, and brushed the hair from Horatia's face. The house around them, apart from the creak of boards, was quiet. She sat with a hand on the child's head, gently scratching her scalp.

'What do you dream about, Fatima?'

'Me?' She kicked off her slippers and pulled her feet up onto the bed. 'I dream of Alexandria. Of the wide blue water, and the feluccas and the fishermen. Of the wide enormous sky and the sun.' She paused, her hand flat on Horatia's cheek. 'But all the time when I am dreaming it,' she said, 'I know that it is not a dream, and I am there. I can smell the streets, and I can see the small cracks in the stone, and colours and patterns that no mind can dream, only see.' In the night outside, owls called in the forest and the fields. Somewhere in the dark, something was being eaten. 'I think to myself, this is no dream, for how can I dream of such smells as mud and spices and *kofta*? I think I am still with Afra Wahid, or Mrs Cassell, and I can walk in that warm sun for many miles. I go to the market, and people know my name. It makes me laugh, that it is true and not a dream.'

Horatia's tears had gone, and she could feel Fatima's hand on her cheek. She wanted it to stay there and never move. 'Who was Afra Wahid?' she said. Their voices were low and even in the circle of light.

There was a hesitation, like a shrug. 'A man. I worked for him first, when I was very young. Before I had bosoms, even.'

'Was he kind to you?'

'Kind, no. He was all right, though.'

'And Mrs Cassell?'

'She was kind. I worked for her next, as a maid. She taught me to speak English. Hat, mat, cat. Her house looked out over the bay, and at night I slept on the roof. Big sky, big stars. When that great battle came, with Lord Nelson and the French, we could hear the guns at Aboukir. We didn't sleep one minute. Bang, and then bang, and then bang. When *L'Orient* was blown up, we could see the bright light on the sky. After that, there were no guns for many minutes. We thought it was over, but it was not. It went on until morning, and in the next day, too. When it was over, Lord Nelson had won the battle. He had a big wound on his head, but he was all right.'

'He had a scar, like this.' Horatia traced a line on Fatima's brow.

'He did.' For a minute they were both quiet, listening to the owls and the shifts in the old house. In her room across the corridor, Emma had begun to snore. 'One man came ashore to Alexandria,' Fatima went on, 'to see my mistress. His name was Block or Black – I don't remember what, or what ship he was on. After, Mrs Cassell told me he said that Lord Nelson wanted a maidservant to take with him to Italy for Lady Hamilton.'

'Did he know her then?'

Fatima smiled to herself. The same questions, over and over again. The same answers, too. 'He knew her a bit, not very well. He went there to Naples one time when he was a captain, maybe five years before. I don't know why, but he came in his ship and met milady and Sir William, and the King. Then on his way to Egypt to find Bonaparte he stopped again at Naples for food and water, but he never saw milady that time. He did not leave his ship. She wrote him letters, though, and helped to get provisions, what the King did not want to give him. That were a big help for him, so he thought that he would bring her a gift. Me. Mrs Cassell said I should go because I was good, and I could speak French and some English. Me, I said I didn't want to go, no, but she said I must.'

'You spoke French then?'

'Always. My mother worked for a French lady in Alexandria when I were small. We lived in the house with her. I don't know what her name were, just Madame. Everyone in that house spoke French, and me too, more than my own tongue.'

'You'd never been away before.'

'Never. And I never had been on a boat. A small one took me out to the ship one week later. That was the *Zealous*, I remember now. Then one other small boat took me to the *Vanguard*, which was Lord Nelson's ship, at Aboukir. There was French ships there, what was left of them broken to bits. I looked down into the water in the bay and I thought of what was at the bottom of it. Cannonballs and buttons and shoes. Lanterns and barrels and ships and men.'

The marines who rowed her out had described the battle,

full of the puzzled fatigue of men who found themselves still alive. They had not seen a woman, of any colour, for months. They had been eighteen hundred miles across the Mediterranean and back, looking for the French. It was not until August that they learned they were in Egypt. Napoleon had landed at Alexandria, and his army had taken Cairo. His fleet had moved a few miles east to Aboukir, at the mouth of the Nile, and they found them anchored by the bow in a curving line inside the bay, protected behind by sandbanks and invisible shoals. There, they told Fatima, and there and there. Where now she saw only still water, and gulls and a single fishing boat. Nelson had attacked immediately, at sunset. The first five ships went in behind the French, risking the shallow waters without proper charts, without pilot boats, with the dark coming down. At ten o'clock, while Fatima lay on a roof in Alexandria, fire reached the powder magazine on board *L'Orient*, and the French flagship blew up; masts and yards and cannons and bodies and blazing wreckage were thrown up into the sky, and rained back down on the ships around it. When the battle was over, no one knew how many had died.

Fatima sighed and scratched the side of her face. How many strange and different worlds a simple, ordinary person could pass through, she thought, in a single, ordinary life. 'Lord Nelson's ship had been damaged in the battle,' she went on, 'and I was afraid to be on it. I thought it must be full of holes, and we would sink. Then we got in a storm out to sea, and it was very bad. The ship got more damaged, and some men lost their lives. Me, I cried because I thought I, too, would lose my life. I saw Lord Nelson one or two times.' He had looked, she remembered suddenly, unremarkable. A little man with a white face walking the deck after the storm. A constellation of badges, ribbons and distinctions on his chest. 'He had that big gash on his head, and two black eyes and only one arm.' It had seemed strange to her then, for the first time, that a man

54

who looked so small, so ill and so tired could have laid waste to so much.

Horatia stretched her legs under the covers. The man she saw in her own mind was tall, with a low voice and one strong wrist, bearing the scars and medals of victory.

'After that battle,' Fatima went on, 'he were tired and ill, and have to rest. Also his ships were so damaged that they must come to Naples to be repaired before they can sail any more. When we got there, there was bands playing, and boats and barges came out to the ships. Hundreds of boats. Milady came out on one, though I did not know it was her, or that she would be my mistress. I was on deck, waiting by the rail, and I saw her. Beautiful.' In the candlelight, Fatima smiled. Beautiful, and huge. Her round face and sweet, full lips, her big blue eyes, her great big bosom and big fat legs. The coxswain on the boat that brought her out had wanted her off before she sank it. She had leaped on board the *Vanguard*, and thrown herself into Nelson's arms. His arm. She had nearly flattened him, crying out to God almighty, and landing as if she had fainted on his chest.

'The King and Queen was there, too, and Sir William. And even though they had all only met him one time before, he had defeated the French at Aboukir and was a great victor, and a bosom friend. They took him to the Palazzo Sessa, which were Sir William's house. And me, I went there too. When we came to the shore, many hundreds of doves were released into the sky from cages by the fishermen. Lovely. Then we come to the house, and there was three thousand lamps lit in it that night, so I thought it was on fire. I were very nervous after being in that ship and because my life was so changed, and I did not know what may happen to me. Plenty, as it turn out.'

Horatia saw the villa, standing on a high hill above the sea. Its shape was white against the dark and cobalt night, its windows and doors ablaze with light. Open carriages drove up to its steps, and dukes and princesses stepped out in their silks and sashes. They were watched, from the piazza below, by the *lazzaroni*, tall strong men of the street who raised their hats and called out Nelson's name.

There was a scuffle somewhere in the chimney, and a shallow fall of soot. 'Fatima, what happened at Naples?'

'Go to sleep.'

'Tell me.'

'Nothing happened there. The Frenchies came, and went away again. There was some rebels, too, but they was sorted out.'

'How? What happened?'

'Nothing, only talk.'

'My father was there. He saved the city.'

'He did, *chère*, that's true. No more talking, now.'

'Are you going to stay with me?'

'Five more minutes.'

FOUR

Night after night for seven days, boxes of jewels and barrels of gold and trunks containing clothes and treasures were brought from the palace to the embassy in covered wagons. Linen, pictures, coins. From the embassy, they were smuggled down in the dark to the ships. Nelson had been in Naples for four months, recovering, under Emma's tender care, from the wounds and fatigue of battle. In November, the French had taken Rome and declared a republic. Nelson had sailed to Leghorn with five thousand troops to cut off enemy lines of communication, while a Neapolitan army, with the King at its head, marched north to retake the city. The Neapolitans went in, the French retreated, and Nelson had returned to Naples. But then came the news that the French had turned round and come back, with reinforcements, and routed the liberators. The Neapolitans had withdrawn, taking with them as much plunder as they could carry, and the King had run for his life.

Now, at the beginning of December, the French were advancing at a steady pace on Naples, and the city was filled with rebel sympathisers waiting to greet them. The royal family was in full flight. Nelson and the Hamiltons were organising the evacuation, and leaving with them. Sir William's own pictures, and his precious collection of ancient vases, had been sent on board the *Colossus* to England. Vases he had dug from the earth, had lifted out of opened tombs. Never in the world would such a collection be made again, and never, if he could help it, would the French get their hands on it.

Everything was done in the greatest secrecy. If the *lazzaroni*, faithful to the King, should get wind of the fact that he was leaving, they would do whatever they could to stop him. Already they were roaming the streets of the city, threatening blood. Fatima had seen them, a mob half naked and covered in tattoos, carrying knives and clubs. They came up from the catacombs where they slept, snarling their hatred of the French. A royal courier, an old man, was mistaken for a Jacobin spy, and beaten to death beneath the palace windows.

In the middle of a dinner held by the Turkish envoy, Nelson and the Hamiltons excused themselves and slipped away. The Hamiltons made their way on foot down to the quay, while Nelson walked rapidly to the palace. He entered it through hidden doors and secret passages, and climbed the dim stair-case to the Queen's rooms. With dark lanterns, cutlasses and pistols, he brought the royal family out and down to the boats at the jetty. Fatima, sent with Mrs Cadogan to accompany the royal children, lost a slipper on the stairs.

Three barges and a cutter were waiting for the fugitives. As they pulled away, everything was silent on the shore. At midnight, they reached the ships. The King and his family climbed aboard the *Vanguard*, followed by his confessor, his surgeon, servants, nurses, two cooks and a priest. Others – lesser princes, cardinals and ambassadors – were taken on assorted Neapolitan vessels. All were under orders to sail at dawn for Palermo, the second capital of the Kingdom of the Two Sicilies.

There was a war going on, yet Nelson had devoted himself exclusively to the protection of the Queen of Naples and her family. Why? Fatima did not know why. She was only glad to get out. She did not know who had entrusted to him the charge of the kingdom, but no one else, it seemed, would save them from the French. It is the duty of the strong, she thought, to protect those who are weak, and the Queen had trusted no one but him. The King took with him all the gold of the kingdom, which he had confiscated to pay for the war, and his favourite hunting dogs.

They did not get off at dawn. The sea was whipped by a cold north wind, and it was blowing too hard to leave the bay. The ships twisted on their moorings, and the passengers began to be sick. In their crowded quarters – stinking of fresh paint, and kitted out with canvas cots and hammocks run up by the sailmakers – the sleepless royal party threw up over everything. They spent another night and day in the bay before setting sail, but a storm was howling towards them, and struck the ships on their first morning at sea. It blew so hard that the *Vanguard*'s topsails were blown to pieces. The King's confessor broke an arm falling out of his bunk, and one of the princesses cut her head open on a sideboard. Everyone thought that they were going to die; they clung to whatever they could to stop themselves sliding across the cabin floors, and cried out to God in their fear.

Only Emma was not sick, and Fatima. For the five nights that they were on board, they did not sleep. Emma gave the royal family her own beds and linen, and the two women tended the ill and held the children. They cleaned them, nursed them, spoke words of comfort in the cramped and stinking quarters below decks. Emma wrapped the Queen's feet in a cashmere shawl, and lifted her hair from her face while she was sick. She did it, in spite of her exhaustion, with a glow at her own significance, and with a capability learned in younger days for sponging faces and soothing fears. Mrs Cadogan looked after the King and his men who, when they weren't losing their stomachs, prayed on their knees in the wardroom. On Christmas Day, the Queen's youngest boy, the six-year-old prince, died of convulsions in Emma's arms.

Palermo, when they reached it, wasn't comfortable. They arrived in driving snow, and the Hamiltons' villa, while it had privacy and a fine view of the bay, was damp and had no chimneys. It was gloomy, dark and cold, and possessed almost no decent furniture. Fatima, when she had time to wonder, wondered at the hand that had brought her from Alexandria to this. Royal personages had been sick over her and had begged her to save their lives. She had seen storms at sea where men had been killed and a child had died. She had heard the King, as he abandoned his people, as the fleet prepared to sail, talk of how the strong north wind would bring in the woodcock, and of the sport that they would have in Sicily. She had been washed up, with the hero of Aboukir, a British ambassador and a woman famous throughout much of the world for her beauty and exuberance, on a cold dark island in the middle of winter. They were all ill, and Emma spent much of her time weeping with the Queen over everything they had lost.

News reached Sir William that the *Colossus* had been wrecked off the Scilly Isles, and the only part of the cargo to be salvaged was a coffin bearing the pickled corpse of an English admiral, taken on board at Lisbon. His pictures, and two thousand ancient vases, every one of them catalogued and carefully wrapped, were at the bottom of the sea.

2

In Naples, all hell was let loose. The *lazzaroni* took over the castles, sacked the palaces, let prisoners out of the gaols, and murdered anyone they suspected of rebel leanings. When the French arrived, they fought them bitterly, losing four thousand of their own men before the city fell.

The French declared a republic. They appointed a government of lawyers, poets, speakers and professors. A tree of liberty was raised, and street names were changed. Then they moved north, leaving behind a garrison of five hundred men and the remaining Neapolitan sympathisers in the castles by the waterfront. In their wake, an army of irregulars, bandits and convicts, led by Cardinal Fabrizio Ruffo, moved into the city from the south and east, and gave themselves up to slaughter and pillage. Ruffo had been given powers of life and death by the King and orders to put down the rebels, to execute summary, military and exemplary punishment. In fact, his troops made up a holy mob that he could not begin to control. They joined forces with the *lazzaroni* and dragged out anyone suspected, even by their clothes, of Jacobin sympathies, and shot them. Men were roasted in the streets, and ears and fingers taken for trophies.

Nelson, with Sir William and Emma, sailed back into the Bay of Naples on board the *Foudroyant* on 24 June. This time it was Nelson who had been given powers of life and death by the King. Their Sicilian Majesties remained in Palermo, two or three days away by letter. Fatima went with her mistress, and was given a small cabin on the poop deck. The air in there was close, and the boards creaked like shots in the heat, making her jump. The *Foudroyant* was a third-rate of eighty guns, launched in Plymouth the year before. Nelson's great cabin had been furnished with bits and pieces from various ships captured at St Vincent and the Nile – four muskets, a flagstaff, a tricolour wooden plume. Standing upright behind his double easy chair was a coffin made for him from the main mast of *L'Orient*, so that when the time came he might be buried in one of his own trophies.

'I heard it, when that ship got blown up,' said Fatima.

The men were on deck, and Emma was using Nelson's desk. She looked up, first at Fatima, then at the coffin. 'I wish he'd keep it somewhere else,' she said. 'I don't like it there.'

'Milord has black looks on his face, these days.'

'He's ready to batter down the whole town, Fatima. It's going to take some work to cool him off. His hatred of republicans is savage. On the other hand, they have to be dealt with.' She put down her pen, and fanned the air with a hand. 'I wish to God it wasn't so hot in here. Can you see if there's anything cold to drink?'

There had been a treaty, signed by Cardinal Ruffo and by Captain Foote of the Royal Navy, allowing the evacuation of the city by the remaining French garrison and their sympathisers. Enough was enough. They were to be allowed to embark on ships in the bay with all their effects and the honours of war, and to return to their homes in the city or to sail for France. Nelson annulled the treaty and then, two days later, stated that he stood by it. The rebels came out of their strongholds but, instead of being allowed to leave, they were taken prisoner on their own boats, then hanged in the city by the mob.

Week after week, the executions went on – the cream of the city's intellectual and artistic life strung up in the market square by the *lazzaroni*. From the bay windows of the great cabin they could see, at night, the lights of the town and the flames of riot. They could smell the stink of the smoke. The traitor Caracciolo, commander of the Neapolitan fleet, was hanged like a common seaman from the yardarm of his own ship.

What Fatima heard, she heard in pieces, with her own ears in the great cabin, or from Lady Hamilton or from sailors. She knew that the rebels had been deceived, but she did not know by whom. Lord Nelson was acting on behalf of the King, yet he was full of his own impetuosity and retribution. She saw hatred on his pale face every day, along with the signs of fever and exhaustion. Hatred of the French, hatred of rebels. It was he who had ordered, after summary trial on board the *Foudroyant*, the execution of Caracciolo. He had allowed the rebels out of the castles to embark, but instead of letting them sail, he made them prisoners. Had he told them they would not be able to sail? Did they know that they were walking out of the forts to death or imprisonment? No, they did not. The King wanted vengeance: he had made it clear that the opposition in Naples must be eliminated. But this? She heard from one of the midshipmen that the republicans who remained imprisoned were sweltering on the boats, without proper food or shelter. Young women whose families had been murdered were raped and left to weep on the decks. The midshipman was weeping himself; he wanted to kiss her, and she let him.

By day, there were letters and petitions from Emma's friends in Naples, begging for the lives of brothers, sons and cousins. Men she had known for many years were thrown into prison or killed. She made lists, sent reports to the Queen in Palermo, and acted as her deputy, her mouthpiece. Nelson spoke no French or Italian, and she became his interpreter in the negotiations. She moved about the ship, in the shadows cast by the sun, or in the evening lamplight, full of her own importance. She made her lists as if she had forgotten that she had known the people on them, and rejoiced in feeding their names to the Queen, whom she served, she said, with her heart and her soul and, if necessary, with her blood. What had she become, this woman of such great beauty? On shore, men were dying, unarmed men and women, hung from a rope in the Piazza Mercato, their bodies cut up and dragged through the streets, and she, Emma Hamilton, had a look of serenity on her face. When the gun announcing the execution of Caracciolo was heard, she had risen with a glass in her hand and thanked God for the death of a traitor.

Fatima had seen him, only hours before, as he was transferred from the *Foudroyant* to an Italian frigate. With a long beard, pale and half dead, he had knelt on the deck and said: 'I am condemned unjustly.' He had changed sides, he was a traitor, but to Fatima's mind, and to the minds of half the crew, it was true: he had been condemned without proper trial, and unjustly put to death. She began to feel that she had come to live with monsters. In the evenings, Emma played the harp. They dined on pork rissoles, quail, figs and shellfish. The King had sailed in the second week of July to join them, and had set up court on board the *Foudroyant*.

He held levees on the quarterdeck, and shot at seagulls from the stern.

It was less than a year since Fatima had left Alexandria. She had heard the guns of Aboukir; she had seen the wrecked and wounded ships. What she heard now, every day, were reports of massacre. She carried letters to waiting boats, and felt their weight in her hands. She watched as Lord Nelson walked the deck, and was sure in her own mind that the piece of shrapnel at Aboukir had done something to his head. She had been shown, in the last twelve months, the image of a different world. Not a new world, perhaps, but new to her. The marble floors of palaces, the balls and music and wine. Keys to boxes of jewels or papers, laughter that travelled the length of curving stairways. Men in government, women in silk. Now this. A ship baking in a still bay, and men from another country directing the fate of a small kingdom. Her mistress deciding who should live and who should die.

3

After six weeks in the bay, the *Foudroyant* sailed back into Palermo. Naples had been restored to the monarchy, though the executions continued and it was still not safe for the King to set foot in the city. They were greeted with three days of festivities and showered with presents. Nelson was given the dukedom of Brontë and the King's own sword, with a jewelled hilt. Sir William got a thumping yellow diamond, and Emma received two coachloads of dresses and a miniature of the Queen set in diamonds.

'Look,' she said to Fatima. 'Isn't it beautiful?'

The Queen had an ugly face, but the diamonds were very fine. 'Beautiful, milady,' she said.

Winter came, and spring. Sir William wasn't well, and frequently had to go back to bed. Nelson didn't like sitting around in Palermo, and the Italians depressed him. His commander-in-chief, Lord Keith, had gone off to chase the French and Spanish fleets into the Atlantic, and Nelson had been left with all the paperwork. The King went from one country house to another and shot large numbers of small birds. He refused to go back to Naples and form a proper government, mostly because he was frightened to. Emma grew fatter, and more fond of gambling; while Nelson sat half asleep by her side, she helped herself without counting from the large piles of gold on the table in front of him, playing with up to five hundred pounds of his money in one night. News reached them that in February Charles James Fox had stood up in the Commons and said that the city of Naples had been stained by murders so ferocious and cruelties so abhorrent that the heart shuddered to hear of them, and that, if the rumours were true, England was not free from blame.

Lord Keith, on his return to Italy, told Nelson that he wanted to leave him in charge of the blockade of Malta. It was an order, but Nelson begged off. He was too ill, he said, and wanted to be with his friends.

They needed a holiday. He made off with his own ship, and by the middle of April they were cruising – Nelson, the Hamiltons, Mrs Cadogan and Fatima – from Palermo to Syracuse, and from Syracuse to Malta, where they moored off the main port, Valetta.

There was a small French garrison in Valetta, left behind by Napoleon on his way to Egypt. It was besieged by the Maltese, and tightly blockaded by a squadron of British ships in the bay. The *Foudroyant* anchored at night, in view of the lights of the town but out of range of the guns. In the early hours the wind changed, the ship dragged its anchor, and at dawn they found themselves within range of the French batteries and under heavy fire.

Nelson flew up on deck. He had pulled on his coat in a hurry, and his right sleeve swung free. He was in a towering

65

rage, and he yelled orders in every direction while shot sang over his head, or landed with great splashes in the sea off their hull. In the middle of it all, Emma Hamilton stood on the quarterdeck, looking out over the open rail.

Nelson swung round on his heel. 'Lady Hamilton!' he roared. 'What in God's name are you doing? Go below. Fatima, make her go down.'

Fatima had come up to do exactly that, and was getting nowhere. She was terrified. The air was full of the sound of guns, and of the slap of sails being set. Men ran up and down the deck, and climbed the ratlines to the yards, where they cast off the ties and hauled. Everything up, and in a hurry. The rattle of the anchor chain, the blue half-light of dawn.

'Look!' cried Emma. 'Another one, and another . . . If you count from the flash—'

'This isn't a thunderstorm. Go down, now.' The *Foudroyant* had started to beat to windward, but they were still sitting ducks. 'I don't want to tell you again. We're under fire from the French. These are bombshells.'

'I want to see! I saved this island from starvation. I sent corn from Palermo when they had no food.'

'You'll see it when we're not being shot at. Do as I say.'

A group of shells, directly in their path, sent up four high plumes of water. Above the battery on the shore, four more puffs of smoke rose into the sky and drifted inland over the town. Nelson took her arm and made her look at him. 'You're in the way. You'll get your head blown off.'

'Don't shout at me.'

'I will shout at you. I am captain of this ship.'

She gave him a smile full of solemn tenderness. In the middle of all that chaos, a solemn, tender smile. 'Yes,' she said. 'And look at you.' She took the empty cuff of his sleeve and fastened it to a tunic button. Fatima watched the light and steady touch of her hands, and she knew that in any other place Nelson would have trapped her fingers in his own and lifted them to his lips. She had watched this as it began and grew, in the airy rooms of the Palazzo Sessa, through the weeks of nursing after Aboukir, through the months of war, the heat and the strain of the Bay of Naples. Through the bleak and chilly winter in Palermo. She had watched it and waited, and here it was, the smile, the hesitation of a longing touch. A shell flew over their heads, and slammed through one of the sails. 'Now!' he barked. 'Go! Fatima, go. Take her with you.'

Mrs Cadogan appeared, then, at the top of a companion-way. She had pulled a robe on over her bed gown, and a white cap over her head. 'Emma,' she said.

Emma turned. 'Ma, look—'

'I know, I can see. I can hear it, too. Come with me, please.'

She started to object, but Mary Cadogan fixed her with small, implacable eyes. Emma cast another look out over the rail towards the batteries, then, followed by Fatima, she allowed herself to be shepherded back down the companion-way. On each side of the ship, fish lay exploded and belly-up on the surface of the water.

An hour later they were sailing south along the coast, with a shattered topmast and punctured sails. They anchored in the small bay of St Paul where, for another week, repairs were made and dinner parties were held on shore and at sea. There were no guns on this side of the island, no French, no war, only days of ease and nights of pleasure. They took a house outside the town, and the Hamiltons rode out over the scrubby, flat-topped hills, looking from high sea cliffs over terraced slopes and the sea. Nelson didn't ride: he didn't trust horses. He said that he felt old, that his heart knocked against his ribs as if it had messages for him; his head was splitting from the wound at the Nile, and his eyes, even the good one, were filmy. Mrs Cadogan kept Sir William company as he read his books on a vine-shaded terrace, or took himself off for walks. In the evenings they played cards and sang and drank champagne. They strolled under skies of shooting stars and listened to cicadas in the trees.

'I sent them corn, Fatima, when they had no food.'

They were on the balcony of Emma's room, looking down at a small group of men with walnut faces who were mending the road below the house. A year ago, the people of the island had been dying fast, and no one would send them food, though there had been plenty of corn in Sicily. Letter after letter had come to the King, begging for supplies, but the King did not care if they starved. Then, in December, several merchant ships had arrived in Palermo, full of grain, and Emma had sent money from her own pocket so that they might be diverted to Malta. Thirty thousand people had been saved, and there below them was living evidence of her work. Short but sturdy, breaking stones. Fatima pulled in her bottom lip. How could it be the same woman, the one who had sent money to save strangers who were starving, and the one who had sent her own friends to die?

'I have brought him to life, Fatima.'

'Yes, milady.' Who? Nelson.

'He has sailed all over the world, but he has never known that such a place existed as the one that I have shown him.'

Malta? No: love.

Then, as May drew to a close, they rejoined the ship and set sail again for Palermo. There, a letter was waiting for Nelson from the First Lord of the Admiralty, telling him that it might be a good idea to come home. He would be more likely to recover his health and strength in England than remaining inactive at a foreign court, however much everyone there might love him for what he had done. Sir William, too, was recalled. From the newspapers, he learned that his replacement had already left England.

4

By the middle of June, they were on their way home. Lord Keith had told them they could travel in a small frigate or a

68

troopship. Napoleon had just won the battle of Marengo, and it looked again as if he might soon conquer all of Italy. Keith wanted the *Foudroyant*. He needed all his ships. He put his foot down. They could take it to Leghorn, but after that they were on their own. If they did not want the frigate or the troopship, they would have to make their way overland across Europe.

The Queen of Naples, who was by this time on bad terms with her husband, had decided to go to stay with her daughter, the Empress, in Vienna. Nelson had brought her on board for the first leg of the journey. The *Foudroyant*, as a result, was crammed once more with royal servants, trunks of clothes and jewels, crates of plate, the crown prince and three princesses. The royals were, at that moment, braced against the beds in their cabin, crying out that they were finished, as the ship pitched and rolled.

'Always bad weather for them,' said Fatima.

'I ought to go to her,' said Emma. 'She'll wonder where I am.'

'I can go. You lie still.' Her mistress, for the first time in her life, was seasick.

'I don't know what's wrong with me.'

'No, milady.'

'You might see if you can find Sir William. Make sure he doesn't shoot himself.' During the last storm, Sir William had been found in his cabin with two loaded pistols, determined not to die with salt water in his lungs.

At Leghorn, the Queen set off for Vienna by way of Florence and Ancona, struggling across Italy with fourteen carriages and three baggage wagons. Nelson and the Hamiltons went with her. It was boiling hot, but they kept the carriage windows shut tight on account of the dust. More than once, their road passed within a mile or two of enemy outposts. When at last they reached Ancona, they had to wait for three weeks until a passage could be arranged across the Adriatic to Trieste.

They drove through Laibach, and through the mountain passes to Klagenfurt and Graz. By the time they reached Vienna, they were all worn out. Here, though, was another new world. Nelson was cheered in the streets, and women brought their children to touch the hero of the Nile. His health was drunk with trumpets and the firing of cannon. They went to the theatre, to banquets and receptions, to breakfast in the garden of the Augarten Palace. There was fishing and shooting, fireworks and concerts. Nelson was received by the Emperor, and loudly cheered as he drove in an open carriage down the Prater. At night, Fatima lay under quilts in turret rooms, and remembered the feel of her bare feet on dusty streets, the sound of the muezzin, the bleating of goats in narrow alleys.

From Vienna to Prague, from Prague to Dresden, Dessau, Magdeburg. Their progress was a spectacle. At every meal, Emma sat next to Nelson and cut his food for him. People came to watch her do it; the doors of the dining room in Magdeburg had to be opened so that they could, and the landlord charged a fee to look in. To Fatima, it seemed as if they were all on stage, a company of travelling players whom everyone had paid a price to watch.

During the final weeks, they caught up with the English newspapers. 'There is a terrible scene to be unfolded,' said the *Morning Chronicle*, 'of what has passed in Naples these last twelve months. The British name has suffered a reproach.'

On his return to London, Sir William learned that his precious vases had not been lost after all. A few had been sent on the *Colossus*, and had gone down with it off the Scilly Isles, but many of the best ones had been put on board another ship by mistake, and had made their way to England safe and sound.

FIVE

The rain came in the night. Berthe went to the village for bread and fish wearing wooden sabots and a cloak. Beyond the windows, the day became invisible. Emma and Horatia worked in the sitting room. There was a fire, but the logs were unseasoned, and smoked. For an hour, they looked at Spanish words and phrases, then turned again to Roman history.

'Titus Vinius,' said Emma.

'We did this yesterday.'

Emma raised her head to look at her. Horatia's eyes, in the shadow cast by the dark day, looked like elliptical coins. She had grown during the summer, and her shape was changing.

'You don't remember,' said Horatia.

'I do. We did this yesterday.' Doubt and evasion swam in Emma's face. 'We didn't get very far, though, did we?'

Horatia was surprised, though only briefly. It was a guess, but not a bad one. Something inside her collected, waited, and wore itself out. 'No,' she said.

'You find where we left off, then. Start again from there.'

A sudden squall sent the rain against the windows, as if it had been thrown from a shovel. 'How old was I when we went to Margate?'

'Darling, concentrate. Titus Vinius. Read.'

'I will in a minute, but how old was I?'

Emma rubbed the back of her wrist. 'You were a baby. You were two years old, not even that. Mrs Gibson took you down, and I came to see you, with your father, while we were staying at Ramsgate.'

Janot wandered into the room, looked at Emma and Horatia in turn and, when they took no notice of him, dropped in front of the fire. He had been out and was still wet. Fatima came in after him with a towel.

'I remember Margate,' said Horatia.

'I don't think you do.'

'I remember I nearly drowned.'

'You did not nearly drown! Don't be ridiculous. I was there – I wouldn't have let you.' She lifted her head and stretched her neck. 'Fatima was there. She can tell you.'

'We nearly lost you,' said Fatima. 'I remember that.' She shook the towel into the fire, and left the room.

Emma's face struggled as she found herself, briefly, in the streets of Margate, nearly flattened by helpless stupidity. She saw her husband, too, sitting in an upstairs room six miles along the coast, sick to death of everything and telling her not to spend so much money. 'Let's talk about something else,' she said. 'Titus Vinius, what happened to him?'

'Dead,' said Horatia, pensively.

Emma found this terribly funny, and hooted. The sound sent the dark air scattering, and Janot opened his eyes, like small church doors. 'I know what we'll do!' she shouted. 'We'll do some Attitudes. We haven't done any for ages. Agrippina! That's how to learn Roman history.'

In Naples, performances of Emma's famous Attitudes – where she had represented, in the manner of *tableaux vivants* or in mime, statues or paintings from antiquity – had crowded the rooms of the embassy. With a few shawls, a chair and some vases, she could present a range of characters – playful, alluring, threatening, anxious – matching the fold of a veil to each successive mood. Hebe, Juno, the Bacchantes. They had gone down well in London, too.

'You can be the Romans. I shall come before you, with the

ashes of Germanicus, my husband, in an urn.' Emma stood and lifted an arm, a supporting hand. 'I've come to move your passions on behalf of your favourite general and to excite you to revenge.'

'All the Roman people?'

'A large crowd, anyway. You can do different faces. Sad and angry, mostly. We're going to have to find a golden urn. And a coronet, and a veil. And then, at the end, you can be my daughter. You can bid me farewell as I leave for exile on the island of Pandateria where I will die of starvation on the orders of Tiberius.'

'We got dinner at two, on the orders of Berthe,' said Fatima, entering the room again. 'Cod.'

'Fatima, we need a golden urn.'

'Yes, milady.'

'And a coronet,' said Horatia.

Fatima looked at the girl and smiled. 'You going to supplicate them gods again?' she said.

'And you and Berthe,' said Emma, 'are going to watch. We've got to put on our thinking caps.'

Fatima screwed up her face.

'It's an expression, woman. Horatia needs a robe and a girdle. And something round her head.'

In the kitchen, Berthe was preparing the fish. Heads of cod lay on the chopping board, slit open, cleaned and scoured with salt. Strings of blood lay on the board beside them, and a dull glitter of scales.

'Berthe, I need a vase.'

'Yes, miss.' She wiped her hands down the front of her apron, and Horatia felt a sudden rush of tenderness for her. As far as she knew, Berthe hadn't been paid in weeks. She was good at her work, though everyone in the village liked to pretend she wasn't. She smiled at Horatia, and led her through to the larder. There was a sense of alteration in the house, of laughter and something almost reckless. Horatia's feelings sat

73

in thin layers of possibility in her chest and, beneath them, a rubble of dread.

Berthe opened a cupboard. Half a dozen vases stood on shelves, perfect for flowers and useless for ashes. 'No,' said Horatia. She made a shape with her hands. 'Like that,' she said.

Berthe took her back into the kitchen, knelt in front of a low cupboard, and brought out a small but heavy casserole.

Fatima's feet went up and down the stairs. Bedcovers, shawls, drapes and belts. The sitting room became, piece by piece, a stage.

Emma smiled at the dish, then frowned. 'Horatia, these are the ashes of a great military commander, not a *cassoulet*. And it's frightfully heavy. Where did you get it? Let me go and have a look.'

From the kitchen, Horatia heard the banging of pots and pans, and the *thop* of the cork coming out of a bottle. She heard the wine being poured into a glass, and her skin became, once more, tender with anxiety.

'I'm going upstairs,' said Emma, coming back into the room with a lidded storage jar. 'Look. Perfect.' She put the jar down on a table. 'I'm going to change. You'll do as you are, I think, you don't need to take that off. Put a sheet round you, and buckle it here.' She put a hand on Horatia's waist. 'Try to make it drape a bit – look at you! You've got no waist.' She raised her arm, and made a fat but graceful fist in the air. 'I did Agrippina at Fonthill, once. When we went there for Christmas. William Beckford had just finished building it, the abbey. Fatima remembers it.'

Fatima made a face. Beckford's house had beggared belief. Not the house, the abbey. The house itself was a grand mansion in the Italian style, but the abbey was a monster, a massive mock-ecclesiastical folly with a huge tower that you could see from miles away. Beckford himself had frightened her. He was perhaps the richest man in England, and had built

74

the abbey, in the depths of his beautiful estate of wooded hills and lakes, for the purpose of entertainments that were lavish almost to the point of madness. She had seen many things in Italy, but even the King and Queen of Naples and Sicily could not match William Beckford for extravagance. 'It was something to see,' she said.

'And people wept, you know,' said Emma, 'as I left the shores of my home for the island where I was to die. They really did.' She lowered her arm again, and prodded Horatia's shoulder. 'You,' she said, 'weren't even born. It was that long ago. Ancient history.' As she crossed the room towards the door she paused. 'Actually, you were born. You were very tiny, though.'

Horatia heard her go back into the kitchen, and then, slowly, up the stairs. The room, now hung with old covers and curtains, made her think of the mole-catcher, dusty and held together with string. There was a yelp from upstairs, and then a bang. Fatima's slippers in the passage, a press being opened and closed. Outside the rain fell harder, and a single roll of thunder trod across the plain. The room grew darker and the fire grew brighter.

She saw the abbey at Fonthill, and her father arriving with the Hamiltons at dusk. Thick woods of pine and fir, with lamps in the trees and flambeaux moving with the carriages. The volunteers played solemn music, and drums beat in the hills. In front of her, above the walls and battlements of the abbey, Nelson's flag hung from the great dark tower. Inside, curtains of purple damask, ebony tables and ivory-studded chairs. There was a Christmas fire of cedar and pine cones, and dinner was served on silver dishes. Emma and Sir William entered the hall, with Nelson and William Beckford. A staircase was lit by living figures in hooded gowns, a library by candlesticks of massive silver gilt. Spiced wine, and sweets in gold baskets. Music died away to silence, and Lady Hamilton appeared from behind scarlet curtains as Agrippina, bearing the ashes of Germanicus. She moved with classic grace and perfect ease. The lift of her hand, her chin, the movement of the urn, an arm. The seated guests were awed and silent, and tears ran down their faces.

Suddenly Horatia saw another image, and this time the memory was her own. She stood, aged three or four, in stockinged feet on a polished table. Emma held her, making sure she did not slip, while she reached up to pull the string of a wooden doll that hung on the wall. Where? Merton, it must have been. In a small room, somewhere, on one of Horatia's visits to the house. When she pulled the string, the arms and legs of the doll moved up and down. Emma had called her clever, and she had turned in her arms and pushed her face into the soft, sweet-smelling bosom. Her feet slid on the table beneath her but she didn't fall, because Emma held her.

'We need candles in here, Fatima. Ask Berthe.' Emma stood in the doorway. A veil covered the top of her head and fell to her shoulders, and her dress was a simple calico chemise, with loose sleeves and a low bodice. 'Well?'

'Very good,' said Horatia.

'You haven't done anything, you've just been sitting in the dark. Come here.'

She allowed herself to be draped like a column in white cotton cloth. Berthe brought candles, and Fatima placed Emma's glass on the table with the urn.

'I don't know,' said Emma, standing back to look about her. 'It's not right, not yet.' She surveyed the Roman people, and drank from her glass. 'Fatima, I know it's raining, but what we need is a crown of ivy. There's plenty by the back door.'

Horatia started to object, but Emma's look was suddenly proud and dangerous. Her chin stuck out like a promontory, and her eyes were fierce. 'Shoes,' she said, prodding Horatia's foot with her own.

Horatia slipped them off. 'Where was Lady Nelson?' she said.

76

'When?'

'When you went to Fonthill.'

'Oh, God. London. She wasn't asked.'

'Not asked? She was his wife. He'd just come back after three years at sea. She'd been waiting for him.'

'They knew she wouldn't like it, darling.'

'Why not?'

'She was a frosty, cold woman, Horatia, and stiff like an old tit.' It sounded as if there was something in the back of Emma's throat – spit, or hatred.

'But he married her. She can't have been so bad.'

'Oh, can't she?' Emma raised her chin, as if to address a crowd. 'Her soul was black and she made your father's life intolerable. She never loved him for himself and when he came home maimed and scarred and covered with glory, she stuck up her nose at his wounds and made a scene because he had found a more lovely and more virtuous woman who had served with him in a foreign country and who had her heart and senses open to his greatness. Me!'

'You?'

'I was his friend, Horatia. I gave him what she could not.'

They heard the back door open and close as Fatima went out into the rain.

'She must have loved him.'

'She didn't. She left him, for heaven's sake. She stood up one morning at breakfast and walked out and never came back. And she never thanked him, either, for the money that he sent her. That's not love, Horatia.'

She opened her mouth to ask another question, but Emma continued, with a wave of her hand, 'Every day there was something different wrong with her, and when your father went to sea she sat and fretted and wished that he wasn't so brave and that he'd forget his duty and come home to her. He wanted someone to love and to be loved by in return but all she ever thought about was herself.' Her hand found the glass

77

beside her, and she lifted it to her lips with elaborate care. 'She turned his whole family against him,' she said, 'but in the end she was her own worst enemy. Anyway, listen.' She shook her head and frowned. 'The light's all wrong in here. We need the candlesticks from the dining room. Where are you going?'

'Kitchen. I'm thirsty.'

The fish kettle simmered on the stove. Berthe had removed one of the heads, and was standing at the table, lifting out the bones. The jaw, the long bones and all the gills; the skull bones and the eyes. Beside her, a pile of roe lay on a plate. The back door opened, and Fatima returned, a loop of ivy on her arm. Raindrops sat in her springy hair, and her skirts were wet.

'She's . . . ' Horatia pursed her lips.

Fatima put the ivy down on the table, and made eyes at the cod's head. 'I know,' she said. 'Make a crown.'

Every day there was a point at which Emma became more precise in all her actions, and then, soon afterwards, the moment when she became incapable of careful movement. Horatia counted the bottles, and what she felt as she counted was fear. Fear because she could see that this would never get any better, because it was pulling everything apart. A bottle in the morning, a bottle in the afternoon. One in the morning, two in the evening. She felt that she was measuring time, and that she was measuring it in bottles of *vin de pays*. With each one that went away empty, another small bit of Emma Hamilton vanished as well. 'I feel stupid,' she said, lifting the circle of leaves.

'Do it, and then we can have dinner. She'll have a sleep after that.'

Emma took over everything. Whatever they did, whether it was her idea or someone else's, she took it over and commanded every stage. She put herself in the centre, and moved the others around her with all the weight of someone getting steadily more drunk.

In the sitting room, however, she looked suddenly stranded. She was sitting on the covered sofa, her face fallen and searching. There was something mute and confused in her eyes. Pity climbed Horatia's ribs, and made its way down again, meeting rising anger. Water slid from the ivy crown on her head, and the jar on the table, though a simple household object, seemed to have got there by an act of madness.

Emma looked up. 'You see?' she said. 'I was right! Very Roman. You look lovely, darling. Now, let me see you angry. Germanicus has died in Antioch. Murdered by Tiberius, poisoned at his own table. The people of Rome come out into the streets to see his ashes being carried . . .'

Horatia screwed up her nose. She could see them, herself and Emma, through the eyes of a stranger entering the room. Two mad women, dressed as Romans in tablecloths, in a room draped like a catastrophe. Her limbs felt like twigs as she tried to express something more in dramatic gesture than an ordinary but growing dismay. The smell of stewed fish and garlic drifted from the kitchen.

'You look as if something's bitten you. Watch me.' Emma stood. Her anger, her vengeance, her grief, were swift and accurate. With a lift of her head, the turn of a palm, the lowering of her eyes, she moved between them with facility and grace. In spite of the drink, in spite of her massive size. 'Now you,' she said, sitting down.

'I can't do it like you.'

'You can if you try. You used to like doing this.' Suddenly her face was grim. 'Don't go and spoil things,' she said.

'Me? I'm not.'

'Just try, make an effort. It's not that difficult.'

Horatia stared into the fire and watched a thin, anxious pillar of smoke escape from the crack in a log. She felt removed, as if the two or three glasses of wine that Emma had already drunk had placed them in separate worlds. Her stomach rose, and she put a hand to her mouth.

'I don't know,' said Emma. 'Sometimes I think you're really an old woman. Try.'

79

'I feel sick.'

'Try!' Her face was hard now. 'My God, Horatia, I'm not having this again, not today. You're going to make an effort. Come on, stand up.'

The room stood waiting, its walls leaning inwards.

'Stand *up*!' Her voice was like a raised fist.

There were swift hot tears in Horatia's eyes, tears of something more elaborate than hurt. On another day, a day that was not half wrecked already by drink, she would have stood in her bare feet and raised her fists to the gods. She would have done it and enjoyed it and earned herself words of praise.

'I'm waiting.'

Slowly, she got to her feet.

'Now. Angry. The Roman people. Anger and grief.'

'I can't!'

Emma rose from her chair, and fell back into it, as if someone invisible to them all had whacked her over the head. There was the sound of a small crack deep underneath the cushions. Her eyes closed, then opened again, widened and fixed.

'Milady?' Fatima was beside her.

Emma waved her hands in front of her face, and breathed in slowly through her nose with a whistling sound. She pushed herself out of the chair and lunged forward on her feet. She trod on her robe and stumbled, her hands looking for a solid place in the air. The table went over, and her almost empty glass, and the ashes of Germanicus. The glass hit the carpet, then, with a thin hairline sound, cracked against a wooden sofa leg. The volume of Tacitus fell too, and opened itself on the floor. Emma shouted with shock, then laughed. It was a high, preposterous sound that rang with fury. 'Oh, don't look at me like that,' she said to Horatia. 'Nothing's broken.'

She was swaying, her great bulk making everything else in the room seem delicate. Horatia shut her jaw against a wave of shame. Like the Roman people, grief and accusation. 'If you're not well, you should go to bed,' she said, sitting down again.

'A table went over, that's all. You're the one who's looking green. We'll eat,' Emma commanded suddenly. 'What you need is food. We'll eat, and then we'll do this afterwards.'

She staggered out, her hands in front of her as if she were pushing a chair from one room to the other. Fatima followed. Horatia, sitting like a block of wood, heard them go into the dining room. Without knowing that she was doing it, she picked up the book and began to pull its bent corners straight. She heard Fatima take out the pot from under the sideboard and then, after much grunting, the sound of Emma pissing into it.

In the kitchen, Berthe was roasting the boned fish – dredged with breadcrumbs and stuffed with roe – over the fire. She had made a sauce with the fish water, and beans were simmering on the stove. 'Five minutes?' she said, when Horatia put her head round the door.

'Thank you, Berthe.'

When the meal arrived, Emma talked as she ate. Food stuck to her teeth, or flew from her mouth when she spoke, and what she did not eat she pushed around on her plate until it was pulp.

2

Her mind is never still. It pulls her this way then that, so she can start with something ordinary – the design on a plate, the sound of bells – and in two or three or seven stages find herself imagining an argument in a street in London, or being led onto the Thames to skate. She can smell the cold and hear the cut of the ice. She can feel the brief glow, as she sails past, of a brazier, and see the circles she has made. She holds discussions with men whose faces she cannot see, and explains to them her circumstances, and how she has come here and who is to blame. Time is slow, and levelled by boredom. She can only believe that it will pass, and in passing take her from one point to another, from this place to another one; in the meantime she must sit and endure. She must wait: for a letter, a man on a horse. For something to lift them out and take them away, give them peace or another chance. There is, strangely, something tedious even in her fears. Her shoulders are hitched to the sides of her neck by the constant strain of being alert, of listening. Glass, bottle, cork. In her head, she yells at Emma and begs her not to drink. She pleads, she uses tears and reason. She hits her on the face and head until she promises not to do it any more. She removes every bottle from the house and breaks them in the stream. She extracts promises from the wine merchant, from every supplier of wine and spirits in France. She sits on her own in a room and shakes with fear at the things that go through her mind and will never be said or done.

She fits her knuckles against her eyes and presses as she says her prayers. In his hands are all the corners of the earth, and the strength of the hills is his also. The sea is his, and he made it, and his hands prepared the dry land. Out of the dark come moving colours – reticulated browns, sharp bursts of red, spilled lines of dun and black. Distant spots of growing light, and suns that spread and shrink like fists. Inside them is the cavern of her skull, a room behind her eyes, and she thinks, Is this the place where my spirit lives? A room within her, dark and light. The thought of her spirit makes her think of Janot, and Janot makes her think of a dream in which they are walking together down a hill, a troupe of children coming towards them the other way, carrying sticks and Chinese lanterns. And she thinks about how in China they bind the feet of young girls with bandages, so that they will never grow. How the feet of the women are no bigger than the feet of children, and they walk with small steps, like children's steps. This is what makes men fall in love with them, their tiny feet. And she thinks of love, and of her father, and once again she prays, though now her prayers turn to tears, and she weeps for love. She weeps for the mother she has never known, whoever she is, and whatever became of her. All Horatia has been told is that she is dead. She tries, as she has tried over and over again in her short life, to imagine what she looked like – her hands, her face, her hair and her clothes, and how she died.

She can hardly remember being told, but she was, many times. By Emma or Mrs Cadogan or Jane Gibson. Your mother is dead. She came to London, she had you in October, and by December she was dead. Your father as well. He was at sea, and then he perished. Very young, what a shame, never mind – we're here. Lord Nelson is your godfather, and Lady Hamilton is your godmother; they will always make sure that you are looked after and cared for and loved. Now, off to bed and no more questions. She remembers that: no more questions.

When she was five years old, she learned that it was not all true. Her father had not been a poor seaman in Nelson's command, but Lord Nelson himself. She learned it when Nelson had died – too late. From the time that she was old enough to understand at all to the time of his death she had been told a lie. Because he was a great man, and to preserve his reputation while he lived. Because she, his daughter, would have brought shame on him and his family for being born to a woman who was not his wife – though it was also true that she had never been made to feel the burden of that shame. But who was she, this woman? If they had lied to her about her father, had they lied, too, about her mother? Was she alive somewhere still, in a far and foreign place?

She remembers things she would rather forget; that she has tried, over and over, to bury. Mrs Cadogan's voice, raised for once in anger: Really, Emma, anyone would think that the child was your own daughter. And Emma: Perhaps she is my daughter! It is a memory, but it is preposterous. These voices fill her head, and strut around in it like crows, all fear and sharp edges. She remembers, in spite of herself, the days when she was little and wished that her beautiful godmother was really her mother. Her soft cheek, and the lovely ring of her laughter on the lawn. The wild excitement every time Mrs Gibson told her that Lady Hamilton was coming to Little Titchfield Street, or that they were going to Merton to see her. The bright, loud songs, the stories under a shady tree; Emma's bedroom, and her jewellery case. Being held by her as they walked through the tunnel under the road on their way to look at the cows. Or Emma, standing on the promenade at Worthing, a ribbon at her breast and a gold chain round her neck.

Beautiful Lady Hamilton. Now Horatia knows it is unthinkable that Emma is her mother. She presses her hands, again, to her face. Never, never, never. Emma Hamilton is not that person any more, and never could be her mother. This woman, this ugly, shouting, selfish person, whose words are stuck to the sides of her mouth, who has brought them here, to this, and cannot take them back again? No, never. It's impossible. She thinks of Emma's great big belly, the folds of fat beneath her clothes, and she tells herself, No, that is not where I came from. There is nothing in their build, in the colour of their hair, their eyes, nothing in their characters to link Emma Hamilton and Horatia by blood. They are opposite in everything, connected only by the man who was friend to one and father to the other. It is inconceivable, too, because of who Nelson was: her father would never have practised such a long deception on Sir William, the friend whose roof he had lived under, and who had lived, at Merton, under his. No honourable man could do it, and it was Emma herself who spoke, every other time she mentioned him, of Nelson's honour; it was she, time and again, who insisted on the purity of her own friendship with him.

Not Emma Hamilton. But who?

SIX

I

In September 1801, ten months after her return to England, Emma bought a house for Nelson. It was called Merton Place, and it was seven miles from London, in Surrey. Nelson himself was off the coast at Deal, depressed and cold and seasick. In August, he had launched a disastrous attack on Boulogne. The strike had depended for its success on the element of surprise – the cover of dark, in silence, with muffled oars, boarding the French ships with cutlasses, pikes and tomahawks – but the enemy had been waiting. Only a fortnight before, Nelson had sent his bomb-ketches in to throw a few shells at the ships moored in the harbour, and the French were on their guard for a second attack. Not one of their ships was taken or burned. It was a catastrophic failure, and Nelson's boats had limped back to Deal. Forty-four of his men had been killed, and a hundred and thirty wounded.

Now, at least, he had somewhere to come home to. The surveyor pointed out that the house was badly built and that a dirty black canal ran through the grounds and kept the whole place damp, but Emma bought it anyway, with nine thousand pounds of Nelson's money. She did up the interior with glass doors and wall mirrors, so that the house was light but also confusing. There were portraits of Nelson everywhere, a bust in the hall, and pictures of his battles, models of ships, flags and honours. Maps in frames, and plans and charts. Coats of arms and pieces of plate and the flagstaff of *L'Orient*. In the mornings there was a mist sometimes, cold and grey and low, and when Fatima looked out of the long glass doors, she knew that she had come to a strange and distant place. There were verandas outside the parlours on the east side, and lawns and statues, and a wide stream and a small lake. Gravel paths, flower beds, ornamental trees. From a mound near the shrubbery you could sit and look out over unbroken countryside towards Wimbledon Hill and Wandsworth. On the other side of the road were the stables and the cows.

Since Boulogne, Nelson had been kept in the Channel by the Admiralty, but in October an armistice was signed between Britain and France, and he was released from active service. He came in the night, at the end of the month, on his own and through the leaves; when his coachman asked him the way to the house, he couldn't tell him because he didn't know. Emma jumped out of bed when she heard that he had arrived, and ran downstairs with almost nothing on.

He was pleased with everything, but exhausted. His niece, Charlotte, had been fetched for the weekend from her boarding-school in Chelsea to welcome him, and on the night of his arrival fireworks were let off over the lake. On Sunday morning Charlotte helped him to put on his overcoat before the morning service, and turned the pages of his prayer book. For as long as he could remember, Nelson had wanted a quiet family life to come home to and now, apparently, he had one. He and Sir William fished in the stream, which they called the Nile, and talked about new statues for the garden. 'I'll leave it to you,' said Nelson. 'You're the expert.' The rain came down in sheets across the low hills, and the fish rose in the lake when they thought that the raindrops were something to eat.

Charlotte's father was Nelson's older brother, the Reverend William. He had just been made a doctor of divinity at Cambridge, and wished always to be addressed as such, to the point of being downright pedantic.

'His head's the size of a melon,' said Nelson. 'What does he want to be a doctor for?' They were in the drawing room.

Fatima was standing next to Emma's chair, helping her to sort out a box of ornaments that had not yet been unpacked.

'Have you written to congratulate him?' said Emma.

'No, but I will. The fat'll be in the fire if I don't.'

Emma was William's staunch ally. He was a vain, loud and selfish man, but he was on her side, and she was on his. He had told her, more than once, that her image and her voice were always there before him, and that it was no wonder that his good, great, virtuous and beloved brother was so attached to her after such a long friendship. His wife, Sarah, also stood firmly in her camp, and in the letters that passed between the two of them, Fanny Nelson was traduced as a false, proud, bad woman, whose cold heart made everyone wretched and whose own wickedness would be her punishment. 'He ought to be in Lambeth Palace,' she said.

Nelson's face broke with laughter. The sound was strange, at least to Fatima, who thought, when she heard it, of a night animal, wounded or startled. 'With you behind him, he probably will be, one day. Can you imagine? I wonder if he'll put on weight. All they ever do is eat and drink, those bigwigs. Eat, eat, eat. Anyway, I hope this stops him badgering me for a while. I love him, but he's a nuisance.'

'And write to your father, will you? I want to know when he's coming.'

'Next month.'

'I know, but when?' She scratched the side of her arm. Edmund Nelson, a frail and elderly Norfolk parson, had been knocked sideways by Emma's relationship with his son, not least because of his own affection for Fanny. Fanny was his friend, his daughter, his nurse, and he had let them know, in his own way, that it was thanks to her he was still alive. For months he had been in an agony of indecision as to whether to come to Merton at all. Now he had made up his mind and Emma, who on the one hand had been damning the man for conspiring with Fanny against the saviour of the country, and on the other had written coaxing letters asking him to come, was dreading his arrival. She had limited experience of country clergymen but she could guess, without really trying, Edmund's views on domestic fidelity and the sacred permanence of marriage.

'Put yourself in his position,' said Nelson.

She leaned back in her chair and chewed the end of her thumb. 'Put yourself in mine. He loves Fanny, they spend half their time together, and she doesn't sit there singing my praises. She's had months to say what she wants about me and to turn him against me and make me his enemy. By now he must think I'm a monster.'

Nelson lowered his face and looked at her from under the green shade over his eyes. 'He's said he wants to come, and he's coming. He'll love you. As a matter of fact, I wish he'd come and live here. I don't know how he still has the will to go on, spending so much time with her. She's got no soul, she really hasn't. Anyway, we'll cross that bridge when we come to it.'

In the event the visit, for ten days at the end of November, was an unexpected success. Emma found the old man irritating and feeble, but he was gentle, too, and had the merit of dropping off to sleep all the time.

In March of the following year, the Treaty of Amiens was signed by Britain and France. To Nelson, the terms seemed outrageous – the enemy got everything, Britain next to nothing – and he still wished all Frenchmen to the devil. He worried all the time about what people were saying concerning his failure at Boulogne; from what he could tell – from the papers, from the gossip – he was not much liked at that moment by either officers or men.

Then his father died. Nelson wrote to his brother-in-law, George Matcham, telling him that the body should be sent from Bath to Burnham Thorpe for burial, and that he would pay the expenses. He did not go himself. He pleaded ill health, and went to Fatima's christening instead.

2

Nelson had come home determined to have Horatia established at Merton. He wanted her to be christened, too. He had wanted it done as soon as she was born, at St George's, Hanover Square, but Emma had put her foot down. There was too much at stake to risk the questions of a London clergyman. She was still against it. While Sir William lived, and while she performed, flawlessly, the part of Nelson's innocent friend in front of everyone, appearances could be maintained. For that reason, Horatia's existence had at all costs to remain unknown, at least for the time being. The way had to be prepared. For a start, Charlotte would come to stay often. Emma planned to give her polish and make her a lady, to teach her to sing and dance and flatter. To lift her chin and lower her eyes.

'I'll give her an education, a better one than Whitelands School on the King's Road, Chelsea. I'll make her into the right kind of girl for the niece of the nation's hero.' This was addressed to Fatima, as they sorted out Charlotte's clothes. When the girl could walk in and out of the room in a hoop, Emma would go with her to Court and to the other grand entertainments of the social season, to which she herself still had not been, and would not be, invited.

'This?' said Fatima, holding up a large willow hoop by the straps.

'Yes, that.'

'She's going to wear it?'

'She's going to wear it, yes. What else?'

Take it in a boat and fish for lobster with it, she thought. Or sharks, dolphins, a small whale.

'That hoop will open many doors.'

'Yes, milady.' Wide ones, she thought.

Not only that, but when the time came, the girl's presence in the house would make the introduction of Horatia all the less noticeable. If Emma could have one girl in the house, she could have two. She would tell everyone that Horatia was one of her many relations, and they would be none the wiser.

For now, whenever the coast was clear, she wrote to Mrs Gibson and told her to bring Horatia to Merton. They came in a chaise over Clapham Common; rugs were laid out on the lawn, and Mrs Cadogan made lemon cakes.

Mary Cadogan watched the child as she ran from them, and ran back again, and it seemed to her that she could hear another child's laughter, not across lawns, but over time. We do what we must, she thought. She felt in her breast the terror that comes when we cannot sidestep Fate, when it removes us from things or people that we love, however hard we pray. Whatever we do, we have to stay alive. My grandchild, she thought, though she had never said the words out loud. That the world would never know was one thing, and not a tragedy, but that Horatia would never call her Grandma was a source of great sadness to the old woman. How unwittingly children can break our hearts, she thought. But she smiled and lifted her chin and gave Horatia a big kiss because here she was. If it were not for Nelson – if it were not for the battle of the Nile, and damaged ships and illness and fatigue – then there would have been no child at all. Sir William could not give Emma one.

And Mrs Cadogan adored Admiral Lord Nelson. He was thoughtful, courageous, melancholy, fair. He was generous, and gave with an open hand to anyone who needed it. Family, friends and strangers. When former shipmates appealed to him, it was never in vain: he sent money, or tried to get them advancement. And he was always kind to Mrs Cadogan: he called her Signora Madre, and never failed to ask about her health. He had brought Emma great and unexpected happiness, and if Mary Cadogan sometimes feared the consequences, she had always approved of the relationship. Now, if only Sir William could close out his long life, and if Fanny Nelson would die of one of her interminable, dreary illnesses, then Emma and Horatio would be free to marry. The old woman caught herself thinking this, and placed a hand on her heart. She was fond of Sir William, too. How could she have wished him dead?

Nelson played with his daughter for hours, floating galleons on the stream and darting out like a lunatic from behind trees and bushes. 'I'm coming to get you,' he shouted, striding through the house and gardens, and she shrieked and ran and hid behind a tree or the piano. He said, 'I don't know, she's gone, she's disappeared,' and her laughter burst out of her. He tucked her into the crook of his arm, and told her stories long before there was any hope of her making sense of them. He watched her stagger away from him on short mad legs, making her way towards the water without a backward glance, laughing at the beauty of her own mischief. He made her yell with astonishment, even though she knew that it was coming, when he grabbed her on the bank to stop her throwing herself in. They sat, for anything up to an hour, under the dining-room table together. Then, as if the stroke of three were the stroke of midnight, she was bundled back into the chaise and whisked off to London again. Sir William, on his return from his club or from fishing on the Thames, would hear no mention of the child, not a word, nor see any sign that she or anyone else had been there. Her visits had doors – open, shut, open, shut.

3

In September 1802 Nelson, Emma and Sir William went to Ramsgate, where they had rooms that looked out over the sea on two floors of a lodging-house. Mrs Cadogan stayed at Merton. Unless she was needed in London, she spent all her time there now. Nelson had been ashore for eleven months. He had occupied himself with walking in the garden at Merton, going to London to the Admiralty – or to sit for another portrait, or to attend the House of Lords. He had fought for peace, and though he might not like the terms, he was enjoying it.

They had only just come back from a long tour of Wales where, in spite of Boulogne, Nelson had been acclaimed by crowds of thousands as the conquering hero. Never before had an Englishman so seized the imagination of his country. London had taken him to its heart, but most of Britain knew of him only from newspaper reports, prints and ballads. This all changed as they went west to Oxford, then Gloucester, Ross-on-Wye. Through Wales, and back via Worcester, Birmingham, Warwick. There were cattle shows, honours and feasts. Bands, parades, cathedral bells. Emma had burst into songs of praise whenever she got the chance – every one, it seemed, to the tune of 'Rule, Britannia' or 'God Save The King'. Tunes that nailed themselves to Sir William's brain, and made his foot swing like an idiot's whenever he sat down. Even now, Nelson was glowing with public fame and recognition, with the love of the masses. After six weeks, it was irritating. Sir William himself had been fractious throughout the trip, and a background figure in the blazing light of celebrity. Then hardly had they set foot back in Merton when Emma declared that she had to go to the sea for her health, and the packing had started all over again. Sir William had not wanted to come, and he was sorry that he had. He was feeling the passage of time and the encroachments of age. Not only that, but his wife was in a filthy mood and not prepared to explain it.

Nelson was finding her scratchy, too. 'What on earth's the matter?' he asked her. They were in a bright, under-furnished parlour on the first floor of the lodging-house.

'There's nothing the matter! I wish you'd find something else to do than ask me that all the time. Both of you.'

The truth was, they had come here at Nelson's insistence. He had decided that Emma and Horatia needed a holiday by the sea, and Emma had written to Mrs Gibson to tell her to take rooms at Margate, six miles along the coast. Nelson and Emma would take themselves off for a few hours here and there to visit them, leaving Sir William to read or walk. Now, however, Emma had lost the directions that Jane Gibson had sent back. She had an address of sorts in her head, but no idea how to get there. For obvious reasons she could not tell Sir William this, and if she told Nelson, he would think her negligent or stupid, or both. She had turned all her clothes and brushes, perfume and books out onto the bed upstairs, and left them in a dreadful mess for Fatima to clear up. She had been through her pockets, her portmanteau, her writing case. It was nowhere, and now Nelson was champing at the bit.

She ordered the carriage to take her to Margate, where she sent Fatima up and down the town, into shops and boarding-houses. Past the assembly rooms, the theatre, the pier and the parade. After an hour, she was hot and thirsty and fed up. There was no sign, anywhere, of a single woman with two small children, and no one seemed to know their way around the town. In the end, Emma sent a message, and hoped that the carrier would have better luck. He did: later that day a letter came from Mrs Gibson with clear instructions. Emma and Nelson drove over while Sir William stayed behind with a book.

Horatia wore a cotton dress, with a cap on over her curls, and they bounced her down the steps of the bathing-machine into the sea. Fatima stood on the beach with Jane Gibson, and together they looked out over the water. Where it met the sky, they could not see its distant edge. The sails of fishing-boats stood out like birds on its surface. Behind them, Mary Gibson filled her fists with sand and let it dribble onto the breeze. Mary was six now, with big hazel eyes, though the hump on her back made her look wary, as if she were trying to hide behind something too small to conceal her. Above them, gulls hung and tilted. The water moved in ripples, reaching the shore with a low *whump*, and a whisper of sand and shingle. A lace of foam stood out on its edge, and sank in white and vanishing bubbles. Laughter from the people in the water seemed to have had the breath knocked out of it.

Nelson sat on a step of the bathing-machine with his feet in the sea, while Emma held Horatia. The child hung on with small fists, her chin lifted, her laughter aimed above the bobbing water. A wave caught and doused her, and she came up spluttering with a cry that swerved from fury to joy.

'She loves the water,' said Fatima.

Mrs Gibson nodded. She could hardly trust herself to speak. Even silent, she wondered why they could not see on her face what had happened. How strange, she reflected, that you couldn't see inside someone's skull, even when it was ringing with near disaster. The day before, when they had settled themselves in their lodgings, and found that there were no instructions waiting for them, she had taken the two girls down to the beach. The journey from London had been long and uncomfortable, and the children had refused to sit still. They had been tired when they arrived, but still excited. And Jane Gibson, in a way, too. In all her life, she had never seen the sea. She had stood, as she stood now with Fatima, looking out at the bathers and the gulls and the endless water. It was like standing up to God, she had thought, here on the edge of the ocean. Her heart felt cowed and lifted, all at once. Perhaps it *was* God, the sky and the sea, the great still sweep of grey, the frill of sound at her feet. She had felt the calm and awe of a great cathedral around her, the calm and awe of a pair of arms. And while she thought these thoughts, while she considered the immensity of the sea and of God, Horatia, with almost impossible speed, had tottered past her and into the water. Somehow, in the space of a moment, she had landed, bottom down and feet up in the shallows; while Jane Gibson's body launched itself towards her, a long fat ribbon of sea lifted her an inch from the sand and broke behind her. Her bottom went out from under her, and she toppled to one side. Mrs Gibson grabbed her, lifted her on to her hip and struggled back up the beach, sopping wet, her terror swerving inside her. She had closed her eyes for seconds.

As they clambered over the stones, a small dog limped past them. It was an old fox terrier, not very good on its legs. Horatia's head swivelled round to look, and her crying stopped. The dog was followed by an old man in a topcoat. He lifted his hat to the sodden woman with a wide hem of sand on her skirts. Jane Gibson kept her eyes on the ground in front of her. At the sea wall, she sat down on a wooden bench, with Horatia in her lap, and did not move until Mary made her do so. A day later, she was still shaking. Yards away from her, Lord Nelson and Lady Hamilton were playing with the child she had nearly allowed to drown. Even in the very moment of pulling her out of the water, she had seen herself motionless in front of them, trying and failing to find the words.

'I think she gets it from her godmother,' said Fatima. 'Milady loves to swim.'

Mrs Gibson smiled. She liked Fatima. 'Yes,' she said, as if this piece of logic were not, at face value, absurd. Her daughter said something, and she turned. Mary had made a small mound of stones and sand, and was idly pushing it over again with her foot. 'What, darling?'

'Can we keep her?' said Mary.

'Who? Horatia?'

'Horatia, yes. Can we keep her?'

95

Her mother lifted her eyes again to the sky. 'Not for ever, no,' she said.

When her teeth were chattering and her nails were blue, Horatia was carried safely to the steps, and Nelson hoisted her up. The bathing-machine smelled of hot wood, of resin and salt and sun-peeled paint. It was a little house, with curtained windows and clothes hanging up. Horatia sat on Nelson's lap and pointed at one thing, then at another. My lady, wearing earrings in the sea. Drips of water on her fat arms. My lovely lord with no medals today. And no arm in this sleeve. Look again. No, not there.

They bundled her in a bath sheet and wrapped it round her so that everything but the top of her head was hidden. She sat on Emma's lap, and was plunged into darkness as two faces – one fat, one thin – met over her head. Above their murmuring, she could hear small waves slap the sides of the bathing-machine. Then she could hear them breathing, and a sound like fishes eating. She opened her mouth and yelled.

The sound of breathing stopped, and there was light above her head again. 'God, what a noise,' said Emma. She tipped her in her lap and kissed her tummy.

'She looks like you,' said Nelson. 'Have I said that before? The top part of her face, here and here.' Horatia gazed at him as he touched her eyes, the bridge of her nose. He closed his fist and ran a knuckle over her cheek. 'What a monkey,' he said. 'I'd shoot anyone who tried to hurt her.'

At their lodgings, Sir William wasn't happy. 'What on earth's the matter?' said Emma, turning the tables on him with a scowl. 'I can see you don't want to be here. It's written all over your face. For God's sake, fix a time for going, and go.'

'Don't be silly.'

'I thought you wanted to be quiet for a while. There's nothing else to do here except be quiet.'

96

Sir William frowned. 'Well, I do wish to be quiet. I've only got a short time to live, and every moment's precious to me. I'm in no hurry, and I want us to do everything we can to make Horatio happy, but the question remains how to do it in the best way for everyone.'

'I have to come here for my skin. Look!' She held out a bare arm, striking a gesture that was almost naturally classical. Her elbows, as well as her knees, were covered in nervous rashes.

Sir William sighed. 'I know, and bathing does you the world of good. I can see that, and I want you to stay here. I am only saying that I'm sorry, while the weather's right, not to be able to do a bit of quiet fishing.'

'Then go home and fish!'

He was sitting in a chair at the bay window, his back to the view. He stretched his legs and straightened his breeches. 'I want to be with you, and with Horatio. I would just like to be my own master sometimes, and pass the time the way I choose, instead of rampaging around the country all the time.' He scowled, but his voice was firm, and his back, even sitting, was straight. 'I knew when we were married that I'd be old when you were still young. We both knew it. That time has come, and we must make the best of it for both of us. Sadly, our tastes as to how we live are very different—'

'Oh, well, if you want to live in solitary retreat—'

'Please don't turn this into another fight. Of course I don't. But at home we have twelve or fourteen people to supper every night. It's worse than Italy, and that was beginning to get on my nerves. Apart from anything else, I'm not made of money. You never stop to think how it all mounts up. You lived for a long time with some very grand people in Naples, and your ideas run a long way ahead of what I can afford. We don't have to have the table groaning with food every night, we could live just as well on pickled salmon, some pigeon, cold lamb and tart. A good bottle of port.' He sighed again, at the thought of lost and simple pleasures. He was paying a third of

97

the household expenses at Merton, and still maintaining the house in Piccadilly, complete with servants. 'I'm not complaining, but all your attention is given to Horatio and to Merton.'

'My friendship with Horatio is completely pure!'

'Yes, I know. I know it is, and I never want to make him uncomfortable by talking about separation, but I'm old, and I would just like to do the things that please me without you jumping down my throat.'

4

There were new rumours of war. If it happened, Nelson had been told that he would be given the Mediterranean command; for the time being, he was going backwards and forwards to London for meetings with the Prime Minister and the First Sea Lord. He was also busy trying to get medals and prize money out of the government for Copenhagen, to get his pension increased, and to obtain a deanery for the Reverend Dr William. November brought the opening of Parliament, and he had to go up to speak in the House of Lords. Whenever he had a spare hour, he went to see Horatia at Little Titchfield Street, to play with her on the living-room floor. She lifted her hands in the air when she saw him, or dropped things for him to pick up. He got down on his hands and knees to look for them under the table; she crawled under there with him, and they held conversations away from the world. Spoon, cup, button. She watched every move and gesture that he made, with a solemn concentration that made him laugh.

Then it was Christmas. Charlotte came to Merton, and her brother, Horace. Nelson's sisters, Susannah and Kate, sent two or three children each, and Mrs Cadogan was run off her feet. Horatia stayed where she was, in London. There were huge meals, a lot of running up and down corridors, dancing, music, and the rehearsing of plays. Books were left lying everywhere, opened at pictures of foxes and geese. Shoes were found under chests and tables, and splinters were drawn out of small feet after skating sessions up and down the dining-room floor. At New Year there was a ball that went on until three in the morning, with children lying asleep where they had fallen, like coats thrown off without thinking. When they had all been packed off home again, the household moved back and forth between Merton and 23 Piccadilly, which was warmer and more convenient for the Admiralty and the House of Lords.

It was a far cry from the quiet life that Nelson had longed for, that he had dreamed of out in the stormy ocean or stuck in a distant port. The fire in the hearth and domestic tranquillity, the occasional neighbour and a glass of good wine. It was costing him a fortune, too. Bills for food and drink at Merton regularly went over fifty pounds a week, and total expenses were more than double that. After the money he gave to Fanny, and to other members of his family by way of gifts and pensions, he had less than eight hundred a year to live on. He was generous, but Emma was spendthrift. Her entertaining grew more lavish, and it was nothing to her to invite a hundred people to Piccadilly.

She couldn't stop. As if she was afraid that the centre would fall away, that they would cease to be, or vanish from the crowd if she did, she spent a fortune, time and again, on light and music, on brilliance and glamour. Flowers: carnations, lilies, roses; red, pink, white and gold. Centrepiece, sideboard, over the fireplace. Silver candlesticks, and glass. Another leaf in the dining-room table, the double damask cloth. Extra staff, and logs for the fires. Chicken velouté, clear turtle soup, purée of barley and carrots. Roasted ham, braised goose, veal in cream and tarragon sauce. Invitations went out far and wide, to fat Italian hangers-on, to actors, singers, theatre people. To the Dukes of Queensberry, Abercorn and Sussex. Generals, captains, naval cronies. Wives and mothers and mistresses. Hosts of people, witness to her triumphant role as Nelson's devoted friend and true companion, pulled up in their carriages in front of the house and filled the rooms like a sort of gale. There were days when Nelson did not know half the men or women with whom he was sitting down, or what to say to them when he found out who they were. He did not try to stop her, though; partly because he didn't want to, and partly because he could not. She was compelled to do it, just as he was compelled to go broadsides to a French ship when he saw one. It made her happy, and if there was something frantic about her happiness, he did not see it.

For Sir William it was too much, even though, as he staggered towards the end of his days, he kept going in spurts of last-minute activity. While Merton filled up time and time again, he went fishing on the Thames, and to his London clubs. He went to the salerooms in Pall Mall and Covent Garden, and to meetings of the Royal Society in Somerset House. He pottered about in the British Museum. But it was a fag getting up and down to London, and he wasn't well. He began to drift, and by the end of March it was clear that he did not have long to live. Emma and her mother nursed him day and night, but on 6 April 1803 he died quietly in Emma's arms, at 23 Piccadilly, with Nelson by his side. He was buried beside his first wife, Catherine, in Wales. It had been her wish, and he had had no objection. He had said that the sea was undermining the church at Selbeck, and that one day they would roll together into Milford Haven.

A month later, England declared war on France. Nelson had been home on leave for eighteen months.

He went to see the Prime Minister, who gave him the Mediterranean command. On 18 May he left for Portsmouth, where he hoisted his flag on the *Victory*. Before he went, he arranged, finally, to have Horatia christened. Mrs Gibson took her to the church of St Marylebone, where Emma and Sir William had been married. It was the smallest Anglican place of worship in London, with the largest parish. Baptisms and burials were conducted in groups, and there were times when as many as eight coffins were piled up in the pews, waiting to go into the ground. Not today, though. Today, candles burned on the sills and lit the varnished wood, the grey stone walls and the lectern. There was a fusty smell of clothes, and the murmur of people waiting. Seven other infants were baptised with her, all born within the last weeks or months. Seven bundles of white lawn, seven sets of parents and godparents, smiles and hats and handkerchiefs. Horatia was nearly two and a half years old. Mrs Gibson led her up to the communion table, then stood with a hand resting on her shoulder. The church had no font, and the children received the sign of the cross from a bowl of water. Neither Emma nor Nelson was at the ceremony. Mrs Gibson had instructions to give the clergyman and the parish clerk a double fee, and to bring back a copy of the register, which did not give the name of either parent. The child's name was put down as Horatia Nelson Thompson, and the date of her birth not as January 1801 but October 1800.

When Nelson had gone, Emma was desolate. Her husband was dead, and her beloved had gone to sea. She threw herself into widowhood. She told her friends that she would never be consoled, and played spanking tunes on their pianos. She bought mourning jewellery for a hundred and seventy pounds, and cut her hair in the fashion for widows. She wrote to George Rose at the Treasury, a friend of Nelson's, and an influential one. The government must give me a pension, she said. I did more than any ambassador ever did, even though their pockets were filled with secret-service money. I served my country in Naples, I arranged the refitting of the British fleet at Syracuse before the battle of the Nile, I sent corn to Malta. I used my influence with the Queen and I spent money from my own pocket. Rose wrote to the Prime Minister, Addington, and told her that he saw no reason why it should not go through.

SEVEN

I

Horatia took a bag and went into the village. After a hundred yards on the road, she broke into a run, pelting over the thin mud on the impulse of nothing more, or less, than youth and the frantic side of misery. Above her the sky was low with cloud, a wide and dreary grey. When the first small houses came into view, she slowed. The clock was striking eight. Bread, meat, wine. There were three steps down from the street into the bakery. She wrenched the handle and pushed the door; a bell jangled over her head. She jumped the middle step, and landed in front of the counter. That morning, as always, Francine Caillois was frowning as she weighed the bread. Her husband was in the back of the shop, looking after the ovens. Behind the counter, wide flat loaves stood in wooden racks; on top of it there was a tray of brioches, and another of cream-filled pastry horns. *Bonjour, Madame, bonjour, Madame.* Francine looked up. 'Oh, it's you,' she said. 'You look out of breath.'

Horatia shrugged. 'Not really. I ran.'

'In a hurry?'

'No.'

'Give me one second.' Francine wrapped the loaf she had weighed in a square of paper. The shop smelled of bran dust and warm dough, pillowy and sweet. 'Have you given Berthe the sack?'

Horatia grinned. 'No. We locked her in the cellar. She'll be all right so long as it doesn't flood.'

'*Bon*. Don't forget her, though. It's easily done.'

The door opened again, and the bell tinged, and a pair of feet clad in sabots appeared on the steps. Madame Joubert. *Bonjour, Madame, bonjour, Mademoiselle*. Madame Joubert was thin enough to get through the door at the top of the three steps without slamming it against the wall and having to make a dash through the gap before it swung back into its frame. 'Dry today,' she said. She did not look at Horatia. She was a grim little woman, whose lips moved even when she was not speaking, as if there were a crowd of prayers or secrets in her head that she must silently repeat.

'Fingers crossed it stays that way.' Francine wiped her hands down the front of the apron tied at her waist. 'A kilo of bread and six brioches?'

'Please.'

Francine smiled at Horatia. 'You don't mind, do you?

'Age before beauty,' said Madame Joubert, with a narrow expression of attempted wit.

As soon as she had been served, a young man clattered down the steps and nearly ran into the counter. The door banged behind him, and the bell rang twice. To Horatia's surprise, Francine served him, too. He was a builder, and his clothes were covered in paint and plaster dust. Horatia had seen him several times over the summer, on a ladder outside the notary's house. It was being done up from top to bottom, and for over a week the fireplace had stood outside on the street.

'Now,' said Francine, when the shop was empty again, 'just a loaf today, or some brioches as well?'

'Just a loaf, thank you.' Francine handed it to her, and wrote the price down in her book. There was a look on her face that made Horatia wait. A hesitant movement in her eyes, a flinch of concern. She looked as if she was going to say something else, something she had been working herself up to and that could not be said in front of other people, but she didn't, and Horatia left the shop.

At the butcher's, she stood in the background while the people in front of her were served. Strings of sausages and sides of beef covered with yellow fat hung from hooks on the wall. The chemist's wife came into the shop and stood beside her in front of the counter. *Bonjour, bonjour.* Over the smell of blood and sawdust, Horatia caught a prickly drift of quinine, and of something dusty, like hay. The chemist's wife spoke to her, the usual string of pleasantries. As she talked, she made darting sidelong glances at the girl, but her eyes were mostly on the butcher, Monsieur Grangé, moving with him as he cut and weighed and scribbled and wrapped. 'And how is Lady Hamilton?' she said. 'I hope she's feeling better.'

The words shocked Horatia not because they had been spoken but because they came out with their real meaning clear. Even in French, it was there to be heard, and she understood. How is Lady Hamilton? Is she drunk again today? It's no way to live, a woman like her, there's no excuse. It was there in the tone, the tight-fisted sympathy, the refusal to meet her eye.

'She's well,' said Horatia. 'Thank you.' The line of women, all dressed in black, shifted with a common righteous twitch. Fidgety gestures were made against sleeves and baskets. Horatia studied the floor. Humiliation beat small fists against her ribs. The whole village knew, and was contemptuous. She could feel it in the silence, the swift exchange of looks. Narrow, black-clad women with yellow teeth, standing like crows in judgement. These are the people, she thought, that my father wanted to kill.

'Calf's liver,' said a woman in front of her.

The shop was moving; it was beginning to turn. Knives, cleavers, a bone saw, all circled the edge of her vision. A goose, hung by a string round its neck, swung on a hook and bled quietly from its bill. She pressed her fingernails into her palm until it hurt. Her heart was thudding, and she felt as if a large animal had landed on her chest. Her body swung in a quarter-turn towards the door, her left foot almost off the floor. Turn and run, run and go. The door was not far behind her. She swung back, stood where she was. She heard the hiss of old skirts, the wet slap of liver on the block.

'Ah, it's you,' said the butcher, when her turn came. 'One minute.' He disappeared into the back of the shop, and returned with a folded piece of paper. 'It's nearly two months,' he said. 'Perhaps Berthe lost the last one on the way home. She'll lose her own head one day, though round here I dare say someone would find it for her. Put it back on the wrong way round, no one would notice. The end of the week is fine.' He gave the bill to Horatia and turned to get the sausages she had asked for. Behind her, the chemist's wife crossed her arms and made a pebbly sound in the back of her throat.

The wine merchant decided to try his luck as well. 'Have a word with her if you can,' he said. 'She's had I don't know how many reminders.' He smiled, but the smile wasn't kind. His bill was for more than eight hundred francs, nearly forty pounds.

When she got home, Emma was up, and in a good mood. 'We've had an invitation!' she declared. 'General James wants to show us something. He's coming at two to pick us up.'

'Show us what?'

'I don't know, Horatia. It's a surprise.'

'Here.' She thrust the bills at her. Emma looked at them and made a face, then placed them on the writing desk.

'You have to pay them! And Madame Caillois, too.'

'Let me worry about that. Go up and change – you look as if the cat dragged you in. You can't go out like that.'

General Robert James came from Essex. He and his wife had been guests at Dessein's hotel when Emma and Horatia arrived in Calais. It had been their plan to go on to Paris, and then to Rome, but Mrs James had been ill after the crossing, and she had not been able to face sixty hours in a three-horse mail coach. She was still, nearly three months later, working herself up to it. In the meantime, they had moved out of the hotel and taken lodgings on the rue Dorian. They were a kind pair, who made occasional and sudden dashes of generosity at Emma and Horatia.

The carriage, hired with a driver in Calais, drew up at two o'clock. The general got out to make a fuss of Janot, and to hand the ladies up. They rattled out of St Pierre under a sky of ranked white clouds and over a plain of shadows. A wind had blown up, but the road was still damp and there was little dust. Emma talked and laughed, and returned the general's kindness with attention and vitality. Sometimes, thought Horatia, she has the constitution of an ox.

The general smelled of old age and an overseas career – cigar smoke, lime water, wool. He was small and round with a dancing walk and, though he looked like a military man from top to bottom, Horatia could not imagine him on a field of battle. His chest was shaped like a cask, and every now and then he seemed to have difficulty breathing. His wife was not with him today. She had stayed at home, dosed up with calomel and cinnamon, opium and senna.

They drove through mile after mile of flat French countryside. Birds flew up out of the hedges, swerving on the wind. They passed woods and copses and little ruins; church spires, farmhouses, cider orchards. They came to the village of Guines and drove through it, scattering boys and chickens. At last, when it seemed as if they would never stop, as if the general meant to take them all the way down through Picardy, the carriage pulled up beside a rutted gateway.

'Look,' he said, leaning away from the window so that they could see out. Fields. Windblown, empty fields, and the first fat drops of rain.

'Rain,' said Horatia.

'Really?' The general leaned forward again, so that their heads, for a moment, were almost touching. 'Well, rain. But look at the fields.'

This was what he had wanted to show them? An empty horizon, naked trees. A line of poplars, still against the white, advancing cloud.

'The Field of the Cloth of Gold,' said the general.

He had gone mad. The field of dug-up turnips, the field of ragged stubble.

'Shall we get out for a minute?' said Emma. 'Have a proper look, stretch our legs.'

Someone had left the gate open. Gusts of wind blew at them from the west, and crows strutted in the field with the fat air of ownership.

'Henry the Eighth,' said the general. 'He came here nearly three hundred years ago to meet the King of France. He brought his wife, and practically the whole English court.' He gave them a moment to take this in, then went on, 'The balance of power in those days was shaky, with France on one side, the Holy Roman Empire on the other, and England in the middle. The idea was to forge an alliance with the French, though not much came of it.'

'Here? In a field?' asked Horatia.

The general nodded vigorously. 'The castles in the villages were falling down,' he said, 'so the valley was levelled, and they made their own. They built a palace out of canvas, and painted it with artificial stones. Huge, life size. Fantastic waste of money, the whole thing. Pavilions, gilded tents, chapels. Three weeks of it.'

As he spoke, Horatia saw noblemen and courtiers, bishops and princes. Horses, kitchens, canopies and rugs. She saw dancing men and women, and fireworks exploding against the sky. Entertainments, feasts and jousts. Women stepped in golden slippers over wooden boards to masques and balls and banquets. A royal salute was fired from the canvas castle, and the swans on the water flew up in fright, their great wings beating like sheets in the wind. A gilded fountain poured claret and spiced wine.

The rain came down harder, and they hustled back into the carriage. The field became a field again.

'Well, I think that's fascinating,' said Emma, leaning back in her seat. She was straining for the right note, but it was the thought that counted. The old general wanted to please them, and here was a piece of their own history in a foreign place, if a dull one. 'And a wonderful idea to bring us here.' She leaned forward and placed a hand on one of his. 'Thank you.'

'I don't know,' said the general. He looked as if he was himself struggling against a creeping sense of disappointment. 'I'm afraid there's nothing really to see.'

'But you've just described it as if you were there yourself! We'd never even heard of it, had we, Horatia? The Field of the Cloth of Gold. It's a piece of history. We spend too much time in the ancient world – you'll have to lend us a book. Good God, just imagine how they used to live!'

Horatia's tummy was rumbling, and the day was growing darker all the time over a perfectly ordinary, vaguely dismal landscape, but it was a good day, for all that. A day that smelled of rain and woodsmoke and leather upholstery, and not of illness and drink. She turned from the view to smile at the general.

It was, he thought, a strange smile. A smile of misfortune and distance, of something deep, like complicity, and he was, for a moment, floored by it. He wanted to give her something, something found in a pocket, but he had nothing in his pockets. A handkerchief, grubby. 'I remember when Lord Nelson was in London,' he said. 'It was the only time I ever saw him. I've told you this ten times.'

'Tell us again,' said Horatia.

'Well, I was in the Strand.' It broke his heart, that was what it was. Her smile broke his heart. 'I was buying books. Kicking my heels on half pay. This was when he had come back from the Mediterranean and, quite honestly, he couldn't move in London without collecting a crowd. Every shop he went into, the door was jammed with people until he came out. Every sort of person, didn't matter who. And it was the most extraordinary thing, to stand among such wonder and ad-miration. I know I've never seen anything like it. I couldn't get anywhere near him. I saw him, though. Dark coat, medals glinting in the sun. Very handsome.' The general winked at Horatia. He wished he could spin out the story for her, but really there was nothing else to say, and in fact the figure of Nelson had been disappointing. Tired, thin and mutilated, he had not seemed to the general like a man who had scattered destruction among the fleets of France. One arm, one eye. Still, he had been, above all, instantly recognisable in his blue coat with its empty sleeve, its spray of stars and medals. A national hero in his lifetime, who had fought alongside his men and who had the wounds to prove it. If he had looked tired and ill, it merely went to show that though his feats at sea might seem more than human he was only a man after all.

What had they done with the arm? Ridiculous question, but it had come into his head, all the same. Someone would have taken it up, covered with a cloth, and thrown it overboard. That would be some claim to fame. Useless waste of a limb, and a useless waste of life, that whole adventure. Ill-advised, at the very least. Bloody Navy, trying to fight a battle on land. Why take Tenerife? It was no use to anyone: it was too far away for a British base. The general could remember where he was sitting, months later, when he read the accounts in *The Times*: Cape Colony. August, and winter, and stormy. A smell in the air like coins. Seventeen ninety-seven. Nelson had just come, basking in praise, from the battle of St Vincent, and hand-to-hand combat at Cadiz. He was centre stage, but he did not have the army. He had asked for soldiers, but was not given any. The whole thing was mad. Mad – and, in the end, a disaster. He had wanted to act the general, to take the city of Santa Cruz in a land attack, then seize the ships in the harbour. The first attempt had come to nothing, and he had led the second himself, which put a rear-admiral and five post captains in the thick of battle. In military terms, it was like sending in a major general and five full colonels with a single battalion of men. He must have known it was futile, but he had gone in anyway, for the honour of his country, or for the sake of his pride. Pride, most likely. Many of the men never got ashore, and those who did faced being mown down by the Spanish batteries. Nearly half of them had been killed or wounded. Nelson's right arm, as he stepped ashore, had been shattered by grapeshot above the elbow. It took them half an hour to saw it off and bind the stump. Where on earth had he heard that? From anyone – it was common knowledge. And the blade the surgeon used was cold; always, after that, Nelson had made sure that the surgeons warmed their knives. But he should not have been there. It was not his proper duty, and it had done the state no service. How strange, really, that such a disaster should have lived on in the minds of men as something magnificent all the same.

'You're right,' said Emma. 'He would talk to anyone, anywhere.' It was not quite what the general had said, but it was no less true for that.

'There was something about him,' he offered, 'his courage, of course, but not only that. He was loved by everyone who knew him, and by millions who did not.' Many a leader, he almost said, would give his right arm for that.

Horatia seemed to wait for something more to be said, and when it was not, she turned her face to the window again. Dreaming. She looked to the general as if she had gone to a place miles beyond the dark, rain-soaked avenue of trees that they were driving through. Whatever will become of them? he thought. Whatever are they going to do?

2

No one had told her. Until his death, she had not known. No one knew. Not in the Strand or at the Admiralty or in Norfolk. She herself had thought he was someone else; and that she was, too. The nation's hero had a daughter, and no one was aware of her existence until he died. He had put it in a letter, once, but she had been too young to understand. *Victory*, October 1803, My dear child, here is the first letter from your loving father. If I live, it will be my joy to see you growing up, but if I die, Lady Hamilton will take care of you. I have left her as your guardian, and I beg you on the value of a father's blessing to do as she tells you and listen to what she says. May God almighty bless you. And then, on the morning of the day he died, he wrote the same thing in his pocket book. Had he known he was going to die? Had he *known*? In his strong, crabbed hand he had written it down: She will use the name of Nelson only.

She sat with her chin in her hands. It was late. Fatima was ironing. Spit, hiss. A candle burned on the wall above the stove.

In the pocket book, in a codicil to his will, he had left Lady Hamilton as a legacy to his king and country, as well as his adopted daughter, Horatia Nelson Thompson, who should in future use the name of Nelson only. These are the only favours that I ask of my king and country, at this moment, when I am going to fight their battle. Horatia Nelson Nelson.

Owls, and the wind. The quiet and rhythmic thump as the iron came down on the board. The flick of water from Fatima's long hands.

In London, when the codicil was published in the papers, those who read it knew. They knew that he was in fact her father and somehow, though she could not remember when, at what point, so did she. They had wanted to see her, to meet the dear little interesting being who had been in his final thoughts.

The smell of women, of mourning dresses and tears. So this is her. What a sweet little thing.

In the same document, Nelson had officially entrusted his daughter to Emma's care, to be brought up in the paths of religion and virtue until she was eighteen years old, and to have passed on to her all the accomplishments that so adorned Emma herself.

The door rattled on its hinges. Wind. Fatima crossed the room and shot the bolt. She laid a hand on Horatia's head, and went back to the ironing-board.

> *Victory*, 19 October 1805, My dearest angel, it made me so happy to get your letter, and I'm glad that you're being good, and that you love Lady Hamilton, who loves you, too. Give her a kiss from me. The combined fleets of the enemy are now reported to be coming out of Cadiz, and I want to tell you that you are uppermost in my thoughts. I know I have your prayers for my safety, victory, and speedy return to Merton. Be a good girl, do as you're told. Receive, my dearest Horatia, the loving blessings of your father.

It was only then that she understood. If she had known before that, would she remember more now, or differently? He was one thing, and then he was another. Would she have loved him in any other way if she had known at the time who he was? Something important had been neglected. Memories of when he was there, alive, slipped like wraiths through her mind, dusting it with images. She had learned, when he was dead, that she had been his secret, hidden between the walls of Little Titchfield Street. She had learned then, too, that somewhere, in Naples or the Mediterranean, he had loved, if only briefly, a woman who was not his wife. Had loved her more than anyone, more than his own life. Only the call of his country had forced their separation, and only her death had compelled it to last. She had returned, alone, whoever she was, for her confinement, and he had travelled across Europe to see with his own eyes that everything was done well and right when she died.

The country had never given him what he wanted. Horatia was here, now, in this place, because the government had never given him that. They knew that she was his daughter, they knew she had not been adopted, and that he wanted them to provide for her, and for Emma. It was not such a strange thing to ask. He had been in the service of his country all his life, and had given his life for it; Emma had done some service, too, which should be recognised. Horatia was part of his posterity and, with his lifelong sense of service and reward, he had left the two of them as a legacy to the nation, for the nation to look after when he no longer could. But the government had chosen to spend its money on other things. Why? She did not know.

'Ssht.' Fatima lifted the side of her hand to her mouth. She licked the burn, still moving the iron with her other hand. Janot, in front of the dying fire, shifted in his sleep. Somewhere deep in one of the kitchen walls something loosened and fell. A small sound, unimportant.

Had he known? He had gone below with Hardy and Blackwood, and asked them to witness the codicil. They were about to go into battle: such documents were being written all over the ship. But had he known, anyway? Get in touch with George Rose at the Treasury, he told them. He knows the ropes. Then, when he had walked the deck one more time, he went below again. He prayed. He prayed for a great and glorious victory for his country and for Europe, and resigned himself and his just cause to God. Amen, amen, amen. He wrote the prayer in the pocket book, too.

In Norfolk she had been hugged to the breasts of generations of a family she had not known was hers. She had fleets, suddenly, of cousins. Death had taken Nelson away, and had given her a father. It gave her long journeys in carriages, and aunts and children and dogs and gifts. It gave her, now, a sort of fury.

'I should have known,' she said.

'Known what, *chère?*'

'When he was alive. That he was my father.'

Fatima put the iron down on the stove. Then she turned, and leaned her back against the wall. 'You think it would have been different?' she said. 'You was four years old when he died. It would not have been different.'

3

Emma woke up. She looked about her as if something must have happened that she did not remember, as if she were uncertain which country she was in. Fatima placed a tray on the table by the door. Emma told her to take it away, and when she did not, she thumped the bed with her fist, groaning in anger. She asked where the general had gone.

'It's morning,' said Fatima.

Emma smacked her lips, as if there was a foul taste in her mouth. The room smelled, too, like something attacked by rust.

She sat on the side of the high bed. Round knees like boulders under her bed gown. Feet broad and veined, the nails hard and yellow and short. Hands tucked into the folds of her stomach, arms dimpled, elbows raw from scratching. Rashes, too, on the backs of her knees. Face puffed up as if someone had left it in the low oven overnight to rise.

'It's still dark.'

'Rain, milady.'

'*Rain?*'

Each morning it was as if, until she managed to remember, she had ceased, in the night, to be. Because without memory we do not know who we are, and since yesterday she had forgotten everything. Only, dimly, that the general had been there.

Fatima watched her struggle as the objects in the room

reassembled themselves, the washstand, the chair, the tray. A line of grey light beyond the shutter, the idea of daylight and rain. She moved to open a window, but Emma stopped her with a hand. She used the pot, and got back into bed. 'Have some breakfast,' said Fatima.

'Just leave it. Go away, take the pot. I'm not getting up.'

'Yes, milady.'

She closed the door behind her and waited. In her hands, the chamber pot was warm. For a moment, there was no sound. Then the bed creaked, and the floor, and she heard the cork come out of a bottle. And, having heard it, there was nothing to be done. With one hand, as she went downstairs, she held her skirts away from her feet.

In the early afternoon, they heard her stir. For an hour she crashed around upstairs, but when Fatima went to see what was going on, she shouted at her to leave her alone. They heard her opening and closing drawers, and talking to the things they contained. Admonishing, angry. The air in the house seemed to ring with the chime of a glass struck lightly on its rim. Horatia sat with a book on the table in front of her, holding her stomach as if there were a pain below her ribs. Another stumbling, angry hour. Then Emma's door crashed open and they heard her feet on the stairs.

'Ah!' she said, in the doorway of the sitting room, as if she was mildly astonished to see them there. She pulled her mouth into a bow, a child's mouth set in an old face, an expression of self-conscious charm, of calculated appeal, which made her look both cautious and sly. 'What are we all doing?' she said.

This cannot go on, thought Horatia, though the terrible thing that she knew to be true was that it could. There seemed to be no end to the suffering that Emma could soak up, and no limit to the changes she could undergo. She was, in the different faces of her illness, indecent and frightening. In her swings between incompatible moods, in the effects of her manipulations, she was a sort of tyrant. There was no way of knowing how it might end, unless it ended in her death. There was no way of telling what might be about to happen now, in this room, only that it would come out badly.

'I thought,' said Emma, stepping further into the room, 'that I would have a look through the inventory.' Her expression, though it had hardly changed, now made her look like someone searching for the right note in a matter of propriety. 'The list,' she said, 'that the landlord gave us. Monsieur . . .' She blew through her mouth, defeated by a name. 'I know what he's going to do, and I intend to stop him before he does it. He makes the great mistake of judging other people by his own shortcomings.'

'Coudert,' said Horatia.

'What?'

'His name is Monsieur Coudert.'

'Really.' She sat, putting a hand on the arm of the chair, and letting it take her weight as she lowered herself. 'Coudert?' she said. 'Oh, well.' Within a minute, though, she had forgotten the landlord and the inventory. She sent Fatima to get a bottle of wine from the cellar, and settled back in the chair. 'Your hair's getting long,' she said.

Horatia's hair had not been cut since they came to France, and it had grown down below her shoulders. Fatima called it her crowning glory, and she was waiting for the day when it was long enough to sit on.

'Go and find some scissors.'

Words of objection rose in Horatia's throat, but she saw where they would take her, and closed her mouth again. Today, now, she knew that she must think about every word, must try to chart the probable progress of anything she might say against the lie of Emma's mood. 'We can do it tomorrow,' she suggested. 'There isn't a sharp pair in the house.'

'There must be.'

'No, he comes tomorrow. In the morning.'

Emma's gaze was level, frowning, curiously still, as if there was a game of cards between them, and she knew that Horatia was cheating. 'Who comes tomorrow?'

Fatima returned with a bottle of wine and a glass. Emma was wearing her bed gown still, under a large woollen shawl. The smell that came off her was rank; upstairs, in her room, she had been drinking brandy. In their company, on a normal day, she drank only wine, and she drank it in the broadcast confidence that wine, unlike spirits, was not intoxicating. To Fatima, this deception, and the deception practised on days like this when they were supposed to be unaware that she had been getting through the best part of a bottle of Cognac in the privacy of her room, was not so remarkable. We believe, she thought, what we want to believe, or what causes least pain, and if it is not possible to believe it, then we agree to pretend. They knew, and they did not know. So long as nothing found its way into words, the denial was tacit and collective. On the larger stage, she understood that this also went some way to making sense of the assertion, and the common acceptance, that Lady Hamilton's relationship with Nelson had always been pure. It only needed the right effort to be put into a pretence for it to exist as the acknowledged reality, even when the evidence was all against it. They knew it, and they did not know. The fact, the extraordinary fact, that no one had ever suspected that Horatia was Lady Hamilton's own daughter only proved the point and, to Fatima's mind, to an almost preposterous degree.

But why had Lady Hamilton never told Horatia? How could this go on and on? Was it because Emma still hung on to the hope that one day there might be some money, but only while the government, and Nelson's family, continued to believe that Horatia was another woman's daughter? She had worked hard and for a long time to make and keep her role and reputation, and though they had long since collapsed in ashes, she would destroy herself before she destroyed the fiction that she had created. There was, too, though Fatima doubted it, the possibility that she was doing it for Horatia; perhaps there lurked in her mind the understanding that Horatia would be better off in the world not knowing who her mother was, and that the world would treat her more kindly if it never learned that it had been deceived. But to live with your own child for all these years, to watch her change and grow under your own nose, and never reveal to her who you are? There were days when Fatima believed she understood the reasons for it, but many more days when she could not remember why she had thought that. Surely there was not, now, so much to lose? Or was it shame – shame for everything that had gone before, and for what she had become? If that were the case, then nothing would change, because the shame was compounded every day, and the lie went down deeper and deeper.

She wondered, too, why Lady Hamilton did not send Horatia home. Back to her uncles, her father's family. She could go to Sussex, to Norfolk. She would be welcomed with open arms and open hearts. But it seemed to Fatima that Lady Hamilton regarded Horatia as her one remaining possession. Not loved, but clung to. Her last possession, and her last weapon in the battle for prize money. She had lost the fight in England, and had been sent into exile with only this one thing of value. In the letters that still went back and forth across the Channel, the child was nothing less than a hostage, held up to view although no one was looking. There was no one left now for Emma to fight, except Horatia. I will blow up all your boats, thought Fatima, and all the men in them, if you do not submit.

Dimly conscious that she had been distracted, Emma fought her way back through whatever muddle had formed in her head, and demanded scissors again. Fatima had no choice but to find them, and a sheet.

'Please!' cried Horatia. 'No.'

'Don't make a fuss.' Emma was standing now, with the concentration of someone who knows there is a certain distance between her head and the floor, and that this distance must somehow be preserved.

'I don't want it cut.'

Emma swung round like a boat at anchor, and lifted, in one fluid movement, a round bowl from the top of a small painted cabinet. The bowl was green and white and blue, and contained pot-pourri. She flung it against the wall, beneath a picture of pollard elms, and it exploded in a shower of china shards and petals. All the scent had gone from them, and much of what fell was dust.

'When I tell you what to do, you do it, do you understand?'

Horatia stared. Her lips felt swollen.

'Do you?'

She nodded.

'Say it! Speak, use words.' She leaned forward, pinching Horatia's chin between finger and thumb.

'I understand.' It was said without moving her jaw or her lips.

Another great expulsion of air. Like a dragon, thought Horatia. When she spoke again, though, her voice was calm. 'I'm only going to do the ends,' she said. 'This much, look.'

'Less than that.'

'All right, less. This much, almost nothing. Half an inch.'

Emma lowered herself back into her chair, and Horatia sat on a stool at her knees, the sheet draped over her shoulders. Fatima would not look at her. The power that Emma held over them was the power of the mistress, the guardian, the power of the sick, and of the very drunk. Emma brushed out Horatia's hair, leaning forward over her own great bulk, and pulling it until tears came into the girl's eyes. Horatia said nothing. She was filled now with hatred, with injustice, and as her hair fell in long strands on either side of her, she wept. She had surrendered, and the only hope in her heart was that Emma would die soon and go to hell. The scissors were blunt; Emma made her turn on the stool, and turn again, as she pulled and sawed.

EIGHT

I

At Little Titchfield Street, Horatia emptied the kitchen cupboard and surrounded herself with pans and tins. 'Story,' she said. Mrs Gibson stepped through the mess with a pile of mending in her arms. 'I haven't the breath to be telling you stories. No more breath in my poor body. Never speak a word again.' She had to peer over the mending to see her feet.

'Story.'

'Don't get anything else out, then. I've only got to put it back.'

'Blanche.'

'Yes, all right. Blanche.' She put down the mending, and began the tale of Blanche Heriot, who saved the life of her lover during the Wars of the Roses. Herrick Evenden is fleeing the King's men, running from the scene of battle in Barnet. He is running to his lover, Blanche, in Chertsey, only a few miles from Merton. But when he reaches the town he is captured by King Edward's soldiers, and sentenced to death at curfew. The rider who carries his pardon is delayed at the Laleham ferry; the pardon is in his saddlebag, but the ferry is on the wrong side of the river. Soon the curfew bell in Chertsey Abbey will ring the signal for Herrick's execution. Dong, dong, dong. His head will be cut off, and the market square will run with his blood. All is lost. But no, all is not lost! Knowing that her lover will die if the sound of the bells is heard, Blanche Heriot runs to the abbey. She climbs into the belfry and hangs on to the clapper to stop the curfew being sounded. She swings forwards and backwards, forwards and backwards, and never lets go, though her arms are ready to break.

Why, wondered Jane Gibson, is it always the same stories? Why do they never want to hear anything else? Blanche Heriot and Horatio Nelson. Outside in the street she heard a row begin. Someone was refusing to back up, and the road was blocked. It happened every day. Carriages, wagons, there wasn't room for them to pass each other, and someone always flew into a rage. She got up out of her chair and leaned down to pick up a small pan; she put it back in the cupboard looking, as she did, for signs of mice. Horatia glared at her. It was true, the story wasn't finished yet.

'She hung on for dear life,' said Mrs Gibson, 'her feet in the air and her skirts flying out. The bell-ropes were pulled, but Blanche hung on, swinging and swaying. If she fell, her neck would break and she would die a terrible death. The ferry reached the other shore at last, and the rider spurred his horse. He galloped to the abbey courtyard, his face black with mud, and the pardon from King Edward in his hand. The bell never sounded, and Herrick Evenden was reprieved.'

'Again.'

'Not on your life. Bedtime.'

Horatia was on her feet in seconds, navigating the remaining mess on the floor. Out of the room, into the living room, under the table. Here we go, thought Mrs Gibson. 'Five minutes,' she said.

'Nelson,' said a small voice, from under the table.

'Not here,' said Mrs Gibson. 'Gone to sea.'

'Why?'

'To look for Frenchmen in their ships.'

'Why?'

'To sink them and burn them and send them to the bottom of the water.'

Silence.

'He is waiting for them outside their ports, so that when they come out he can pounce on them, like mice. He's the cat and they are the mice. Squeak, squeak, bang, dead.'

2

Nelson wrote from the *Victory* off Toulon. His orders were to take, sink, burn or otherwise destroy all French ships he might encounter, and to prevent the French, Dutch and Spanish fleets joining forces. Darling one, thank you for your letter, and for the lock of beautiful hair. Here is a bit of mine, and a pound note to buy a locket to keep it in. Listen, I didn't promise you a dog, you're making that up. We have no dogs on board ship. I forgot I promised you a watch, but I've sent to Naples for one, and will send it home as soon as it arrives. Be a good girl and I love you for ever.

To Emma he wrote about the house, about contracts and architects, materials and money. He wrote of footpaths and passages, and about putting netting around the stream so that Horatia would not fall in. Promise me, he said. Let her come and live with you, it's high time she did. I want to be able to think of the two of you together. She needs more than a nurse now, and Mrs Gibson spoils her. Tell people that she was left to my care by someone in Italy, and that you fell in love with her and promised to look after her. From Naples he wrote to tell her that her old home was now a hotel, and that her servants had run wild. The Queen has given us up, he said. She has no use for her former friends.

For weeks, between ports, there would be nothing from him. Even so, every day, she waited.

'Fatima.'

'Yes, milady.'

'I'd like some porter. I'm exhausted. And please don't just stand at the top of the stairs and shout.' Emma had been drifting between Merton and London, as well as visiting

Nelson's family in Norfolk and Canterbury. She was restless, and pregnant again. Her ankles swelled and her rashes came back. Sir William's estate – true to the promise made seventeen years before – had gone to his nephew, Charles Greville. Emma's debts were paid off, and she had eight hundred pounds, as well as another eight hundred a year. Greville had told her that he wanted her out of 23 Piccadilly in a month, and she had moved to a smaller house in Clarges Street. Mrs Cadogan was, as usual, at Merton. The baby was due at the end of December.

Fatima twitched her nose. 'Are we going to Merton this week?' she said. It was hard to keep track of simple things. Clothes, shoes. They were in one place, or they were in another. Many things were still in crates marked *bedroom*, *dining-room*.

'I suppose so.'

They could hear Charlotte downstairs, having a singing lesson with Mrs Bianchi. Charlotte Nelson had grown into a pretty girl, with dark curly hair and eyes set wide in a heart-shaped face, and she was already in demand. Emma went everywhere with her, to balls and parties, concerts and dinners, and each invitation to a grand London house was for her a personal triumph. Out of her own pocket she paid for language tutors, music teachers, dancing masters. She had taken Charlotte over completely, and her plan to enter the highest circles as chaperone of Lord Nelson's niece was succeeding beyond her expectations. The girl's parents were delighted, even if Sarah was worried that Charlotte was learning to drink and to gamble, and was eating far too much. Thanks to Nelson's efforts, William had been given a prebendal stall at Canterbury, and had moved his family to a house in the close. It had puffed him up like nobody's business.

'Actually, no,' said Emma. 'There's too much to do here.'

'Yes, milady. You want your blue dress for tonight?'

She screwed up her face while she thought. 'I don't know.

What do you think?' She straightened her back, and put a hand on her great high stomach. 'I don't want to go at all. I hate these grand affairs, I don't honestly feel like it. What's Charlotte wearing?'

'Don't know, milady.'

Emma nodded. 'I think we'll get that sorted out before I decide.'

There wasn't, in fact, much choice. Of all the spacious garments in her wardrobe, only one or two still disguised her pregnancy; only one or two still fitted her at all.

'Miss Horatia coming home soon?'

Emma raised her head and looked at her with a weary frown. 'Why do you ask that? No, she's not. Look at me – use your head. And, Fatima, if you could find time between now and Christmas, I asked you to get me some porter.'

Fatima sniffed and left the room. Lady Hamilton had not seen Horatia for weeks; she was much too busy doing other things – dinner at Lady Cawdor's, dancing at the Cholmondeleys', performing her Attitudes at Lady Abercorn's, in spite of her enormous size. The Devonshire set, the Countess of Macclesfield. Every other evening she dined with her neighbour, the Duke of Queensberry, who lived round the corner from Clarges Street. Ancient, deaf and immensely rich, Old Q was a disreputable ruin and a firm friend. He had had so many women under his protection in his day that even those who knew him best had lost count. Fatima happened to know that he took a milk bath every morning when he got up, then sat on a cane chair on his balcony to watch the ladies on Piccadilly and wink at them. In the summer he went to his house in Richmond and sat by the river, where naked girls danced for him. He was extremely fond of Emma, but she was not the only woman in London, not by a long chalk, who was in a state of tension about his fortune and what he would do with it when he died.

She began to fill the house with other children. On the point of giving birth in secret again, she had decided to keep the place crammed with activity during the Christmas holidays.

'You're going to wear yourself out,' said Fatima. 'All them children everywhere.'

'It gives the impression of normal busy life, Fatima, and, anyway, I love children. Do I look worn out?'

'No, milady. A bit.'

'It works though, doesn't it? With the house full, I've got a good excuse to refuse any more invitations. I can stay here and put my feet up.'

Fatima looked down at her mistress's feet. They were enormous, like fishing-boats. They stuck out from under her skirts as if they had docked there in a storm.

Mrs Cadogan came up from Merton, and went through the rooms working out where they were all going to sleep – Charlotte and Horace Nelson, and Nelson's other nieces, the Bolton girls. The weather was dreary and cold, one grey day after another. For two days it snowed, and the streets turned to slush, stained with mud and horse manure.

Then Horatia caught smallpox. For two weeks they didn't know if she would live or die. Mrs Gibson wrote every day. Fatima kept her mouth firmly shut.

'Good God, woman, don't look at me like that.'

'No, milady. Like what?'

'As if this is my fault!'

Fatima shrugged. Nelson had asked Emma more than once to have Horatia inoculated, and what had happened? Nothing. 'It's God what send the smallpox,' she said, 'not you.'

'I don't know what to do.'

'Nothing, milady. Wait.'

It was true, they could do nothing but wait. With each letter that came, the child was worse. They were written at dead of night, and always in an exhausted hand. They traced the course of the rash, the violence of the fever. Dullness, thirst and sweats; fits of cold and heat, headaches, vomiting and convulsions. Pustules, filled with a thick white matter, then yellow. The doctor ordered bleeding, blistering and purging, Jerusalem bark and syrup of lemon, senna, prunes and rhubarb. Emma was beside herself. Horatia was the key to Nelson's heart if it was, for some reason, ever closed to her, and even with another child on the way she was afraid that if they lost Horatia she might lose him. And if she lost him now, she would have no one. She kept herself going on porter, and felt increasingly ill.

She took to her bed and stayed there. If there were any suspicions as to why, they were dispelled by the fact that several young people were rampaging around the house, learning dances, eating goose and roast potatoes. No one would choose to have a baby in that sort of noise; it would be madness. At the end of December, though, she gave birth to another daughter. The labour was difficult, and the child was weak. She lived only for a few days. Once again, Fatima and Mrs Cadogan made the sad and secret march, with a small bundle, to the local burial ground.

Then Mrs Gibson wrote to say that Horatia was out of the woods. She was fragile still, and it would be some time before she got back her strength, but the worst was over.

'Out of the woods?' said Fatima.

'For God's sake, girl, it's an expression. It means she isn't going to die.'

'Thank almighty God for that.'

3

On board the *Victory*, Nelson was writing letters and making lists. My dearest Emma. Two dozen Yorkshire hams, six Gloucester cheeses, twelve sides of beef, four kegs of sauerkraut. *Smallpox?* Thank God it's over, thank God we had her inoculated. Think what might have happened otherwise. I wish I could have had it for her, but at least it was short, it was over before it was serious. Last night I dreamed I heard her call Papa. Twelve quarts of chilli vinegar, six boxes of mangoes. He himself did not eat much at dinner – a chicken wing, a small plate of macaroni, vegetables. He was sick and tired of patrolling the Mediterranean. He longed for the French to put to sea, so that he could go after them and destroy them. Until they do, he wrote, it's one long monotony, with a hard gale every week and following swells. He didn't feel well and his eyes were getting worse. I want to come home. I want to spend Christmas with my daughter. Onions, leeks, pumpkins, sheep and oranges. Frigates. Then again, if he went home, they might send another admiral out instead of him, and he would never get back. He changed his mind. Bonaparte had made himself Emperor of France, and Spain had declared war on Britain again. The times are big with great events, he wrote. Soon the French fleet will break out and I will follow it, as I followed it to the Nile. I will have one more good race of glory. In the meantime, he would put up with the gales and the swells, with the pain in his side, the night sweats and his eyes.

Then the French did escape from Toulon. The French admiral, Villeneuve, slipped past the British fleet in the dark, and sailed off into a storm. Nelson tried Sardinia, then Naples, then Malta, but they were nowhere to be seen. They were not in Alexandria, either, and it wasn't until the third week of February that he discovered they had been driven back by gales to Toulon. No one, he wrote to Emma, can be more miserable or more unhappy than me. All I wanted, after two long years, was to have another go at the French.

At the end of March, they got out again. They slipped through the Strait of Gibraltar into the Atlantic. Once again, Nelson had no idea where they might have gone. He was anchored off the Moroccan coast. He had twelve ships-of-the-line, and Villeneuve twenty. For days the British were delayed by the winds, and then by one of Nelson's ships, the *Superb*, which couldn't keep up with the rest. By the beginning of June, however, he reckoned he was within a week of the enemy. Pray for my success, he wrote, give me a kiss for all this hard fag, and in a few days I shall be immortalised. But Villeneuve was not to be found. Reports from St Lucia said that a fleet had been seen sailing south, perhaps to Trinidad. He went to Trinidad and found nothing. He sailed north to Grenada and Antigua. From island to island, no sign. They had missed him. Nelson set sail across the Atlantic again. Villeneuve was in front of them all the way; two of his fleet were captured off Finisterre in a skirmish with another British squadron, but he managed to get the rest into port at Ferrol, on the north-west coast of Spain.

4

Emma was at Southend. The house in Clarges Street was being painted, and she had to get away from the smell. Also, she was covered in rashes again, and needed sea water. She had taken Fatima with her, and Charlotte. Her mother was at Merton.

Funny, thought Fatima, how she always got her rashes when Mrs Cadogan told her that money was tight. And money was tight. The gardener, Cribb, was after the thirteen pounds that he had paid out for the mowers, and there were bills from the baker and the butcher for a hundred pounds and seventeen shillings. Mrs Gibson was owed nearly twenty-five pounds. 'Also, Mrs Cadogan want a bottle of ink and a box of wafers, remember.'

'I know. Where's my bathing dress?'

'On the chair, milady.'

'The other one. And I'd like a drink, please. Porter.'

Fatima put down the stockings she was rolling, opened a drawer and pulled out the bathing dress. When she held it up and shook out the folds, it looked like a dark blue Berber tent. She decided to pretend, for as long as she could, that she had not heard the last request. Her mistress was drinking too much. On their last visit to Canterbury, in July, she had finished off the Reverend Dr William Nelson's stock of expensive champagne, and her manners had been so bad that invitations to the family had explicitly left her out. 'Shall I see if there is any post?' she said.

'Yes, do. And see what Charlotte's up to.'

Charlotte was outside in the garden. She was eighteen now, and reading a lot. The garden was perched on a steep hill, and looked out over the road and the sea. The early sun had been thinned by haze, but now it was getting hot, and bees were buzzing in a straggling yellow bush. 'You put your hat on,' Fatima told her, 'or you go black, like me.' On her way back through the house, she picked up the letters that had come for Emma. Big noise in a minute, she said to herself. One here from milord, I think.

There was a big noise. Nelson was at Spithead, and would be travelling to Merton in the next day or so, as soon as he was out of quarantine. He had been away for more than two years.

'You going to have to move like the devil,' said Fatima, when the shrieks of joy had died down and the threat of a fainting fit had passed.

'Get my writing case. Oh, God, he's coming home!'

Wearing a morning dress that had seen better days, she sat down to dash off several letters. 'And order the coach,' she said. 'And pack.'

Horatia had to be brought from Mrs Gibson, and the family summoned. She wrote to Nelson's sisters, Kate Matcham in Bath, and Susannah Bolton in Norfolk, to Sarah and William Nelson. Her long campaign of vilification against Fanny had succeeded to the point where all his relations – even, after her latest visit, the William Nelsons – were now her bosom friends. No one even spoke of Fanny Nelson any more. She wrote to her mother at Merton, telling her to order pork tenderloin, beef, fish, oysters and veal. Gammon, asparagus, grapes. Wine, champagne, brandy.

'Is Charlotte packing?' she said to Fatima.

'Yes, milady.'

At last she put down her pen and stood. 'Good God, I can't go home in this!' She stripped naked, and made Fatima dig through the bags she had just packed to find a dress to put on. 'Two years!' she cried.

'Long time.'

'It's a century, Fatima. An eternity.'

'Nearly over now.' Fatima held out a sleeve. 'Put your arm through here.'

'He's coming home! He's coming home, Fatima.'

'Stand still, milady. Breathe in.'

NINE

Fatima found Horatia sitting by the window in Emma's room. There was a fire in the grate, but the shutters were closed and the room was otherwise dark. Emma was motionless in bed.

'I found this.' Horatia held up an empty brandy bottle.

Fatima stood for a moment, then nodded. 'Come downstairs,' she said.

'Fatima . . .'

'Nothing you can do. Come down.'

The rain was beating steadily on the roof of the porch. Janot lay on the floor in front of the stove, and watched with dark eyes as they came and went. On the other side of the kitchen, a large fireplace was set deep into the wall. Berthe had been to the village, and her cloak and skirts were wet. She put more logs on the fire, and soon the room smelled of drying clothes and drying dog.

'There's nothing you can do.' Fatima lifted Horatia's chin, and looked into her eyes. 'I know this.'

The girl's chin began to tremble.

'What can you do? Nothing. I am here to look after her, and Berthe is here, and that is all.'

Horatia drew her head away. 'She lies there as if she were dead. When she talks, I don't understand any more. She mutters at the furniture and shouts at me.' She placed her fists, knuckles down, on the table. 'She stands and looks at the chairs as if they've let themselves in without asking, as if they've come here to tell her something she can't understand.

135

Sometimes I think she's forgotten what they are. I want to shout at her, *"This is a chair, this is a table."* There are times when I think some other person has come to live in her head.'

'She's unhappy, *chère*.'

Horatia nodded. Emma had been overwhelmed by misery, and it had come to overwhelm everything, like mistletoe on a tree. It was hers alone, and yet it darkened all their lives. It drew attention to itself and demanded every last thing that they could give, even as it forced Emma to remove herself to one room, to her bed, to a place no one else could reach. It called them to witness as it wrestled her to the ground and said, *Do you submit, do you submit?* It pointed its finger at them, morning, noon and night, and showed them how helpless and small they were.

'Today is bad,' said Fatima. 'Tomorrow will be better.'

There was nothing to be done, and nothing to do. Berthe lit a fire in the drawing room, and Horatia sat there with a book. Fatima had done what she could with the mess that Emma had made of her hair. It reached her ears, now, like a boy's. The words in front of her were made of lead and would not leave the page. She lifted her face and watched the raindrops on the window. One here, one there, sliding with the apparent pain of being almost weightless. This is what happens, she thought, this is how people die of boredom. Their blood slows until it can't go on any longer, until it's silted up like a stream, with mud and twigs and leaves. She wondered if she would know when the moment came, and if she would tell anyone when it did. She imagined meeting such a death with indifference, with little more than a long sigh in an empty room. She put her legs up on the long low stool in front of the fire and looked at them. Legs, skirt, stockings. My legs, she thought, with an absence of wonder. She stared at them as if, given time enough, they might turn into someone else's. Someone else, the same age but different. Then she imagined them useless, lamed in a dramatic accident. She had to be carried everywhere. She wore white, mostly, and friends wrote letters to her from one end of the year to the other, enclosing poems and pressed leaves. Once or twice a week they heard the sound of an approaching horse, the rattle of a carriage on the drive. Young strong men carried her to the lawn, where chairs had been put out and books lay on the grass. On the other side of a wooden fence, horses flicked their tails against the flies. Then it was the seaside she saw, and her cousin Frank Matcham holding the reins, leading her donkey along the fringe of sand between the pebbles and the sea. She was less lame now, though only slightly. On the sea wall, Frank's brother George stood watching, a look of proud reflection in his face. Then, miracle of miracles, she could walk again. She made her way across the marble hall of a stately house, over carpets of dark red wool, past windows open to the breeze and the last light of a long day. Through oak doors to a ballroom where the music, out of sheer astonishment, stopped. Then a waltz, lightly played and lightly stepped. Uniforms and dress coats. Slippers, dresses and jewels.

One raindrop becomes another raindrop. All the raindrops become other raindrops. A spider hangs on the inside of the window, indecisive, thinking. Up or down? Down, and then down. She is in the farmyard, suddenly, at Merton. She can smell warm straw, and cowpats flattened by the sun. Her father, in a black coat, runs towards her from the barn and touches her face with his hand. *What's the matter, little one?* There is green still water in the trough, and cloven prints in the baked ground. There is a tremble on her lips of a wild, abrupt fear. *No more tears.* He stands her on her feet and turns her round to inspect her. The back of her dress is wet and green. *You are my darling child,* he says. *Can you remember that?* Then she is walking beside him, holding his hand, and he is telling her a story. Once there was a boy who went to sea when he was twelve years old to join his uncle's ship. His mother was dead, and his brothers and sisters stayed behind. It was a cold winter's day. His father took him as far as London, and put him on the coach for Chatham and the docks. He travelled alone, and when he arrived, his uncle wasn't there to meet him, and no one had heard of him or his ship. The boy made his way down the cobbled streets to the dockyard, asking sailors if they knew where he should go. A kind officer took pity on him and gave him something to eat, then found a boat to ferry him across the river. There was the *Raisonnable*, a sixty-four-gun ship, moored in the Medway in the final stages of fitting-out. The boy climbed aboard the warship at last, but still his uncle was not there, and he paced up and down the deck in the gales and the squalls and the snow, thinking he was in a dream.

She could not remember, without looking, what book lay on her lap. '. . . for he did not think, with Caliph Omar Ben Abdalaziz, that it was necessary to make a hell of this world to enjoy Paradise in the next.' *Vathek*, by William Beckford. She saw again the abbey at Fonthill, the walls and turrets and battlements, the great tower vanishing into the gloom above. There was Beckford himself, wandering through the monumental ruins, with a terrible eye that no one, when he was angry, could behold; anyone on whom it was fixed fell over and died. Not Beckford, Vathek. She bit the inside of her lip. If she couldn't read, then the day would never end. She tried again. 'The palace of Alkoremi, which his father, Motassem, had erected on the Hill of Pied Horses . . .' The house was quiet. She could hear a log hiss, and a steady drip outside from the gutter. Berthe and Fatima were talking in the kitchen, and a saucepan lid was lifted and put back. Clunk. She had no idea of what she had just read. A caliph, a palace, wine and musicians. It was like trying to stick pieces of paper to the wall with spit.

Merton, again. She is sitting outside, on one of the verandas. She has been there, in that same place, all these years. Certain in her waiting, patient as a stone. She has made herself, day in, day out, imagine them, and they are coming back: Horace, Charlotte, Anne, Eliza. Tom, George, Sarah, Frank. Mrs Cadogan, Cribb. Her father, with his medals and his wounds. Just look at him, hardly changed. Everything that has happened in the time between, including his death, is forgotten – absence, humiliation, lies. Lies and death are the easiest to forget, having been, on the one hand, untrue and, on the other, unreal. There are secrets and toothache, fights between the boys, even though they are older now. There are slow walks to the summer-house, and fishing in the stream. At night there are conversations that last longer than the candles. These are my friends, she says, this is my family. Nelson takes her arm, and walks with her through the house. The upstairs rooms are in a mess, and smell of young people. Clothes have been left lying like the clothes of ghosts, scattered where they were taken off. Splashes are drying on the washstands, and soap has been left in the bowls. Boys, says Nelson. Wasn't I lucky to have a girl? He stands with her by the window, looking out over the lawns. Is that Cribb out there? It looks like him. Let's go down. I want you to help me choose something new for that bed over there; the roses had to go.

Fatima was standing in the doorway. How long had she been there? 'I never have seen a child stare into space so much.'

Horatia sighed. 'Nothing to do,' she said.

'You got a book.' She came and lifted the book from her lap and read the spine. 'That old fornicator,' she said. 'You're not in the mood, that's all. You want to help me?'

'Do what?'

Fatima sat with her for the rest of the afternoon, unpicking the seams of an old dress, taking out the short ends of thread and throwing them on to the fire. Cutting stitches, working backwards.

'If my lady . . .' said Horatia. She paused, her hands still. In her mind, too, she had been working backwards and backwards.

'If milady what?'

'If she hadn't gone to London when she did, we wouldn't be here now. None of us.'

Fatima smiled. 'If . . .' she said. 'If we never were born, then we never would die.'

'How old was she when she did?'

Fatima calculated the fib. 'I don't know,' she said. 'Eighteen. Twenty. Is this what you been thinking about all day?'

'No, just now. Where did she live?'

'My God, I weren't even born. I don't know what happen to milady all them years ago. Scissors, please. You want the truth?'

Horatia tipped her head.

'Well, she was in Wales. Her father died when she was very young, and she went with her mother to Wales, where all the fields are black, and the streets and the trees. That is why she talks the way she do, like someone, a bit, from Wales. That is all I know. They came to London, milady and Mrs Cadogan, and lived with Mr Greville in the Edgware Road.'

Fatima was stepping over stones. Buried stones, in the bed of a stream. She had picked them up herself, over the years, but she had put them down again, making sure that they were hidden. How her mistress had lived as a young woman was something only a handful of people knew, and Horatia was not one of them and never would be. Fatima knew, and did not know. Secrets, letters, mysterious visits. She had learned the value placed on reputation, and that it was something to be guarded with one's life, or the lives of other people. She knew that it was part and parcel of survival, when you were a woman without her own means, or a man who was a nation's hero. When it was gone, there was no one to help you: you were left in the floating mess of an engagement fought and lost. There were times, however, when she doubted it was worth it, or if it was worth it, that it was fair. The one thing she

140

wanted to tell Horatia, she could not, and she told herself anyway that it would break the girl's heart to learn the truth about who her mother was. Better that she lived with the dream of someone good than have to come to terms with what had become, by now, an awful truth.

Horatia was leaning forward, peering into Fatima's face. 'Fatima,' she said. 'She can't have been twenty.'

'Sixteen, then. She came to London when she was sixteen, and stayed with her mama and Mr Greville in the Edgware Road. Mr Greville were Sir William's nephew, and had expensive taste but not much fortune of his own. He also liked minerals and antiquities, like Sir William. They lived very quiet and retired, and milady ran the house with only some money, and tried to be like Mr Greville, and be good to him. She was a big girl, then, but also beautiful and not so fat. People came to see her, and she was painted many times by Mr George Romney, famous painter, and many others too. I seen some of them, the paintings they done. Beautiful.'

'And Sir William?'

'He came there and met her. At the Edgware Road.'

Sir William had been ambassador to Naples, at that time, for nearly twenty years. His first wife had died and he was bereft. He had brought her body home to be buried, and spent a year's leave in London. He was fifty-three years old. 'He thought milady was the most beautiful girl he had ever seen,' said Fatima. 'Mr Greville said to him, "What may happen if I run out of money, and cannot look after her any more? You have her, and I will marry a rich wife." So she went to Italy with Sir William and her mama, and she never did come back, not till after many years. She still thought, when she went, that she would be Greville's for ever, but he have washed his hands of her. He have given her to his uncle, thank you goodbye.'

'Fatima, I don't believe that.'

'Believe it. Listen, he was kind to her, but the money was all gone.'

'He sent her away!'

'Well.' Fatima drew in her mouth, and dimples appeared on her chin. 'Worse things can happen. He have spent all his money on stones and pictures and ancient vases. He thought he must find a rich wife, and went to look for one. Sir William was kind, but it was never milady's intention to become his. She belonged to Greville, she think. Then she find out from Sir William that she did not, that Greville have not made one mention that he will come to Naples to get her back again. She did cry and cry, and said that she would walk barefoot to Scotland to get him, which is where he were at that time. Then she came to love Sir William, and he married her himself.'

Horatia was gazing at the pattern spread over her knees. Sprigs of heather. 'My father met them in Naples.'

'Yes.'

'I wish I had lived there.'

'Well, listen. One day you can live where you want. Marry some lovely handsome man, who is kind as an angel and have a pot of money. He can take you to Rome, to Naples, to Vienna and Paris. He can say, "My dearest beautiful wife, you can take your pick." Also Surrey and London, you choose.'

Horatia grinned and shook her head.

2

She stood in the door of Emma's room. A candle burned beside the bed. 'Who was my mother?' she said.

'Horatia, go away.'

She moved across the room, and sat in a chair beneath the window. 'Who was she?'

Emma still did not move. 'You can't ask me that.' The flame of the candle was steady. 'Now's hardly the time, for God's sake.' Emma pulled herself up and reached a hand, wandering, towards the drink on the bedside table.

'When, then?'

'Not now. I don't know. I'm ill, I'm going to die soon.'

Horatia stood. She lifted the glass and gave it to her. The time would never be right. There was never, any more, a sober moment. 'I'm not going to leave you. Is that what you think? That I'll get up and go the minute I know who she was? For God's sake, you know I won't.'

'What does it matter?' Emma sighed. 'You've had me to look after you. I've done everything a mother would have done. I've spent every penny I had—'

'You're not my mother.'

'And what if I was?'

Horatia turned her face away; a small dismissive sound escaped her lips.

'What, Horatia? What if I was your mother?'

'You aren't, you never could be.' It was whispered, and certain. 'I want to know.' She studied the face of the sick woman. Somewhere in that half-destroyed mind, in that dying memory, was a name. Two or three words. 'It won't kill you to tell me,' she said quietly. 'If you're so sure you're going to die, then at least tell me who she was before you do.' Her eyes burned with the heat of dry tears, and her throat caught on anger. 'Please,' she said.

'I've given everything to you that a mother would give—'

'You aren't my mother! Stop saying that. You could never be my mother, not in a million years.' She lifted her face to the shuttered window. The words she had just spoken swept back through her head. 'I'm sorry.'

'Go and find something to do.' Emma's voice was weary again, and weak. 'I don't know. I don't know who your mother was. Do you think I wouldn't tell you if I did? I don't. Now leave me alone.'

TEN

I

Nelson's carriage turned into the drive. He and Emma had
spent the day in London. He had been to the Admiralty, to the
Navy Office, to his agents, and with the Prime Minister. He
had gone to Mr Salter, a silversmith in the Strand, to order a
knife, fork and spoon with Horatia's name on them, and a
silver-gilt cup. He had been mobbed in Piccadilly, and crowds
had followed him from place to place, from shop to shop.
They had run down the Strand in front of him, shouting his
name and waving hats. Doors and windows had been
crammed with faces, and women had tried to kiss his coat.

'Damn,' said Emma.

'What?'

'I left a pair of shoes in London. I meant to bring them. I
always forget something if Fatima isn't there.'

'You'll live.' His head was half out of the window. It was
August, and hot. He had been ashore for less than a week.
There was some cloud, but it was high and seemingly still.
'There she is!'

Horatia was running towards them across the grass. Fatima
followed at a walk. Nelson called to the driver to stop the
carriage. 'Look, it's you!' he called to his daughter. 'Where do
you think I've been?'

She didn't answer him. She swerved to a stop and looked up
at his face. She was wearing a dress that came to her knees, and
long pantelettes underneath it. 'Get out,' she said. 'Come and
take me in the boat and look for fish.'

He laughed. 'May I go upstairs and change my shirt, first?' Unusually for him, he was not wearing uniform. He was dressed instead in green breeches, a yellow waistcoat, a plain blue coat, and a cocked hat with a green shade over his eyes.

Horatia shook her head. 'Now. Fatima can row us.'

Emma put a hand on his knee. 'Horatio, it's after three, we should eat.'

'Half an hour,' he said.

He climbed down from the carriage, and Horatia took his hand. 'This way.' She tugged him, like a donkey.

'Excuse me.' He dug his heels in and bent low. 'Do I get a kiss?'

She placed one on his face, and set off towards the lake. Behind them, the carriage rolled off to the house.

'Fatima,' he said, as they met her on the lawn. 'You're well?'

'Yes, milord. Thank you.'

'I wish I could spend more time here, instead of going backwards and forwards to London.'

'Yes, milord, I wish that, too.'

Soon, though he did not know when, he would have to go away again. The French and Spanish fleets were still scattered in the Atlantic ports. They were watched by British squadrons, but if they could get out and mass their ships, Napoleon might soon be in the Channel.

Behind them, the house faced east out of bow windows and between the pillars of the twin verandas. Chairs had been brought out, and every downstairs window was open. Inside, someone was playing the piano. The sound was thin and high, as if it lived out here on the still air. Tree-studded lawns sloped down to the river, and behind them stood cedars, chestnuts and oak trees. Copper beech and juniper. Cribb, the gardener, was pruning roses, and Nelson made a mental note to talk to him later. His wife was about to have a baby, he should have some money for a christening robe. He needed to talk about next year's planting, too. Horatia swerved in front of him and pointed. His three nephews were fishing in the stream – Tom, Horace and George. 'Any luck?' he called to them. Horace waved and made a face.

'You can be . . . Lord Nelson,' said Horatia, when they reached the bank above the lake. 'Fatima is the flag captain, and I am lookout.'

'She's bossy, Fatima.'

'I say she should be captain, milord.'

'I agree. Horatia, you should be captain of this vessel. Fatima can be first lieutenant. I'll be your flag captain, if that's all right.'

'Can you speak French?' said Horatia.

'Not a word, no.'

'I can. *Comment allez-vous?*'

Nelson beamed. 'You're a clever little girl. We'll send you to France, and you can deal with Bonaparte. That's what you get for boasting.'

She yelled, then let go of his hand and ran towards the boat, which was moored to a stake in the ground.

'Don't go near the water!' Nelson turned to Fatima. 'She runs everywhere,' he said.

'She does. She falls over, many times. Also, she runs into things and bangs her head.'

'Good Lord! Does she hurt herself?'

'Not so much.'

Nelson scanned what he could see of the grounds through filmy eyes. Paradise Merton. He could smell the warm, dry scent of the grass, the sweet stink of pond weed, the old perfume of lavender drying on the stem. 'It's very fine here, Fatima,' he said. 'It's everything I wanted.'

'Yes, milord.'

They climbed into the boat, Fatima first. She lifted Horatia onto the seat in the stern, and stood to give Nelson a hand. She piped him aboard with a whistle that carried over the still water of the lake. 'Carry on,' said the admiral, and she pushed

147

off, sat herself between the oars, and rowed. Sunlight spun on the water, and the oars creaked; dozing wildfowl blinked at them from the shore. Horatia leaned forward and touched Nelson's brow, the line of the scar underneath his hat. 'Egypt,' she said.

'That's right, little one. I thought I'd been killed.'

She laid a hand softly beside his right eye. 'Corsica.'

'Yes. That was a shell.'

She nodded. Then she moved her hand and touched the stump of his right arm. 'Tenerife,' she said.

'Do you know where that is, Tenerife?'

'No. Sing.'

'Sit still, then. Don't wriggle.'

They sang songs at the top of their voices, and went up as far as the bridge and back. They shot their guns at trees and birds and fish and clouds. They caught leaves in a net, and threw them back. Too small.

They were the long days of August, and the short days of a leave that might end tomorrow. They were sailors, hunters, royal dukes. They crawled under the table in the dining room and set up camp. He lifted two pinched fingers to his lips. 'More tea?' he said. There wasn't a lot of room between the table legs, and he leaned forward on his elbow. 'Shall I tell you a story?'

She nodded. Her eyes were round and her mouth was full of make-believe cake. 'It's a true story, about when I tried to catch a bear.'

'A bear?'

'Yes. The year is seventeen seventy-seven. I am a boy of . . . oh, fourteen, nearly fifteen. I was on an expedition to find a passage past the North Pole to the East Indies. We set off in May. For weeks, there was nothing but fog. Then we saw the sun shine down on the ice hills of Spitzbergen, and they looked like castles and ruins and monsters and whales. White and blue and pink. They looked like jewels in the icy sea. It was so

148

cold that we were given extra pepper and mustard with our rations. Extra rum, too.'

'Mustard!'

'Mustard, yes. We ate it in great big spoonfuls. I'll show you, at dinner. Anyway. We could see real whales, too, sending their fountains towards the skies. Then the icefields, and then the floes. They were like drifting islands, hills and plains of snow and ice, and when we looked, we saw monsters walking on them.'

Monsters. She listened to the highs and lows of his voice, and watched his face, a man's face. She waited while he paused to put his hand to his eyes and rub them.

'Monsters,' he went on, 'with long dripping moustaches and big ivory tusks. They jumped off the ice and crashed into our boats, and would have sunk them if I hadn't chased them away.'

Outside, someone was calling Horatia's name. She shrank down between her shoulders, and kept perfectly still.

'It was a world of ice. The snowflakes came down like icicles, like stars. One night we decided, a shipmate and I, to go out and get a bearskin for ourselves. There was a bit of fog, and we could get off the ship without being seen. I led the way, over great cracks in the ice, a rusty musket in my hands.'

'Two hands.'

'Yes, two hands, then. Soon, after walking for a while in the cold, grey fog, we found a bear. A great big shaggy bear. I fired at it with my gun, but just then, behind us, we heard a party from the ship. They'd come out to look for us. The signal was made for us to go back. My shipmate did, but not me. I fired my musket again, but this time it flashed in the pan. No more ammunition. Big bear, standing up on its shaggy legs, roaring across a chasm in the ice at little Horatio Nelson.'

'Did you get it?' It was a whisper.

Nelson's leg had gone to sleep underneath him. He stretched it, and winced. 'No, little one, I did not. I might have jumped the chasm, and given it a bash on the head with my musket, but I wasn't given the chance. The captain of our ship ordered a blank charge to be fired from one of the guns. It made a huge bang, and the bear loped away. I got into trouble, needless to say, but never mind.'

Horatia's name was called again, this time from inside the house. 'Come on, Captain,' said Nelson, 'time to go.'

2

Sometimes she is a captain in the Navy, sometimes in the Army. She is Herrick Evenden, fleeing the King's men, running towards London. It's the Wars of the Roses, and she can hear the clash of battle. She hears the sound of pikes ringing one against another, of swords and pistols, and of men crying out in anguish. A fierce battle is raging in Barnet, north of London, between King Edward and the Earl of Warwick. Edward's army wins the day, and Warwick's men flee towards London. Run for your lives, men!

'Don't run,' says Fatima. 'That's the second time you've done that.'

'It doesn't hurt.'

It's night. They have to flee through the dark, past the fields of St Pancras, through the streets of London. The men of Lancaster, put to flight. Herrick Evenden is with them. He has spared the life of a Yorkist in battle; he is brave, and chivalrous, too. He has been given a ring as a token, a Yorkist ring, which he wears on his hand.

'Upstairs, please. Face, hands, clean dress. Now.'

Now he is making for Chertsey, his chainmail glinting in the light of the moon. He has lost his shield and his weapon, but if he must die, he will die in the arms of his beloved Blanche. Now he has been taken by the guards, but a rider has been sent to King Edward in London to seek a pardon. Now the rider is nearly home, the pardon in his saddlebag, but he is on the wrong side of the river and the ferry is delayed. Only a mile to go with the news of the King's reprieve, and time is running out.

'Look at me, please, and keep still. It'll hurt if you don't keep still.'

All is lost. But no! Blanche Heriot runs swiftly to the abbey. She climbs into the belfry and hangs on the clapper to stop the curfew being sounded. She swings forwards and backwards, forwards and backwards, and never lets go, though her arms are ready to break.

'Horatia, keep still or I'll smack you. What's your godfather going to say if you go down looking like you've walked through a hedge?'

The Wars of the Roses. She sees an army of roses marching up over Chertsey Mead, their big heads tossing pink and yellow. She hears the clink of their armour, and the shouting of orders. She sees the lines of rose cavalry, and the lines of rose infantry, and hears the sound of their boots on the village street. Camp followers straggle behind and spread without formation. She sees them on a boat for France, saying their prayers, pink and red and white. Ships full of roses, captains and midshipmen, bearing down on the ports, and the loud explosions, and a cloud of petals.

'Look at me, please.' Fatima licks a finger, and wipes a spot on Horatia's face.

'What's for dinner?'

'Wait and see.'

3

That evening, Emma pulled Nelson upstairs by the sleeve of his coat. 'They won't miss us for half an hour,' she said.

'The boys will. They'll run out of money at cards, and their uncle won't be there for them to empty his pockets.' By this time the senior Matchams had arrived from Bath. The William

Nelsons were also there, walking somewhere in the grounds.

'Never mind the boys.' She had bought a large feather bed and feather bolsters, and a new Kidderminster carpet for the bedroom. She unrolled his stockings and kissed his feet. 'William's coming over from Bushey tomorrow,' she said.

'William? He's here – he's outside.'

'Not your brother, the Duke of Clarence.'

'Oh, William. Good. Is he coming for dinner?'

'Marianna's ordered mackerel – it's coming down tomorrow. She's going to cook it with gooseberries.' She kissed his knees. 'From the garden.' Then her hands were on the buttons of his breeches. 'There's a joint, and beans with sack and cream and orange peel. Stewed venison, chicken in wine.'

He lifted her chin and kissed her mouth.

'Anchovy toasts and potato pudding.' She worked her way up the buttons of his waistcoat. 'Who put this on for you this morning?'

'You did.'

'So I did. I missed a button. Pancakes and raspberry fritters.'

'But what if he's hungry?'

'Lift your chin.' She undid the bow of his neckcloth, and pulled it away from his collar. Suddenly, their clothes exasperated them; they came off in seconds rather than minutes, and were thrown down on the Kidderminster carpet. His arm was soon pinned somewhere under her heavy folds, and he had all but lost the feeling in it. The rest of him was singing with grateful astonishment at the things she was doing to him. She whispered a word in his ear, which, if it was not an obscenity, sounded very like one. He laughed, a yelp of joy that came from his heart and from a region deep beneath it. Her hand slid down the inside of his knee, and he felt tiny fists open over every inch of his skin. Never in his life had he forgotten so much of himself and yet been reminded at every moment that there was something exquisite to be felt in every part of his shattered body. He had been to India, Jamaica and Quebec, to

Yucatán and Venezuela; he had sailed to find an Arctic route to the Pacific, but he had never before set foot in such a place as this. She had brought him to life; she was everything he held dear in the world, and he had no other thought but of her, of her beauty and her exuberance. Her perfect mouth. Her beautiful shoulders, extraordinary breasts. He was helpless with love and with sensation, and his heart, which at other times gave him pains in his chest that made him think he would die, felt close to exploding with joy.

ELEVEN

I

Emma stayed in her room. Fatima took food up to her, but
most of it came down again. On her way to her own room,
Horatia stood outside the door, in the shadows of the passage,
trapped by silence. The whole house seemed to be leaning on
its elbows, staring down into the space between, trying to stop
itself thinking. It felt to her that while she stood there, if she
stood long enough, the silence might open a crack and some
small message be slipped through for her. It was not a real
place at all, this or any corridor, where no one stopped and
nothing was familiar except the boards that had come up
under the runner, creaking when they were stood on, and
sometimes when they were not.

It was a fearful place, a passage of ghosts, all of them
strangers, and French. Like the women in the village, they
hovered near her, arms crossed over their hearts. It was a place
where thought became a thin line, barely lit, and where she
herself felt invisible. The door to Emma's room was like the
door at the bottom of a stairway in a dream: there was a
monstrous darkness behind it and the rustle of attention, the
silent exclusion of suffering. Every time that door closed, even
though she knew what lay behind it, her own fears swarmed in
her, her helplessness, her dread.

Janot sat at the bottom of the stairs, his eyes fixed on the
half-landing, waiting for her to come down again.

'Take him for a walk,' said Fatima. 'He's driving me mad.'

It was no longer raining. The sun had come out, scudding

155

between the clouds, and the wind was cold. It came from the north, and Horatia could smell the sea on it. '*Viens,*' she said to the dog. They followed the stream until they were forced off the path by brambles, then cut across a small field of long grass to the edge of a birch wood. The rain of the last two days had filled the ditches at the edge of the trees; she yelled at Janot not to go in, but he did. He came up black with mud and leaf mould, smelling of soggy wood. Then he plunged off into the trees, nose to the ground. She heard the sharp, staggered call of a pheasant, and the *tink, tink* of blackbirds. They walked for half an hour, circling the wood, until they came out onto the lane that led past the neighbouring farm. It was lined on either side by hedges, packed with dogwood and ivy. As they turned a corner in front of the farm, Madame Brigeaud, the farmer's wife, was herding a dozen geese in through the gate. She was wearing sabots, and an apron over her skirt, and carried a stick. She saw Janot first. 'Sit, Janot,' she said. 'Stay. *Bonjour, Mademoiselle.*'

Janot sat. He knew Madame Brigeaud and her flock.

'He's filthy,' said Horatia.

Madame Brigeaud held the gate for them. 'Do you want to come and see where they live?' she said. 'Close the gate behind you. Make sure it's shut.' Janot waited for a signal, then followed.

There were about twenty geese in all. In the daytime, those that were being fattened for St Martin's Day were kept in pens while the rest of the flock grazed the stubble fields. Madame Brigeaud gave Horatia the stick to hold, and hobbled off through the back door of the farmhouse.

The yard was packed mud. On one side stood the house, pink and ramshackle in the evening light, its gutters mossy, its doors and windows painted brown. The paint was flaking, and the roof was sloped by weather. The shutters were all closed, as if someone had died. On the side opposite the road stood a small shed made of stone and wood. Beyond it were the pens, and behind them two goats stood tethered to a stake. Chickens pecked for food on a compost heap. There was a pond, its edges a trodden mess of mud, feathers and droppings.

'Come on, then.' Madame Brigeaud emerged from the low back door with a pail of kitchen scraps in one hand, and of turnips and potatoes in the other. She crossed the yard and set the pails on the ground. The small flock made a ring round her, a quiet gabble going through it like a dozen squeaky doors. They stretched their necks in greeting, and dabbed with their beaks. The old woman ducked down into the end shed and, after banging about inside, came out with a shallow pail of corn. 'Take this,' she said. 'Just throw it.'

Horatia leaned the stick against the shed wall, and took the pail.

'And don't go anywhere near that one over there or he'll try to take your leg off. That's Marshal Davout.'

Janot had learned this lesson already. He had been seen off by Marshal Davout more than once. He took up a post under the wall near the gate, and sat on his haunches, waiting.

'He's very brave,' said Madame Brigeaud, 'and very chivalrous. Unfortunately he went for the mole-catcher last week.' She squeezed her face into a frown. 'I'm afraid that's probably what killed him.'

'The mole-catcher?'

'The mole-catcher, yes. Monsieur Costes.'

'He's not dead! He can't be dead.'

Madame Brigeaud dropped her chin and peered at Horatia, the frown still there between her eyes. 'Well, he can. It happens, you know. Hasn't Berthe been to the village? They found him yesterday, under a hedge. The doctor said a heart attack, but me, I keep seeing him last week, when Davout chased him off the road.'

Horatia could not see him dead. She could see him running, his traps banging against his legs, puffed and terrified, but not dead. They had passed him only days ago; Fatima had said hello to him. He had been there, as much as the trees and the ditches and the crows and the fields, and now he was gone: a hand had come down out of the sky and taken him away and left a gap. She looked up, as if to make a quick inventory of the rest of the world about her.

'Seventy-six,' said Madame Brigeaud. 'Not bad.'

She saw the old man, hung out on a hedge, grey and silky, with his eyes gone, flies circling and buzzing over him. His jaw hung open, and his teeth were small. She threw a handful of grain over the yard. 'Do they always follow you?' she said.

'They would if I let them. They think I'm their mother.'

'All of them?'

Madame Brigeaud turned down the corners of her mouth and nodded.

'But you're not a goose!'

'I know that and you know that.' Madame Brigeaud straightened and stretched her back. 'They don't know it, though.'

They scattered the corn and the scraps over the yard. The geese waddled forward, fighting and pushing for food. 'Now the others,' said Madame Brigeaud. The young ones were almost ready for market. For the last week they had been kept in the pens and crammed with as much corn, oats and boiled potatoes as they could eat. Their faces were full of trustful curiosity, and they thrust their beaks through the stakes of the pen.

Horatia could still see the goose in the butcher's shop, its head hanging limp on its long neck. She wanted to lift the latch and let them follow her out, the way they followed Madame Brigeaud to the fields and back. The young ones, the old ones, Marshal Davout. She walks them through the yard, then the gate, and they troop off down the lane behind her, Janot bringing up the rear. They hold a tidy formation, matching her pace and chatting like children. When they meet the road she

158

turns south, and they all keep going, Horatia Nelson, Janot and twenty geese. They are seen on the outskirts of Amiens, and in fields of cut wheat near Paris. Orléans, Clermont-Ferrand. At night they sleep under the stars, or in the shelter of barns. People begin to expect them; they stand by the side of the road to wait and watch. There, they say. There they are, and that's Marshal Davout. Not fat enough to eat, that lot: too much walking and seeing the world. They've seen just about everything by now, those geese. Further south, and further south. The seasons have run backwards, and at Le Puy the sun shines with the strength of June, and the ditches beside the road are white with cow parsley. They wind their way up grassy hillsides, announcing themselves with gobbles and honks. At a castle high on a hill above the Rhône, they are met by an Englishman. I knew who you were the moment I saw you, he says. Come in, have something to eat, the geese, too. Your father was a great man, he says, and a hero, but also kind and simple. I knew him well. Some men put their manners on in the morning with their clothes, but not him. He was good through and through, and not at all vain.

The farmer's wife emptied the buckets into the pen, and led Horatia into a dry and airy shed. There was straw everywhere, and dust and down feathers, and countless bright green slimy droppings, like small, broken eggs, gone off. Madame Brigeaud forked up the dirty straw, and shook out some new.

'Do they all have names?'

'No, only Davout.'

'Why?'

'You can't eat something that has a name.'

They left the flock to finish feeding, and traipsed across the yard again with the empty buckets. 'Let's see if we can find you some eggs,' said Madame Brigeaud. 'To give to your god-mother.' *Pour ta marraine.*

Horatia felt her chin tremble. It was like a small animal, something she couldn't control attached to the bottom of her face. It puckered, pulling down her lower lip. Without warning, sorrow had flung itself at her, the way a boy flings himself onto a rope slung over the river, grabbing it mid-leap and taking it out in an extraordinary swing. She knew that she had to find the thoughts that had done this to her, to beat them off so she would not think them. The line of women in Monsieur Grangé's shop, the rustle of their clothes, the grey hairs sprouting on their chins, the mean line of their lips. The young goose, sleek and dead. Lady Hamilton, drunk or in bed. Her chin began to hurt, and the sides of her neck, with the effort not to cry. Perhaps Madame Brigeaud had not yet heard the rumours flying round the village. Perhaps she was deaf to them. She turned her face to the pond, the geese, the dust and the mud. She saw Janot, lying on the ground beside the wall, his head between his paws, his eyes on her. She looked up into the sky, her lips closed tight like the neck of a drawstring purse.

'Take this.' Madame Brigeaud thrust a basket at her. Then she took her arm, pinching it above the elbow until it hurt. 'Everybody's got to eat,' said the old woman, and Horatia knew, then, that she had heard everything and knew what everyone was saying. She tried to thank her, but her throat was rigid.

The henhouse was an old cupboard, filled with woodworm, and cleverly extended with planks. The shelves made perfect roosts. Madame Brigeaud scooped handfuls of grain from an apron pocket, and scattered it on the ground. Then, while the chickens made their way over from the compost heap, she rummaged through the wooden boxes that lined the shelves. 'Here,' she said. She held three eggs in her cupped palm, and Horatia placed the basket under them.

'We used to have a farm,' said Horatia.

'You?' She felt around in another box. 'Here, one more,' she said, passing the egg to Horatia.

'My father had one. In England, a small one. Cows and chickens and pigs. I remember it.'

The old woman wiped her hands on her apron. 'Listen,' she said. 'Take the eggs. Tell Berthe to poach them. Nothing gets any easier, but everyone's got to eat. Bring the basket next time you come past.'

It was nearly dark when she got home. Fatima took one look at Janot, and told her to put him in the stream. 'And dry him off properly. Underneath as well.'

2

General James rode over with a volume of Hume's *History of England*. Emma got dressed, came down, and practically buried him in flattery and gratitude. She leaned forward on the sofa and looked at him as if there were a sort of radiance around him, as if he had gathered all the light from the fire and from the windows, and was as a result both bright and unsteady. She poured him a brandy, then another. She spoke to him as to a dear friend, though there were moments, as she peered into his old face, when it seemed she suspected he was someone else, someone to whom she owed money, perhaps. Horatia sat still, almost rigid, as if she were waiting for pain. Nowadays, when she counted bottles, she counted two or three or four. Emma stayed in her room most of the time, the shutters closed and a low fire burning. When she did emerge, she had to be watched every moment, so that she did not fall or break something, or spill wine on the furniture.

'I would have brought it over sooner,' said the general. 'I couldn't get away.'

'Couldn't get away,' Emma repeated, with a quick lift of her head. 'Couldn't get *away*?'

'Thank you,' said Horatia. 'You remembered.'

The general told them that he and his wife were finally set to leave for Paris, and then for Italy. He was making a gift of the book or, to put it another way, he was giving it to them until the day that their paths might cross again – here in France, or in London, or in Essex, if they ever found themselves in Essex. His tone kept swerving, strung as he was between Emma's volubility and Horatia's discomfort. He rolled the brandy in his glass.

'Essex?' said Emma.

Horatia shifted on her chair. 'How long will you stay in Rome?' she asked him.

'For the winter. Not Rome, in fact, Tivoli. Wonderful gardens, extraordinary views. Have you been there?'

Emma leaned forward again, and laid a hand on the old man's arm. 'Listen,' she said, 'I helped him to write that book. I told him everything he needed to know. I gave him money, too. He had a large family, and they were desperate.'

The general frowned. She had helped to write the *History of England*? But Hume was dead. Dead for forty years, more or less. He looked to Horatia for help, but her face was white and blank.

'People said that it was full of lies, but it wasn't. It was the truth. Mind you . . .' Emma looked away into the corners of the room, to one side and to the other, then closed her eyes for moments, as if stuck in the act of blinking. 'He let me down very badly. He stole from me, and he made demands. He . . .' She seemed to give up then, lost somewhere in a backwater of betrayal.

Harrison, the general thought suddenly. The name came into his head like a coin dropped into a moneybox. There was a biography, brought out the year after Nelson's death. He had not read it, but he had read about it. Someone in one of the papers had called it nauseous. Then there had been a book of letters, published earlier this year. Had she seen it or not? Evidently she had, or she had heard enough about it. Many thought James Harrison was behind that, as well. It hadn't done much for Nelson's public character, whoever brought it out, and it had been the death blow for hers.

'I'll tell you something, General.' Her eyes were open now,

filled with tears of desolation. 'The government owes me something. I did them some service, you know. I paid money from my own pocket. I wrote letters. I gave them information. I paid over and over again for corn to save Malta. I secured entry for the British fleet to the port of Syracuse before the glorious battle of the Nile. They would have had no water or provisions if it had not been for me. There would have been no battle, no victory.'

He had begun to feel like a man who had walked in on the scene of an accident, and was incapable of doing anything more useful than sitting by the wreckage and waiting. He had never seen her like this. He had no idea what to say to her. Here she was, claiming to have changed the course of history. Then again, he told himself, perhaps she had used her influence at Naples. By all accounts, it had been hers to use.

'I might have been rich,' she told him, in a low, confiding tone, 'if I'd thought about myself and not about my country. I spent my own money and I haven't had one penny back from the government. They've used me very badly. He left us to the nation, his daughter and his one true friend. He asked them for that one thing, and did anything come of it? They've left us to rot, never mind his dying wishes. He gave himself, his own life, that his country might be spared and nothing, *nothing*, is given back to him.'

It was more than manners that kept the general in his seat, and it was nothing so magical as a spell. It threw him back in his mind to his Army days, and the bullying effusions of drunken majors that trapped him where he sat. The endless litany of things regretted and people loved; the pointed finger that nailed him to his chair. The strange constructions of speech, the small foam of spit at the side of the mouth. Still, it was true: the government had treated them very badly. 'I wish . . .' he began, but then he hardly knew what it was that he did wish, or should wish, and in any case Emma was not

163

listening. She had swerved mentally, and was demanding that Horatia play something on the piano.

It had not been tuned, and one of the hammer shanks had split, but Horatia played it, sticking to pieces that had no words, to tunes that could not be sung.

Emma sat with her eyes closed, as if she were waiting for the world to slow down or change direction. Then she decided that they would dance. She demanded a waltz, and dragged General James out of his chair. Though she had taken him very much by surprise, he managed not to fall over, and placed an arm on her waist. The room seemed to stagger around them as they moved. 'Very good!' cried Emma. 'Excellent! You're a born dancer, General.' Beside her, he was small, easily smothered. Held against her great bosom, he felt as if he were being attacked by a bed. He did his best to steer, but barked his shin on a low table, and knocked a picture out of line. Then suddenly the strength seemed to leave Emma's legs, as if they had remembered something in another place. She slid to the floor, her back against the side of the sofa. The general staggered forward, but managed to let go of her before he was dragged down, too. Horatia stopped playing and went to her. 'Did you hurt yourself?'

'Get . . . off.'

The general was torn between concern and the urge to pretend that nothing had happened, or that what had happened was only natural and common in the middle of a waltz. Also, the brandy was working against him. However, there were rules to fall back on. If she was ill, he should leave the room; if not, get her up. 'My lady,' he said, leaning forward, and offering his hand. She watched it as it remained in the air in front of her, as she might watch a bird that had come for a look.

'Thank you,' she said at last.

Was this a mistake? He was not a young man, and no longer strong. He spread his feet a little, and centred his weight. His boots, he saw with interest, had been splashed with mud on the ride over, which had dried in grey spots. 'One, two, three . . .' he said.

Then Fatima was in the room, standing beside her mistress. She looked at Horatia, and lifted her chin. They each took one arm, and the general pulled from the front.

'I can do this . . . myself,' said Emma, as they brought her up. She wasn't concentrating, and swayed. 'You see,' she said to the general, 'how you knock a woman off her feet!'

He took this, though he was not supposed to, seriously, and felt suddenly defensive. Then it dawned on him, strangely late, that while she had kept up with him drink for drink, these were not her first of the day. She was very seriously drunk, and he should have gone home an hour ago.

When he left at last, it took him several goes to get onto his horse. He struck off towards Calais with an hour of light still left in the sky. Emma went up to bed, and the house retreated into its own corners. Horatia went through every room on the ground floor, looking for bottles. Every one she found, she took outside and emptied into the stream.

Fatima was waiting for her in the kitchen with a lamp. 'Heh,' she said. She put an arm round her shoulders, and walked her to the stairs. 'Listen, *chère* . . .'

'It's all right. I know.' It had been a useless thing to do. A waste of money, nothing more.

3

Late that night, she heard Emma shouting at Fatima. She heard her own name, cried out on the other side of the wall. And then, extraordinarily, a slap. A slap, and then silence. Silence, then the sound of weeping. Weeping, then the voice of accusation again, low and anguished. Emma's voice, flat with rage. Everything had turned to shouting and anger; their days were filled with different ways of giving and receiving pain. All they had was each other, but in Emma this reliance had mutinied and turned to fury. Fatima could not do anything right any more; everything she brought to Emma's room was wrong or badly done – the bread was stale, a stocking was still damp. Wrong, wrong, wrong. They could do nothing right, any of them, not Horatia, not Berthe. Worse, Emma accused Fatima of turning Horatia against her own mother, of feeding her with lies, and teaching her to hate.

Listening to her from her own room, Horatia hated Emma Hamilton with all her heart. She put her hands over her ears and began to keen behind closed lips, so that the sound of her own voice filled her head. You, you, you, she thought. You are no one's mother, you could never be anyone's mother. You will say any monstrous thing to make people look at you, pity you, take your side. You were in Germany when I was born! Your mind is turning to mud, and you say things only a mad person would say. She was weeping now. Emma was not her mother: she had long since settled that in her mind, a certainty. With all her logic and instinct and the force of her great incredulity, she knew. She wept, not because there was any truth in what Emma was yelling at Fatima on the other side of the wall but because she was yelling at her. Poor, loyal, devoted Fatima, who had come from Egypt to Naples, from Naples to Europe, from Europe to London, and here. Who cared for Emma day and night with devotion, and for no thanks. Horatia wished to God that Emma would die. Now, she prayed, tonight. They would take her body back to England and bury her wherever she wished. She and Fatima would go to live with the Matchams, with her aunt and uncle, and George, Catherine, Horace and Charles. Then, terrified, she prayed it all back again.

TWELVE

I

'Tom, George, Catherine. Horace, Charlotte, Anne, Eliza. Mr Matcham, Mrs Matcham. The Reverend Doctor, Mrs Nelson.'

'Marianna and Mrs Cadogan,' said Fatima. They were in the garden, walking under the trees.

'Oh, yes. Dame Frances, Cribb.' The house was bursting with people. There were so many staying with them that it took moments to remember which rooms they were all in. 'Tom and George cut worms into three,' said Horatia, 'and put them on hooks. They don't catch anything. Fish don't like worms.'

Fatima said: 'If you cut up worms, they can grow again.'

'I know. But only worms. My lord had his arm cut off, and that didn't grow again.'

'No.'

'He says my lady is my guardian angel, but she can't be – she's too fat.'

'Horatia!'

'What? She is.' He had told her, too, that she must be obedient and an ornament to her sex. Ornaments are what you put on the mantelpiece and on the piano, and she sometimes wondered if she was going to have to climb up and stand there with the other ones. He was kind to her, and told her she did not have to eat mackerel with gooseberries. Fatima said she did, and if she didn't Lady Hamilton would be angry, and so would the King's brother, who had come to dinner. Fatima said, 'Think of all the poor children with not enough to eat,' and Horatia said, 'All right, they can have it. I'll wrap it up and you can take it to them.' Fatima told her she was a cheeky monkey.

Fatima had her own views on why Lady Hamilton had invited half the world to Merton. She had done it because Lord Nelson wanted to have his family around him, but also so that he might be less inclined to ask why Horatia had not been brought to live there until now, and why Emma was hardly ever there herself, these days, and why she had no money when he gave her more than a thousand pounds a year, on top of what Sir William had left her.

Now, at least, it looked as if the child was going to stay. For some reason, Nelson had got it fixed in his head that Jane Gibson was going to be difficult about giving her up. He had visions of her locking the doors against him and running away with his daughter, claiming her for her own. He would go to Little Titchfield Street and find it empty, and no one would know where they had gone. He had been, one day, almost in tears about it. In the end, he had decided to settle a pension on the woman, on condition that she never had anything more to do with Horatia. The break was already complete.

This is what Fatima thought of Lord Nelson: in London he was one thing, and on his ship another, and at Merton yet another. At Merton he did not dress up in all his stars and orders and medals, but in a black coat or a blue one. He did not talk like a hero, but like an ordinary man. He had a bold nose and a steady eye, and seemed in his face like a conqueror, though his body was a bag of bones. He was a kind man who would not hurt anyone, and yet, at sea, one who was always ready to get people killed. In his face, in his half-blind eyes, she had seen his ruthlessness. In the Bay of Naples, under a burning sun. She had read his letter from Copenhagen. It had been there then, and was not now. It seemed to her, too, that he had been prepared to die in every battle that he fought, and had wished, in between them, that he could. He held, she thought, a constant vision in front of him of a glorious death in battle, and more than a vision: a wish. In his letters to Lady Hamilton he had expressed an expectation, born of his ill health, his wounds and exhaustion, that was almost like hope. Even when he was burning with love, he wrote as a man who was ready to die. Yet he loved his life as well, and longed for love himself, private and public. He sought approval and warmth and a touch. He could never admit that he was wrong, and he was eaten up with vanity, consumed on the one hand by hatred and on the other by love. With Horatia, he was besotted, he was pure joy. Lady Hamilton talked to him as if he were God, and gave him praise and glory for breakfast and dinner. She dug it up the way Cribb dug in the garden, and shovelled it on him to make him grow. She sang and danced and laughed for him, and he sat with small eyes watching her. He loved her with a helpless love, enthralled by her beauty and by her motherly care. He was in many ways a great man, and in many others a baby.

'Fatima, run!'

Horatia launched herself down a steep bank, over the lawn, down to the stream, along to the lake and up to the summer-house. Fatima said there was a dragon in the summer-house, and they walked all round it, looking for signs of smoke. Fatima yelled, 'Aagh, I can see one!' and they ran like the devil. Then Lord Nelson was in front of them. He picked up Horatia with his one arm and carried her like a sack of wheat or a small pig.

'You're always running,' he said. 'Look at your knees. You've fallen over again.'

She couldn't look at her knees because she was a small pig. She was too heavy for him, and he sat her on top of a low wall. He leaned down to look at her. His eyes were filmy, like a dead fish's, and a green shade stuck out from under his cocked hat.

'Watch,' she said, digging a finger into the fob in his waistcoat.

'Mine, too? I've already given you one. I sent all the way to Naples for it, to Mr Falconet. I hope you haven't lost it.'

Her face was close to his coat. There was a strange smell, like tea and salt and brass. For a moment, she was fascinated by his wrist, by its bones, and the dark hairs under his cuff. Somewhere in the distance a gun went off. George and Tom. She swivelled towards the sound, but they were too far off, in a field, shooting pigeons.

'We saw a dragon.'

'Really?'

'We nearly did.' She turned his watch over in her hand. It was closed, and had no face. 'Are you going to stay here?'

'I suppose so, until you let go of me. I'm not going to miss my dinner, though.'

'*Here*. With us.'

The top-stones of the wall were flat and deep; he sat down beside her and let her scramble onto his lap. 'Careful,' he said. For a moment, he considered telling her that he would stay here for ever, that nothing would make him go away again, or tear him from his home. 'No, little one. I can't. The war isn't over yet. I've got to go and look for the French again.'

Horatia punched him. He took her fist, and kissed the knuckles. 'I'll find them as soon as I can, and then come back.'

'Will you kill them?' She pushed a finger into his chest. 'Don't.'

He thought about this for a moment. 'All right. I'll put them all in barrels. I'll put big labels on the outside, and send them back to France. Will that do?'

She wanted to believe him. She did believe him. She nodded.

'Tell you what.' He nudged her off him, and stood. 'To-morrow's Sunday. We'll go to church, and you can say your prayers, and ask God to send me home again soon.'

'Will he?'

'I think he might.'

Emma walked across the grass towards them. She looked like a ship. 'What are you two talking about?' she said. Horatia tried to think: nothing – God. Emma smiled at her, then fixed her eyes on Nelson's face. 'Come and feed the animals,' she said.

He leaned forward and kissed her mouth. 'They've just been fed.'

'Then we'll give them some more.'

Horatia was swept off the wall and through the tunnel under the road. 'Carry me,' she said, when they were half-way through it.

'Frightened?' said Emma, and her large voice hit the walls, got a shock and came back. Horatia was not afraid, but she nodded, and Emma picked her up. She smelled like a pillow. There were wheel tracks under their feet, and grass growing up between them. Sometimes Horatia came down here with Fatima, and they waited for a carriage to go over their heads. It was the French, and they were hiding.

'Don't kick,' said Emma.

They came out into the sun again, and there were cobbles and straw, and a plough and nettles, and the clop of hoofs in the stable. The mud had been dried hard by the sun, and cracked into shapes. Emma put her down. 'You run round for a while,' she said.

Horatia ran and then stopped. She got up on a step next to the trough, and looked down into it. The water was green and insects were skating on it. She wondered for a while how they did that, and tried to sink one, but it wouldn't go under. The sun jumped on the water, and tiny snails stuck to the stone sides. Her face came and went, green and slimy. She put her hand in the water, and her face shuddered, broke and vanished. The pump was hot in the sun. Nelson and Emma had gone inside the barn. She couldn't see them, but she could hear them. A ring of laughter, a bright sound on the warm air. She

171

could smell the hay from here, a green smell that had turned brown.

The pump was dripping. She put her hand under it to catch the water. On the other side of the fence, cows stood staring. Above them, the sky was blue and huge and endless. Cow plops, she thought, land flat on the ground, like pancakes. Horse plops are round, and they land like stones, only soft. She could no longer hear her godparents. They had gone. They had slipped out of the barn, their shoes in their hands, a finger to their lips. They had crept round the barn wall, over the nettles that grew beside it, and off on a path that Horatia did not even know about. Lord Nelson had jumped onto a horse and ridden to the coast and got on a ship without telling her.

Her lip began to tremble as if some minuscule insect had become trapped beneath the skin. She opened her mouth and yelled.

Nelson ran across the yard. His coat and his waistcoat were undone, and his hat nowhere to be seen. The scar on his head was livid, and for a moment she thought it might be alive. 'Little one!' he said. 'What is it?' Bits of straw had stuck to his coat; they looked as if they were hanging on for dear life. 'Did you get a fright?' He set her on the ground and knelt beside her. 'Good God,' he said, 'I thought you'd fallen in. What were we doing, leaving you here? Let's find a handkerchief.'

She found one for him, in his pocket, and he wiped her face. 'No more tears.' He turned her round and inspected her. The back of her dress had gone in the trough, and was wet and green. 'You are my darling child,' he said. 'Can you remember that?'

She wasn't sure what he meant, but she nodded.

'And you're very dirty.'

She grinned.

'Bend over.'

'No!'

'Come here and bend over.' He put her over his knee and

172

pretended to thrash her. She was looking straight down at a hard green cowpat on the ground. He said, 'Smack, smack,' and tickled the back of her legs. She laughed until she had the hiccups. Emma came out of the barn. 'Your hat,' she said, and gave it to him. There was something concealed in her face, like a small hare hidden in a painting of fruit and flowers.

'Story,' demanded Horatia.

'Another one?' he said. 'If I tell you one, will you be good?' She told him she would.

'And do everything that my lady tells you?'

Emma looked at her and smiled. 'It's hot,' she said, fanning herself. 'I'm going to go in. Are you coming?'

2

Sunday afternoon. After the second hymn, the children trooped through to the vestry. The sons and daughters of farmers, tradesmen, army officers. They could still hear, as the door closed behind them, the voice of the Reverend Thomas Lancaster, reading the notices.

'Sit down, everybody.' Frances Washer lived in the village. She cleaned the church, did the flowers, and taught the children hymns and Bible stories. Fatima had come in behind her, and was standing at the back of the room like a guardian angel. There was a smell of old clothes, of vinegar and polish.

'Bible pages,' said Frances Washer. 'Christ rebukes the storm. Nancy Turner, you may start.'

Nancy Turner was a small, brittle child with a grey complexion and a bitter mouth. She sat up in her seat, then dropped forward again to peer at the words on the page in front of her. ' "And it came to pass," ' she read, her finger tracing the line, ' "on a curtain day—" '

' "Certain," ' said Miss Washer.

' "On a certain day, that he went into a shop with his. . ." '

'No, think about it. What does it say?'

Horatia brought her shoulders forward, her fists clasped in her lap. She couldn't help seeing them, Christ and his disciples, riding the stormy seas in a shop. Around them, other shops tossed and pitched. The baker's, the glove shop, a bookseller's. A print shop, a chandlery. While Jesus slept, everything fell from the shelves and tumbled into the waves. Tobacco, bread, books and spoons. Brushes, hats and candles. The shop-keepers cried in alarm, and tried to save what they could. Cakes rolled across the steep decks, and pens and jewels and skeins of wool. Boots and birdcages bobbed on the water, and china vases sank like stones.

'Ship,' said Nancy Turner.

'Yes. Good. That's enough.' She continued to read herself: ' "And he said unto them, Let us go over unto the other side of the lake. And they launched forth. But as they sailed he fell asleep: and there came down a storm of wind on the lake; and they were filled with water, and were in jeopardy . . ." '

There were tears running down Horatia's face. It was not Christ but Lord Nelson, not shops but ships, and the danger was terrible.

'Heh,' said Fatima. She had swooped down from the back of the room with a wonderful rustle, like wings. 'What's this?'

Horatia's fists were closed, poised in the air above her knees. She had to save him. She had to think of a way to stop the water flooding the ship, to make him wake up, and run up to the lifeboats. He could not get his coat on, and there was no one there to help him. Monsters flew up from the deep, and the sky cracked with lightning, then burst with black, rolling clouds.

'Up you come,' said Fatima, lifting her from her seat.

They walked in the graveyard. The sounds of the service rose and fell away. On the other side of the lych gate, the carriage waited to take them back. Horatia spread her arms like a dancer. All her fears were swept away, and she ran

174

round looking for moles and old wreaths. 'What was that all about?' said Fatima. 'I never heard such a fuss.'

Horatia looked at her, then looked away. 'Snail,' she said, pointing at the ground.

'Slug.'

'Snail.'

Fatima pushed a hand through the child's hair. She didn't have a fever, anyway.

The final hymn thumped out from the church, then there was more murmuring and the people all came out. Nelson hurried over. 'What was it, Fatima?' he said. 'What was the matter?'

'Don't know, milord. I think it was a bit strange for her.'

'I was worried.' Horatia ran at his legs, and threw her arms round them.

'Not much wrong with you now,' he said.

3

The house was no longer full of people. Only the Matchams, George and Kate, remained. Beds had been stripped in the children's rooms, and the passages were quiet. At the bottom of the front steps, the gravel had been churned by carriage wheels.

It was time for bed. Her hair caught on a button, and she couldn't take off her shift. It was stuck over her head and she couldn't see anything, except her feet. She ran round the room with her arms sticking out. She had her stockings on but not her shoes, and where the carpet ended, she slid as if she were skating. *Whish, whish.* Ouch, splinter.

'What's going on in here?'

Fatima.

'What on earth are you doing? They can hear you down-stairs.'

'Stuck,' she whispered.

'Come here and stand still.' Fatima turned her round and stood her straight and tried to find where it was caught. Horatia's arms stuck out on either side and she couldn't put them down. She felt like a puppet or an angel.

'How did you get yourself into this state?'

'Ouch.'

'Keep still. I'm trying not to pull.' Fatima fumbled for a while, and then the shift came off over her head.

Suddenly there was a new cry. 'Fatima!'

'I'm standing right here. Don't shout.'

'I forgot to say my prayers. In church, I forgot.'

Outside, there were still hours of daylight left. 'Look,' said Fatima, 'another bruise.' She ran a thumb over the child's knee. Then she pulled a bed gown off the chair and unfolded it. 'Arms up again.'

'Fatima. I forgot.'

'I know, you said. You can remember now. Kneel down and say your prayers.'

'My lord said I must pray for him in church. So that God can send him home again soon.'

Fatima raised an eyebrow. 'He hasn't gone anywhere, he's downstairs.'

'But when he does. When he goes to sea.'

'All right. Listen, you don't have to be in church. Kneel down by your bed. Hands together and eyes closed. God bless my lord, and God bless my lady. Keep them safe, and make me a good girl. Amen.'

'Don't shut the door,' said Horatia, when she was tucked up in bed.

Swifts were still peeling the sky outside. She could hear their small bright screams, and the bark of a distant dog. Then she heard the stamp, stamp of enormous feet. Closer and closer and closer, stamp, stamp. Nobody there, but somebody coming, someone as big as a house. Then the smash of the sea on the side of a ship, and the steady thump of enemy guns.

Frenchmen lay where they fell, heads and arms cut off. My lord with a cutlass in his hand, rushing at them over the deck. Young men in blue coats, crying out as they died. There was blood on their knees and chins, on their chests and in their eyes. Then Fatima was standing in the open door. She looked as if she had been cut out of it with scissors. 'Wake up, *chère*,' she said. She came to the bed and leaned down over it.

'Can you tell him to come up?'

'Milord? He's busy, darling.'

'I haven't said goodnight.'

'Yes, you have. Go back to sleep.'

4

On 2 September 1805, at five o'clock in the morning, a post-chaise drove up to the house. Battle was imminent. The combined French and Spanish fleets were at Cadiz. Villeneuve had left Ferrol and joined with another fourteen sail-of-the-line from Corunna.

Nelson was already up and dressed; before midday he was in London, talking to government ministers about what should be done. The following days were a frenzy of meetings: the Foreign Office, the Admiralty, the Prime Minister. He would leave for Cadiz in the *Victory* as soon as possible. He paid a visit to William Peddison in the Strand, where Emma had bought the feather bed and the Kidderminster carpet. Peddison was also an undertaker, and Nelson had arranged to have sent to him the coffin made from the timbers of *L'Orient*, so that his name could be engraved on it.

He also went to Barrett, Corney and Corney, lace-makers and embroiderers to the King, where he bought silver embroidered stars of the orders of the Crescent, St Ferdinand, St Joachim and the Bath. He came out with five of each, and Mrs Cadogan and Fatima were up all night, sewing them on to his coats.

On what should have been his last day at Merton, he was summoned to Carlton House to pay his respects, through gritted teeth, to the Prince of Wales. He went home to Merton for dinner, where he found Emma in tears. She cried all through the meal, and her tears fell on the table and into her food. For once she could not eat, could hardly drink, and was near to collapse.

'Darling one,' said Nelson. 'Don't cry. Not so much.'

She shook her head, a hand held over her mouth. 'I feel as if I've been in a dream for a fortnight, and now I've woken up and you're going. I don't think I can do this, I don't think I can bear it.'

'Don't cry, though.'

'You might be killed!'

'If I am, there's a song I want you to sing for me, from Naples. I've left the words in the coffin.'

Her face was raw. 'How could I do that?' she wailed. 'What are you talking about? Unless I sang it in madness. If I lost you, I couldn't sing, not a word, nothing.'

'I suppose not, no.'

'Don't go. Please don't go! No one expects you to – you've done your duty, Horatio. Please, stay.'

They drove through the dark and the wind-tossed trees to the church. The Reverend Thomas Lancaster was waiting for them. The small building was chilly, and shadows moved as if the draughts were shifting them.

'Lift up your hearts,' said Lancaster.

'We lift them to the Lord.'

The sound of their voices moved like the shadows, and seemed to drift in the almost empty place. A door banged in the vestry. Outside, a fox barked. Above these sounds, Nelson could hear the words of a West Indian fortune-teller, years ago, who had looked into his future and been able to see no further than 1805.

'Let us give thanks to the Lord our God.'

'It is right to give thanks and praise.'

When the communion was over, and while Lancaster still stood before them, Emma and Nelson exchanged gold rings. 'I have taken the sacrament with you today,' said Nelson, 'to prove to the world that our friendship is pure and innocent, and of this I call God to witness.'

'Don't go,' whispered Emma, on the steps of the church. She could not look at him, and her eyes were lifted to the dark, the wind in the yew trees. 'Please.'

Part Two

ONE

I

He wrote from Portsmouth. He wrote with Weymouth off his starboard side. Four days later, he was in the Atlantic. He wrote off Cadiz, standing out to sea. My beloved Emma, may heaven bless you. My mind is calm. I love you both as much as my own life. Alone in the cabin of his ship, waiting for the French to come out, riding the Atlantic swell. We have very little wind. Kiss her for me.

A scouting frigate saw the topsails of the French fleet, and the signal went along a line of ships to the *Victory*. The nearest point of land was the Cape of Trafalgar, thirty miles west of Cadiz. 19 October 1805. My little one. The signal has been made that the enemy's ships are coming out of port. I know you will pray for me. You are always uppermost in my thoughts. Be a good girl, your loving father.

Fatima prayed. She prayed to one god, and then to the other. She went through the rooms of the house looking for things that had not been lost. One day, quite early, she heard the boom of the guns, all the way from the Tower.

They were at Merton. Emma was not well: she was in bed with a rash. 'The guns . . .' she said.

Fatima went to the window, as if she might from there be able to see their smoke. 'Maybe some victory in Germany. Maybe some news of milord.'

'No, it's too soon. It's much too soon.'

Five minutes later, they heard the wheels of a carriage on

183

the gravel drive. 'Go down, Fatima. Find out who it is.'

His name was Whitby. He had come from the Admiralty. He did not need to speak, and for ten hours after he had left, Emma did not move.

In her room, Horatia stared into the shadows. A lamp had been left burning in the passage. Footsteps went up and down, up and down. She had been woken by a wailing from outside. She leaned over the side of the bed, as if the noise had struck her on the back of the neck. The pattern in the carpet was one rose, and then another rose. The sound outside was like something torn and dying. She knew what it was: cats. They were below her window in the bed of nettles that stood against the wall. They were stuck there with their anguish, whatever it was, and no one would ever be able to get them out because of the tall strong nettles with their stinging leaves. She knew that it was cats, and yet she knew that it was something greater and louder and sadder than cats. The lamp in the passage flickered, and she saw the shadows change on the wall. She turned her eyes to the door, saw the wedge of yellow light. More footsteps, up and down. Fatima, Mrs Cadogan. The sound of words uttered in whispers, not because it was night but because something great and awful had struck them all. The sound of people who had, for the moment, forgotten her.

The whole country grieved, and could think of nothing else. In the streets, everyone wore a black scarf, or a cockade with Nelson's name on it. Every newspaper printed hymns and ballads in his praise, and the print shops were filled from floor to ceiling with engravings. His image was put on plates and cups, on the lids of snuffboxes and jars, on pipe bowls and tea trays; in picture books, on tea canisters, jam jars. People stayed indoors, then realised they could stay indoors no longer. They wanted other people, people beyond the family circle, to talk to as if they had known him. There had been a great victory, but all they could think about was his death.

Emma went to London. Captain Hardy, who had been with Nelson at the end and had heard his dying wishes, sent his belongings to her. She lay in bed in Clarges Street with everything around her: shawls and bracelets, gifts and letters. His hair, and the coat that he had died in. The bullet hole was there, stiffened with blood. People came and went. They sat at the end of her bed as she talked about his virtues and showed them all his gifts. The rooms were alive with grief and with things remembered, over and over.

2

For all the people going in and out, the house was bleak and cold. Emma sat in the drawing room with Alexander Scott. It was January, a week after the funeral. Emma had not attended it: women were not invited.

'I never left his side,' said Scott.

'I know.'

Scott had been Nelson's chaplain on the *Victory*. He was a small man, with a worried face, its creases deepened by his years at sea. He had been with Nelson while he died, and with his body throughout its long journey home, through the vigil and to the interment. He looked exhausted. He was exhausted.

'We don't know anything,' said Emma.

Scott nodded. He had not been looking forward to this, but then, in a way, he had. He had talked very little in the last weeks, as if grief had lodged its frontier in his throat. He had stopped praying almost completely. He found himself on his knees often enough, knocked down by the image of a bullet hole, by a great cry that was trapped in his chest, but all he saw when he was there was the floor, and the dark behind his eyes, pelted by images.

'Tell me what happened,' said Emma.

Scott placed his hands on his knees. He was not, even now, quite used to rooms that did not move while he sat in them. 'We could see them,' he said. 'They had more ships, but we had better guns.' There was a light wind, and the fleet rode a slow Atlantic swell. The sun shone on the sea, and the studding-sails were spread to catch the breeze. On the horizon, the four-mile line of the French and Spanish ships was slowly growing. Scott could see it all in his mind's eye, even to the point of feeling the sun on his face, and the salt, and the tremor of dread. He realised, if he had not known it before, that what he would tell her was only part of what he had seen.

'There were bands playing on some of the ships,' he said. 'We could hear the pipes on the breeze.' Marines sat cleaning their muskets on the *Victory*'s quarterdeck, while sailors sharpened their cutlasses. They were mostly stripped to the waist, their ears bandaged to deaden the sound, when it came, of the guns. Nelson walked up and down and spoke to them, talking of prizes and of victory.

'They all loved him. It's easy to say, but they really did.' Scott was rubbing his chin again, as if it was there, and not in his mind, that his memories resided. 'I've never seen anyone else do that. He could make them love him, and by the time he had walked the deck once or twice that day, they were ready to die for him.'

They were three miles, now, from the enemy line; when they were one mile away they would come within range of their broadsides.

'He had been below, with Hardy and Blackwood. Then he went down again, on his own. He went to pray.' Scott knew this because the signals lieutenant, John Pasco, had gone down to ask him something and found the admiral on his knees.

'He wore his courage and his faith like a hero,' said Scott. And all his medals, he thought, like a fool. His sword had been taken down from its rack in his cabin and put out for him, but he had left it behind on a table. He was, however, wearing half a hundredweight of silver embroidered stars from Barrett, Corney and Corney on his chest. He was a sitting target. All you needed was one sharpshooter in the rigging of a French ship.

'Blackwood wanted him to transfer to the *Euryalus*. It would have been safer, and he'd have had a clearer view of the action, but he wouldn't. He was right, I suppose. I don't know.'

When he lived it over in his mind, it was just as if it were happening again. The room around him, with its fire and its chairs, was miles away on a distant shore, and Scott was on the deck of the *Victory*. Just now, there was a huddle of officers around the admiral. The chaplain turned and looked out over the rail. They were sailing straight at the French and Spanish battleships. Until they split them, they would be under direct and concentrated firepower. Very soon, Scott would be down in the gloom below the water line, talking to the wounded and the dying. The dark down on the orlop deck was deepened by the dark rust red in which it was painted, and by the faint glimmer of horn lanterns. He would be surrounded by screaming men, laid out in rows on strips of sailcloth. He wanted to say something before he went below: someone had to make the admiral change his coat before they came into sniper range. He hovered near him, waiting for a pause in the talk, but before he had a chance to speak, all officers whose duties did not require them to be on the quarterdeck were ordered to their proper stations. On his way past the knot of men, Scott snagged Captain Hardy's arm. He cocked his head at Nelson, and tapped his own chest. Hardy promised to speak to him, and Scott went below.

Soon after one o'clock, they brought him down. His back had been shot through by a sniper in the rigging of the *Redoutable*. The ball had struck his left epaulette, penetrated the shoulder, passed through the lung and severed his spine. The medals still glittered on his coat, even in the gloom.

'He didn't take it off,' said Scott. 'His coat. Hardy spoke to him, but he wouldn't change it.' He rubbed his eyes. Behind them, the scene on the orlop deck dimmed and then brightened, as the concussion of the broadsides above sucked the air from around the lanterns. He could see himself picking his way across the bodies to Nelson's side. 'His first words to me were that I must remember him to you and to Horatia. To his friends, and to Mr Rose at the Treasury. "Tell him that I have made a will," he said, "and left Lady Hamilton and Horatia to my country." '

'Yes.' It was a whisper. She had not moved. 'What else did he say?'

'Just that. To remember him to you, and to Horatia. He had no other thoughts, not then. He thanked God that he had done his duty.' The dying man had been hot, and terribly thirsty. Scott sent for lemonade and watered wine, and knelt beside him, fanning his face and rubbing his chest. Nelson asked constantly for news of the battle, and of Hardy, who had not come down. Above them, timber split by cannon fire crashed onto the decks and into the sea. Lead and iron, cannonballs, grenades. Scott could hear the loud explosions, the thud as blocks and tackle fell. He could see bare feet on the companionway as the wounded were brought down.

'Hardy came down at about half past two,' he said. 'Lord Nelson asked him to give you his hair, and all his other belongings.'

'Yes, he did that.' Emma lifted her face, and wiped the tears from her chin. 'Was the pain very bad?'

Scott shook his head. 'You know . . . the shock.' The man had been in agony. Crying out that the pain was so bad he wished he was already dead. 'His last words were for you. And he asked me once more to remember that he was leaving you and Horatia as a legacy to his country.'

'I know . . . you wrote . . .'

188

'I wrote to George Rose, yes. He put it all down, Nelson, in his pocket book. Rose has seen that, too, I think.'

Thomas Hardy had taken the codicil to Rose on his return to England. Another copy had gone to William Nelson, who took it to the Doctors' Commons. It was not a legal document, and its value depended on how far the government felt beholden to a public servant who had died for his country. William had been advised to take it to the Prime Minister.

'You have the house . . .'

'Merton, yes. I have that.' The house, with its contents and the grounds, had been left to her. The rest of the land was to be sold to pay the legacies and dues provided for under the will. Nelson had also left her an annuity of five hundred pounds. To Horatia he had left four thousand pounds, and his name.

'I never shed a tear for years before that day,' said Scott. 'Now, whenever I'm alone, I cry like a child.'

For a while they did not speak. Scott was on board the *Victory* again. Sometimes he believed that he would never really leave that ship, that he would walk its boards and climb its companionways until the day he died; that the colour of his thoughts would always be the rust red of the orlop deck.

'He never hesitated,' Scott said quietly, 'to lay his own life on the line. Example was everything, and he brought out the best in the men around him.'

The body had been undressed, placed in a cask filled with brandy, camphor and thyme, and lashed to the *Victory*'s mainmast. At Gibraltar, the ship was fitted with jury masts and its rigging repaired, and five weeks later it arrived in Portsmouth. Hardy had orders to sail to the Nore, a point offshore at the mouth of the Thames, from where Nelson would be taken to lie in state at Greenwich. The surgeon, William Beatty, took the body from the cask, removed the bowels, and found at last the ball cartridge, which had lodged in the muscles of the back. It had taken with it a piece of gold lace from one of Nelson's epaulettes.

'The coffin was collected from Peddison's,' said Scott. 'As he had wished.' It had been put on the dockyard yacht from Woolwich, but they searched for three days against a southerly wind before they found the *Victory*, in the channel at the Nore. The body was placed in the coffin, then soldered into another, made of lead, and then in a third, of wood. As the yacht came upriver, all the forts and ships flew their flags at half-mast and fired minute guns.

'It's the most sorrowful sound on earth,' said Scott. 'The sound of guns fired in mourning. All hope is lost when that sound is heard.'

'Lost,' said Emma. Her face was streaming.

'Well . . .' His faith, he understood, must really be shattered, for him to speak of lost hope.

The coffin lay in state for three days at Greenwich. Scott stayed with it. He hardly slept. From Greenwich, it was taken to London in a procession of boats and barges, all draped in black. Thousands lined the banks of the river. It was landed at Whitehall stairs and taken to the Admiralty, where once again Scott stayed with it through the night. By now, he was sleeping on his feet, a few minutes here and there.

The next day, Nelson was buried. Through the silent streets, the slow beat of the Dead March was played on pipes and muffled drums. The heartbreaking sound of the horses' hoofs. It was too much; he could not describe all that to her. She had heard about it, anyway, from others who had been there. The pavements crowded, every door and window; the rustle, as they passed, of hats being taken off. St Paul's had been packed to the rafters, literally – there were boys perched up on the cornices of the dome, seventy feet above.

'I won't go back to sea any more,' he said.

'No.' Emma wiped her hands across her face, and shook out a long sigh. 'I made him go,' she said. 'He didn't want the command, but I told him he must take it. I told him it was his duty. He would have stayed if I hadn't insisted. He would have been alive today.'

There was a table at the end of the room, covered with a piece of patterned cloth. Fleur-de-lis and tassels. On top of it were miniatures in gold and silver frames, a vase of mourning flowers. Underneath it, Horatia sat in the semi-dark. She could see the coast of Spitzbergen, and monsters, and a bear vanishing over the ice. She saw her father's coat, with its empty sleeve and its stars and spangles.

3

Westminster Abbey is a place of whispers and the echo of feet. Tap, tap. There are pillars of stone, and doors through which the ghosts come and go. Candles, shadows and great high arches. It smells of God, a big, empty smell, mixed with wood, beeswax and stone. Just here it smells, too, of smoke. That's because a candle has just gone out. The wick drowned in the wax and sent up a long black thread.

'Come on, darling, keep up.' Lady Hamilton. She has on a lovely dress and a warm coat. They are being shown round by an army officer, who is their guide to the monuments. He has a very long neck, as if God has given him two, one on top of the other, to make sure. He marches them up the north aisle and past the organ loft. 'The main piers of the church,' he says, 'are of solid Purbeck marble.'

Horatia wonders if they are going to look at all the monuments. They're everywhere, hundreds of them. An old man in a long coat walks past them, the other way, and she wants to ask if he is holy. The Reverend Mr Lancaster at Merton is holy, but she thinks they may be more so, in this place. It's bigger, so they should be.

'Here behind the High Altar,' says the officer, 'is the chapel of St Edward. Here is his shrine. Here is the tomb of Henry the Third, and here is his son, Edward.'

'Don't fidget, darling.'

'Edward the First,' says the officer, 'was buried in a simple chest so that his body could be brought out at any time and his flesh removed by boiling, in the event that his bones were needed to carry before an army invading Scotland.'

Horatia wants to know if they would boil him here in the Abbey, or in some other place. She wants to know how long it would take, and what they would do with the flesh when it had come off. She does not, however, ask.

Eleanor of Castile, Edward III, Anne of Bohemia. Tap, tap. Wooden steps, worn by time. Ages, years and centuries. She wants to ask why kings and queens must have the same names, and be the fifth and the sixth and the eighth, and why they don't go up to the tenth or twentieth. She does ask. Emma smiles and kisses her head and says that she is very clever. They don't know the answer. The army officer says that in France they go up to the eighteenth.

Abbots, queens, chancellors, poets and prime ministers. The man in the black coat returns. Emma whispers something to the army officer, and he whispers it to the man. He is the verger. 'Of course,' he says. 'This way.' His teeth are long, and orange in colour.

He's going to show them something. He leads them past men and ladies flat on their backs, hands together and eyes closed. Through echoing arches, past shining pews. Past angels, saints, kings, philosophers and . . . *My Lord Nelson.* My father!

Somehow, since the news of his death, this is what he has become. He is dead, and he is her father. She forgets, and then she remembers. Who is her mother? She does not know, and wonders if she has forgotten that, too. Our Father, which art in heaven. He was her godfather, and then he was her father. This is what may sometimes happen: someone is one thing and then, when he is dead, he is your father.

He is standing in a glass case, and he is very bright. He is wearing his stars and medals, and a sash and his sword. His coat is black and his breeches are white. His right sleeve is hooked to a button on his coat. He can't move. Let him out! cries Horatia. No, she only thinks she does. She can't speak at all.

'Here,' says the verger, 'we can see the wax effigy of the nation's pride. It was commissioned by the Dean and Chapter from Catherine Andras, for whom Lord Nelson sat shortly before he returned to sea for the last time. He was buried at St Paul's, of course, but we felt that we really wanted something here . . .'

Horatia looks up into Emma's face. There's an ache in her throat that fills the inside of her neck. Something makes her lip curl out and tremble, and she bites to stop it. She traps it between her teeth, like a slug.

'That . . . lock of hair.' Emma is speaking. The verger looks at her as if he has made the effigy himself and is highly pleased with it.

'It hung differently, in life. Not like that. It should be . . . I wonder if I might alter it.'

The verger shakes his small head. He is in charge round here. His face is almost as shiny as the face of Lord Nelson in the glass cabinet. You can see his teeth even when his mouth is closed. She wishes that her father would tap on the glass and make them open it. Then he would step out and take her hand in his and say, Come along, Horatia, we must go home for dinner or we'll be in deep water.

'I'm afraid,' says the verger, 'that no one is permitted to touch the effigy.'

Emma smiles. 'When I tell you,' she says, 'that I am Lady Hamilton . . .'

He makes a sound in his throat like a sneeze that has got stuck there. *Ach, ach.* He looks at the army officer, who nods. 'Oh, madam,' he says. His hands come together in front of him as if he's going to beg for money. Horatia doesn't care if he is the verger, he doesn't look holy. 'Of course,' he says, 'this is a great . . . my goodness, yes, of course.' His hands come apart again, and he goes through the folds and pockets of his coat to find the key. It's on a ring with many others, but he picks it out with one quick look. It is the newest one, and small.

Even now Horatia thinks he might come to life, and step out onto the marble floor. It is her greatest wish on earth. But he is dead. He won a great victory, and died for his country. He wrote his will and wore his coat and walked the deck and died.

The glass door swings open. Emma reaches in, and moves the lock of hair. It is not real hair. She has his real hair at home. She was right, though, they had done it wrong. She is trembling, and there are tears in her eyes. Horatia wants to run. She wants to take her hand and run from this place, but you can't run in churches.

'I would like, one more time—' says Emma. She means that she wants to kiss his lips.

The army officer shakes his head. 'I am afraid, my lady, that the colour is not quite dry.'

TWO

They moved back to Calais, into two north-facing upstairs rooms in a small, bleak house on the rue Française. Their landlord was Monsieur Damas, a retired monk. The wallpaper was grimy and peeling and the beds were narrow and uncomfortable. Horatia slept in a small alcove in Emma's room, behind a heavy curtain. Fatima was in the attic, and Berthe had a room downstairs next to the kitchen. In the sitting room there were old armchairs, obscurely placed, fire irons, bookshelves and a solid table with massive legs. An oval mirror in a gilt frame, a worn screen, a rug almost weeping with age and wear. Emma went to bed and stayed there, and never once left the house.

It was October. Their lives were running out like the tide running out beyond the town walls, and the sound in their ears was the sound of every last possession slipping out of their hands. Emma sent Horatia to the *mont-de-piété* with her watch, dresses, a gold pin to pawn. She took, one after the other, her own trinkets, family pictures and mementoes. The pawnbroker was thin, with a sunken chest and a reedy voice. A dog lived under the counter in the shop, eaten up by worms, on its last legs. It stank, and sometimes there were puddles between the counter and the door. The pawnbroker himself seemed to be falling apart, and there was a snow of dead skin on the shoulders of his coat.

'What did he give you?' said Emma, on her return from one of these trips.

Horatia held out a few old notes.

'No, he gave you more than that.'

'He didn't!'

'Then you're incredibly stupid. Do you know where that shawl came from? Did you tell him that once it covered the feet of the Queen of Naples?' Emma plucked at the bedcover; her hands were shaking. 'You don't even try. I don't know why you're so spineless – you don't get it from me. Sometimes I think I've got on my hands a child with no sense and no ability to think.' Her face became slack, suddenly, as if someone had loosened a knot at the back of her head. 'Darling, come here. Sit beside me.'

Horatia stayed where she was.

'I'm going to write to the Queen.' Emma waved her hands in front of her face, batting at the words she was looking for. 'I'll ask her to help us. She will.'

'The Queen's dead.' The news had reached them earlier in the month. Maria Carolina had died in Austria at the age of sixty-two.

'Dead?' Emma's eyes would not fix on anything. 'I know she's dead.' She scowled, an expression slung between uncertainty and anger. 'I'm not an idiot, Horatia. I know she's dead, I've still got the letter.'

'Then what . . .?' Horatia shook her head. It was hopeless, everything. Emma was drinking all day long; it was the only thing she did with any strength of mind. She drank until she was talking nonsense, and then until she was shouting abuse, and then until she could not talk at all. Horatia moved towards the door.

'Where are you going? Wait.'

She turned and put her hands on her hips. One of these days, she thought, she would open her mouth and scream with irritation. If it did not make her afraid or outraged, anything that Emma did or said got on her nerves. The noise she made when she ate, the things she said. Horatia could feel it in her teeth, in her stomach. It made her rude, and because of this, she felt the shadow and press of guilt, the oily surface of her own ingratitude.

'What has Fatima said to you?' demanded Emma.

'Nothing. About what?'

'I think you know what I mean. Come here.'

'I am here.'

'Here, for God's sake. I'm trying to talk to you.'

She crossed the room in two steps and stood by the bed again. 'What?'

'She has told you!'

Horatia sighed. 'I don't know what you're talking about. Tell me what you mean.'

But Emma said nothing more. She lay with her eyes on her daughter, her face locked away again in the privacy of thought and the internal labour of following it. Horatia turned again and left the room. Though not yet winter, it was cold, and she stood by the window in the sitting room and counted chimneys.

She did not want to hear, any more, stories of the past. Not from the lips of Emma Hamilton. Now when Emma spoke of their former lives it was unbearable to hear, either because she was filled with the abject pain of what could never be retrieved, or because she was talking rubbish. She recalled great events she had not been there to see, and wept over people she had despised. She spread her blame and rancour over those who had helped her and forgot that, but for them, things might have been even worse. She shaped and altered the past, and lied with every breath she drew. When she spoke in trembling whispers of love and betrayal, of a glorious existence taken from her by acts of theft, Horatia bit her cheeks until they bled. It was talk that filled her with the fear that everything remembered might be in part a lie, that at most it was a tale that grew or changed with the telling. The stories she had heard a hundred times were her last remaining possessions, stories about a time she herself could not remember, having been too young, or not yet born. When Emma's voice began to slide and she drifted, sodden, through all the old avenues of Nelson's glory, his brilliance and his courage, Horatia put her hands over her ears. Not least because the past was claimed as the singular property of the woman who saw herself at its centre, and was robbed of its true light and dignity. She understood, or thought she did, that Emma had used the currency of grief until it had all run out. She had traded on her friendship with Nelson and on her anguish at his death as if it had all been left to her. And for a time she had received in return the attention of his family, of friends, the generosity of their hearts. She had not foreseen that sympathy can only go so far, that it, too, runs out, or becomes so torn and old that it cannot be used for anything.

Then something happened that was worse than anything else. Emma sent Fatima back to England. Horatia went upstairs to find her one morning, and came running back down again. She all but kicked open Emma's door. 'What have you done?' she shouted. 'Fatima's packing her things. Are you mad?'

'I beg your pardon!' Emma was up, standing, wearing her bed gown and a shawl.

'You're throwing her out.'

Emma lifted a hand, as if Horatia had exploded and was fluttering, like ashes, in the air in front of her. 'God almighty, what's that supposed to mean? Don't you dare speak to me like that.'

'You're sending her away! She's not coming back.' Horatia looked at her with hatred.

'I knew there'd be a fuss. Yes, Fatima has to go. We can't keep her any more. We've got Berthe, we'll manage.'

'What about *her*?' No one had thought this through – no one had seen it for what it was. A mistake, something said and done in fury that should never have gone this far. 'When were you going to tell me?'

Emma's hands were shaking. 'Listen. I've given her some money. Greville sent me some, and I've given most of it to her.'

Horatia's head tipped from side to side, a small movement with its own momentum. 'I can't believe this.'

Emma could not stay on her feet any longer. She sank down on the bed. 'You'll see her again one day. It's not the end of the world. I'm sorry, Horatia, but these things happen. I can't afford to keep her. Blame Fulke Greville if you want to blame someone. Blame the government. After everything I did—'

'Don't start that again.' Tears ran down Horatia's cheeks. It was like learning of a death, of something impossible that could be understood only in pieces. There had been no sign in these two small rooms, in the occasional lift of the curtains or the fall of soot in the hearth, no indication anywhere that everything would fall apart yet again. 'Tell me you had an argument. Tell me you were angry with her, that you didn't know what you were doing. Please . . .' It was a moan, a low cry.

'Listen to me. She's going to take the packet. She'll go to London, and she'll find someone else to work for, someone who can pay her wages. Cribb's in London, he can help her. Good *God*, Horatia, do you think I'm doing this because I want to? Just stop thinking about yourself for one minute and face up to the facts.'

The truth was throwing itself against the inside of her skull. It was unacceptable, it had to be stopped; it had to be brought out and crushed and made to bleed. 'Go up and stop her. Tell her to stay.'

Emma shook her head. 'She's got her life ahead of her, she doesn't want to spend it locked up here with us. Believe me, Horatia, I'm doing the best thing for her.'

Horatia's mouth was dry with shock. In her heart, she knew. She had seen how lack of money had wrecked one thing after another. It had ripped out the walls of their lives, and taken away every single last thing that they loved. It had gone round like a gale under the door, blowing the very dust at their feet. Fatima would go, and Horatia would be left here, alone with Emma and her illness and no one but Berthe to spare them the deadly familiarity of their own company. 'Why can't you give her some of my money?' she said.

'Yours?'

'The money my father left me. Ask my uncle to send it.'

'No. Out of the question.'

'Please! I'll write to him.'

'You will not. That money stays where it is. I've never touched it, and I won't now, and it's not yours to spend until you're eighteen.'

'Not my money, then. He has money.'

'Don't be ridiculous. What do you think he's going to think of me, if you start sending him begging letters?'

'You write to him.'

Emma looked as if she wanted to throw something, but there was precious little left to throw. 'Are you telling me what to do?' she said. 'Let's get one thing straight, Horatia. I'm responsible for you, not your uncles, and I'm not going to go to them cap in hand. Neither are you. I forbid you to write to anyone. For your information, all their money's tied up in trusts, anyway.' She put a hand to her bosom, and let out a heavy sigh. 'You're not old enough to understand, and you're not old enough to tell me what to do. Now get out.'

Horatia spoke through her teeth. 'If you spent half what you do on wine and brandy,' she said, 'you'd be able to keep her.'

'That's enough! Out! You can go next door and stay there until you've simmered down. *Never* speak to me like that.' Emma's face was grey, and its lines, hard and raked, made her terrifying. 'Can't you ever do anything to help? This is difficult for me, too. Look at me! There's not much left of me now, I'm not going to last very long, but at least when I go I'll be able to say that I did what was right when I had to. You'll never be able to say that.' The gesture, the arms, the open palm, might have been addressed to the Roman people. 'You've got to pull yourself together, and I don't just mean now. I don't know what's happened to you but if you don't change soon you're going to be detested by all the world, and when I'm not here to shield you any more then God help you! No one's going to like you, no one's going to help you.'

'I hope you die, I hope you do!' Horatia ran out of the room. She turned round, grabbed the door, and slammed it shut.

That evening, Fatima went down to the harbour, and took the Dover packet.

2

She couldn't go out. She was trapped within two rooms, and there was nowhere to go, and nothing else that she could do. She couldn't step outside the door for fear of someone de-manding money – tradesmen and shopkeepers, the laundry woman, the wine merchant. They were sniffing around, all of them, waiting for what they were owed. Also, she was afraid to leave Emma alone. Now that Fatima had gone, there was no one else to look after her, to feed and clean her, to get her in and out of bed to use the pot. Horatia was terrified that she would fall. If she did, no one on their own would be able to pick her up, not even Monsieur Damas, the landlord. Emma was living in her own world, miles from Calais and from those around her. Berthe did the rooms every day, brought food and water up and took the chamber pots down.

'Wake up,' said Horatia.

They knew no one now, not a soul. The general had gone to Paris, and no one else wanted to know them. The world went on without them, beyond the walls of their humiliation. They heard the bells, the clack of wooden shoes on the street, the sound of hoofs and cartwheels. Beyond the windows was the town, beyond the town the world. They had vanished and were invisible, and their existence meant nothing to anyone but themselves.

She had become Emma's guardian. Her nurse, her sentinel. The world was the wrong way up, and now she was left to look after the woman who had sworn to look after her. In the time that they had been cooped up together in two rooms, the balance had shifted like cargo in a high sea: Emma had slid until she could slide no further, and it was Horatia who had to find heart and courage for them both.

'Wake up, you've got to eat something.'

The only person who came to see them was the priest from l'Église de St Pierre. He was a middle-aged man who smelled of cupboards and incense. 'She may get better,' he said. 'There's every reason to hope.' Horatia scoured his voice for the truth, but could not find it there and, in fact, everything in his manner contradicted what he said. Everything in his manner said: Lady Hamilton will die, and there is nothing you can do. When he left, she watched him from the window, crossing the rue Française. Birdlike, dressed in black.

'What on earth is this?' Emma was staring at the plate balanced in her lap.

'Sausage. *Andouille.*'

'It's got . . . bits in it.'

'It's supposed to.' Horatia felt her heart swing between rage and pity. It was true, the *andouille* looked disgusting. As well as breakfast, Monsieur Damas gave them one meal a day, but what he sent up was usually grey and nearly cold.

'I don't think I can eat it.' Emma lay back against her pillows, worn out. Outside, the rain was streaming down again, hard drops blown from the north that hit the tiles outside the window with a steady clatter. The room was dark, the curtains drawn, the December sky outside black with clouds and the coming night. The only light came from the fire, burning quietly in the grate. Horatia pushed a pile of clothes from a chair and sat. She didn't know what to do any more. She leaned forward and studied the pattern on the bedcover. No one even knew what was wrong with Emma – the drawn-out legacy of jaundice, water on the lungs, drink. The doctors, before they stopped coming, had given her emetics, which made her groan with pain and reach for the brandy bottle. And there was no more money for doctors, now, or medicine. Horatia hugged her arms around her. All the pieces of her life, those that were left, were here in this room. Everything she had ever known was in her head, and yet her head was full of nothing but this room. 'Who was my mother?' she said. Her heart had thrown itself against the wall of her chest, and was knocking as if to be let out.

The plate slid from Emma's lap, and on to the floor. 'Oh, look, I'm sorry. It's all right, it's not broken. Don't eat it, it's dusty.'

'Who was my mother?'

She shook her head. 'We've been through this.'

'I want to know.'

'Pick up the plate, for God's sake.' She reached for her glass, but Horatia got to it first. 'Give that to me.'

'Tell me who she was.'

'Give it to me, Horatia.'

'I will when you tell me.'

Emma's hands flew up in front of her face. Her cheeks were suddenly white with fury. 'God in heaven, why don't you just stop? You're going to drive me mad. You have no mother, you never had a mother. Do you understand? You were a mistake. There's a word for children like you and, believe me, it's not a nice one. Just thank God for who your father was and forget the rest. Does it never occur to you to shut up and leave it alone? There are bastard children all over the world who are nothing like as lucky as you. Just remember that and stop whining. Now get out. I wish just for once that I could wake up and find that you'd gone.' Her eyes closed, and her head collapsed into the pillows. She looked suddenly exposed and disarmed, like a bag that had broken and spilled everything into the road. Horatia placed the glass back on the table. She lifted her eyes to look at the face of the only person on earth who knew the circumstances of her birth, the name and the nature of the woman whom Nelson had, if briefly, loved. The woman Horatia had dreamed of and imagined in every different bed that she had slept in, had looked for in every street she walked and every new room she entered. Emma's mouth hung slightly open, and she breathed with a small flutter at the back of her throat.

She picked up the empty bottle and the plate, and carried them through to the sitting room. She had not lit the lamp, and the fire was low. Crossing the room, she tripped on the hem of her dress and her legs went out from under her. The bottle flew from her hand and shattered on the tiles in front of the fire. As she fell, she saw the pattern in the thin and faded rug. She saw broken glass, and shut her eyes. The breath was knocked out of her, and she heard a strange sound from her own mouth. For several moments she lay where she had fallen, while her mind played slowly over the long spill through the air, the obstacles she had only barely missed. The table, a vertical beam.

When she got to her feet, she looked at her hand and saw blood. She saw it slide through her fingers, and pool in the cup of her palm. The edge of her vision went black. Her legs lost their strength, and she dropped to the ground again.

'*Merde.*'

Her head was in someone's hands. Her fingers were burning, either with heat or with the cold. Everything was the wrong way up. For moments, she had absolutely no idea where she was.

'Stand up, can't you?' The words were in French, and the voice was familiar. Then the hands were under her arms, and the furniture on either side of her was moving, either lifting or dropping. The table slid to one side, as if it had decided to get up quietly and go to another room. The ceiling filled her line of sight, and fell away again. Then she was standing. She swayed on her feet, and the hands came down and gripped her elbows.

'Now sit. Put your head between your knees. And keep your hand up, like this.'

'I'm all right. I'm not going to faint.'

'You just did.'

'I did?' She looked up to see Berthe standing over her. She had heard the crash in the kitchen. Then she looked down, and saw a drop of blood fall onto her dress. 'Blood,' she said.

'Don't look at it.'

Horatia lifted her face again. 'It was a piece of glass. I broke a bottle. It just needs a bandage.'

Berthe lit a lamp, and poured water into a bowl. She washed the wound, found a rag and sat on her haunches next to Horatia to bind it. 'Deep,' she said. The rag was long, and went several times round her hand. 'You're shaking, stop it. Keep still.'

'I'm not. I can't.' Her teeth were chattering, too.

Berthe lifted Horatia's fist to her mouth, and used her teeth to pull the ends of the knot. When she had done it, she went down for a dustpan, and came back to sweep up the glass. 'Does it hurt?' she said.

It was breathing pain: in, out, in, out. Horatia nodded.

'Drink some brandy.'

Horatia shook her head. The thought of brandy made her sick. Berthe found the plate, where it had fallen, and the remains of the *andouille*. 'She hasn't eaten anything,' she said, shaking the glass into the back of the pan before she swept up the bits of scattered meat. When it was done, she stayed on her knees, and stared at the bedroom door. There were days when she was sure that Lady Hamilton was already dead, and that her ghost was wandering the rue Française while the flesh fell away from her bones in the bed next door.

'She wasn't hungry,' said Horatia. Her face felt set with grief and loneliness. 'She isn't well,' she said uselessly.

'Nor are you,' said Berthe, standing up again. 'If you don't mind my saying so.'

'I'm all right, Berthe. I just fell over.'

'I know that – I don't mean that. Look at you, you've no colour in your face. You never go out. I worry about you.'

Horatia said nothing. They were kind words, and she was afraid that in her present state the tears would come and never stop. She would cry and cry, and no one would be able to put an end to it. Berthe put the plates and the dustpan onto a tray and shoved it outside the door on the landing with the water jug. Then she straightened a few cushions, built up the fire, and left the room.

She did not ask again. She feared too much that she would again be given no answer, or that she would be the target of more abuse. She feared the degenerate form of confrontation that had become almost the only way that Emma still spoke to her, the fury her questions provoked. It was not a matter of choosing her time: all their time was drink, oblivion and rage.

She wrote to her uncle, George Matcham. They had almost nothing left to pawn, and she was forced to act. He sent twenty pounds, and told her she should leave immediately for England – get someone in to look after Emma, leave her there and get on a boat.

She couldn't: there was no one else. Who? No one. She had wished many times that she could go back to England, but she knew now that she could not. She owed to Emma Hamilton a debt of gratitude and responsibility, hardly less than if Emma had, indeed, been her mother. It was up to her, and no one else, to look after the woman who had taken her in for the sake of friendship, who had given her food and clothes and a roof over her head. For as long as Emma lived, she could not leave her. She could no longer believe in a life with her uncle, her aunt and cousins, while the person on whom she had so long depended lay in bed in the rue Française. She prayed on her feet, standing in front of the window, looking out onto grey roofs, onto a sky that was washed with light and then with dark. She prayed as she leaned her back against the door to Emma's room, and in the darkness at the top of the stairs.

One day, in the first week of January, she went once more to the *mont-de-piété* with one last small piece of jewellery. The twenty pounds had vanished. Yellow sun fell through cracks in the cloud, and puddles creaked with frost under her feet. Her cheeks burned. There was a strange feeling, too, in her chest, as if the day, or this brief part of it, were something alive and private for once. The simple elation of being outside. She ran past the shops and slipped down alleys. It seemed to her that all the people they owed money to had lookouts on every corner, but if they were there, she ran past them. She smelled the sea, and filled her lungs with the cold and briny air until they hurt. The faster she went, the better she felt. In the market, stallholders smacked their hands together and breathed smoke when they spoke. They leaned out over their stalls to lift out winter greens and salsify. Cheeses, poultry, beef; garlic, sausages, wine. The ground was a bed of leaves and stalks, fish scales and mussel shells. Above her gulls circled and cried. An old man drove a fat white cow through the fringes of the crowd. Over the yelling of prices and the stamping of cold feet she could hear his clucking encouragements, and the lazy tap of his stick on its back.

The taste of freedom was like a taste of something precious. This much, no more. Suddenly afraid that death had come while she was away from the house, she turned on her heels and ran back to the rue Française.

THREE

I

In May 1806 the government, on direct instructions from the King, decided the grants to be bestowed on Nelson's family. William – now Earl Nelson of Trafalgar and Merton – was given an annuity of five thousand pounds, tax free, for him and his successors for ever, with a further hundred thousand to buy and furnish an estate. Nelson's sisters, Susannah and Kate, each received fifteen thousand. At the end of May, Nelson's codicil, written in his pocket book and leaving Emma and Horatia to the nation, was returned by the Prime Minister to William Nelson, and by William to Emma. There was nothing for her. No grant, no annuity, nothing.

'It's his fault,' said Emma. Mrs Cadogan, sitting opposite her in front of the fire in the drawing room at Merton, traced back through a long silence to pick up the thread. William Nelson. It was not his fault, it was the King's. The King had never much liked Nelson, and his dislike of Emma was well known, founded on what he knew of her past. But what he or anyone in government might know about Emma Hamilton, and might hold against her, Mrs Cadogan understood very well – and so did Emma – that it must never reach the ears of Nelson's sisters. The blame for an otherwise inexplicable situation must therefore be put somewhere else: William.

'I don't know how he thinks he can do it . . .' said Emma. 'He won't even let her live here any more!'

This was true. On top of all the other bad news, William had found reasons to withdraw Charlotte – now Lady Charlotte –

permanently from Emma's household. He had whisked her away in January, and they had seen almost nothing of her since. As the favourite niece of the nation's hero, and as a titled heiress, she was now even more in demand, a fact that made the loss all the harder.

'Well, let them refuse me,' said Emma. She picked up Nelson's pocket book, and thrust it into the air. 'I'll go through the streets of London with this bit of paper fixed to my breast and beg. Every barrow-woman will see it and say, "Nelson left her to *us*".'

Mrs Cadogan pulled in the corners of her mouth. Her sewing lay on her lap. The windows onto the garden were open and, briefly, she heard voices raised in song. A sound muffled by walls, carried on the wind. It confused her. For a moment her hands were still.

'He was never meant to be anything more than a village curate, and now he has a fortune and a title. I wish he'd die!'

'For God's sake,' said Mrs Cadogan, 'simmer down.'

It was not William's fault, but it was a disaster. They had been badly treated. There were bills from shopkeepers, tradesmen, the butcher. There was the rent at Clarges Street, and wages to be paid to the staff. The cook, Marianna, was owed for four months. Every time Mary Cadogan turned round, Emma had bought something else, or was arranging another party. Even while they were mourning, she had filled Clarges Street with people, and Madame Bianchi spent half her life at Merton, with other members of the Italian opera and their hangers-on. Why did she still do it? Not for Nelson, now. It was as if she only really existed in the company of others; as if there were no light in the room to see by unless other people were there to surround her. While Nelson lived, she had conquered the world, what she knew of it, by throwing herself into its arms, by giving it wine and food and music. Now it was as if, were she to stop, the world might let go and she would slip from the place she had reached. Mrs Cadogan had spent her life arranging these things, but now they were bringing her down – because of the expense, and because of her own ill health, and because she feared that Emma could not stop herself. 'All the same,' she said, 'you shouldn't get so worked up. Whatever they do to Merton, the house is still yours.' Again, for a moment, her hands were still. Now someone was playing a fiddle, somewhere in the village.

Emma threw herself into a chair opposite her mother with a long sigh. 'Are the others coming back for dinner?' Horatia had gone for a drive with Fatima.

'Of course,' said the old woman. Her voice was always calm, always level. 'Marianna is doing *minestra verde*. And a roast.' She was struggling to see what she was doing. She found a pair of spectacles on the table beside her, and put them on.

'I swear, Mama, I'll go to Naples and live with the Queen. I promised her I would if anything happened. We'll all go.'

Her mother raised her eyebrows, without looking up. Queen Maria Carolina had long since lost interest in Emma. As soon as she had stopped being of any use to her, she had forgotten her completely. She sighed, took off her glasses, and looked at the clock on the mantel. As if that small act had conjuring powers, the front door closed with a smart *thup*, and Horatia came running into the room. 'We saw a wedding!' she yelled.

Mrs Cadogan peered at her. 'Did you wipe your feet?'

'Yes. They were outside, and they danced, like this.' She careered around the room, breaking up the atmosphere of complaint and fury, and risking a couple of porcelain figurines.

'Coat,' said Fatima, in the doorway. She caught the child mid-leap, and pulled her arms out of the sleeves. 'It was Mrs Grant's maid, Julia,' she said. 'They was outside the Bell.'

'She's having a baby!' shouted Horatia. 'She's as big as this.' She spread her hands as far as they would go. 'I don't know why she didn't run away. I would, seeing that squinting husband come into the church. He's ugly, and he's cross-eyed – he looks two ways for Sunday!'

'Come here, sweetheart,' said Emma. 'You funny thing! You're very clever, aren't you? If only your father could hear you.' Horatia threw herself on to Emma's lap, and breathed in the smell of soap and porter.

2

Waiting for the pension that did not come, and refusing to believe it never would, Emma was forced to find another house in London, and moved to New Bond Street. She was still near to the old Duke of Queensberry, and still optimistic that he would leave her a huge sum of money when he died. It was a question, really, of managing one way or another until he did.

They went to Ashfold. The Matchams had recently moved there from Bath. It was deep in the Sussex countryside; the nearest market town was Handcross, three miles away.

'Pease Pottage?' said Horatia, on their way there from Merton. 'Lower Beeding?'

'They're very old names, darling,' said Emma. 'Don't wriggle. We're nearly there.'

In fact they had gone too far, and the driver had to turn round at Slaugham. Horatia settled back on Fatima's lap, her eyes on the rattling scenes outside, and tried to imagine a village made of pease pottage. The houses were green and lumpy, and the gardens knee-deep in a vivid green paste. The people went in and out in boats. What's for dinner today? they shouted to each other. Carrots! they replied. Beetroot!

'Wake up, sweetheart, we're here.'

Mrs Matcham was standing in front of the house, waiting for them. 'I wish you'd stay longer,' she said. 'A week's nothing.'

Emma regarded the house, its doors and windows open to the summer breezes, the parkland stretching off into the haze, the high sound of larks and the chatter of martins in the stable block. Horatia had already vanished in a cloud of children. Kate Matcham had nine: her eldest, George, was eighteen; Charles, the baby, was barely walking.

By now it was generally accepted, without any word being placed with undue weight here or there, that Horatia was Nelson's child. The fact of her existence had been made public when his will appeared in the papers, and everyone wanted to see her. His family opened their hearts to the little girl, who, in their eyes, was something sacred, a relic of the man who had been their darling and their pride, and she was admitted into their circle as a cherished member. The importance of this to Emma was only equalled by the fact that no one, in the family or in the wider world, showed any sign of assuming that she herself was the child's mother. At no time had anyone appeared to doubt her word, and in spite of her known friendship with Nelson, it was accepted by all that there must have been another woman in his life. If the family ever wondered who it was, they did so privately. All sorts of stories had done the rounds; Emma had started several. Horatia's mother had been ill, she had left London, she was dead. Only recently she had let it be put about that the mystery woman was none other than the Queen of Naples. In the end there were too many stories, and half of them too wild, for any to be believed. As for Emma herself, the role of Horatia's guardian, placed on her by Nelson's will, lent her an almost sublime prestige in the climate of grief and glorification.

'Change your mind,' said Kate Matcham. 'Stay a few more days. The sea won't go away.'

The following week they were all, including the Matchams, going to Worthing for a month. Young George Matcham was leaving in the morning to look for lodgings.

'Look at everything!' declared Emma. 'It's a Paradise, like

Merton.' She swept her hand suddenly to her chest, as if a trapdoor were there through which her feelings might escape. 'I still miss him so much. I don't know how to live or what to do.'

'I don't think it's sunk in,' said Mrs Matcham. 'Even now. I sometimes wonder if it ever will.'

'No, never, perhaps.' Emma looked back at the frozen fields and leafless trees. 'I lived for his glory and his great deeds,' she said. 'I was so happy at Naples, but it all seems gone like a dream. I wish you could have seen it. And Europe, too. Everywhere we went there were people in the streets, people in all the windows. Dances and dinners and gifts and prizes. They were the glory days, and I was there. I was always there, for everything.'

The two women were weeping as Kate Matcham led her guest upstairs to show her where she would sleep. 'You'll have to take us as you find us,' she said, as they reached the first-floor landing and she opened a door off the passage. 'Make yourself at home, and tell me if there's anything you want. Your mother's next door to you, through here.'

Emma crossed the room and examined the brushes on the dressing-table. 'It'll do us good to be with you,' she said. 'Even for a few days. It's been so hard for all of us.'

Mrs Matcham was at the window. In this weather, one was drawn to the windows in every room. Below her in the garden, she could see the children showing Horatia a small den in the shrubs. 'She's a lovely child,' she said.

'Horatia? Yes, she is. I don't know what I'd do without her.'

'Tall.'

'She's shot up suddenly. She had chickenpox in the spring, and it's made her tall and thin. A month by the sea will get her right.'

Mrs Matcham smiled. 'I'll leave you to settle in,' she said. 'I'll be downstairs.'

3

Sometimes when Fatima woke up, she did not know where she was. Naples or Alexandria, London or Merton. Now she could hear the sea, and for a few moments she thought that it was Alexandria, and that she had gone home, but it was Worthing. There was shingle all along the beach, and the waves came up, made it rattle and whisper.

Lady Hamilton's spirits went up and down. One minute she was full of life, laughed, sang and took Horatia off to swim, the next she was in the dumps.

'Fatima,' she said, 'come here. Tell me something amusing.'

'Amusing? What?' said Fatima.

'I don't know. Anything. Something must have happened to you in the last few days.'

The amusing ironing, thought Fatima. The amusing mending. Dressing and undressing my amusing lady. Washing her feet and cutting her toenails. That was amusing.

'Never mind,' said Emma. 'Go down and get me some porter.'

She did not mind the work. She did what she was told, and was diligent and did not drink or run away. But she kept thinking, What will become of me?

One thing Fatima noticed: when a person is alive, they may beg someone to do something that they want very much. They say, *Please do this, please do*, and that other person doesn't do it. Then, when the one person is dead, the other does it, whatever it was. Perhaps they think that God is looking down on them, and the dead, too. Lord Nelson had always begged Emma to have Horatia with her, and to take her with her when she went away, to the family or to the sea. And she never had until now. Now it seemed to Fatima that her mistress acted as if Nelson could look down and approve and bless her for doing his wish, and see that she was doing right by the dead.

It rained, and then it stopped. Emma finished her porter and the sun came out. 'Fatima!' she cried. 'The world looks as if it's been born again, doesn't it? Put that down, whatever you're doing, and come to the sea. You can help Horatia look for shells, and blow away the cobwebs.'

They hired bathing-machines. Boys in one, girls in the other, separated by a hundred yards of water. Horatia's uncle, George Matcham, was a tousled, square-faced man of fifty-four, with a broad chest and narrow ankles. He swam as if he might get to Hove and back before dinner. 'Kick!' he called to Horatia. 'I want to see those legs work.'

Horatia, chin tipped like a teacup, grinned. He was behind her and she could not see him. She began a slow circle, paddling with her hands, and swam towards him. Emma kept with her, wading in four feet of water.

'Just look at that,' said Mr Matcham. 'A great big fish, and it's coming towards me! Very good, little one, keep going.' He scooped her out of the water and lifted her. Horatia screamed with the joy of being airborne and the centre of his attention. Then he crashed backwards into the sea, Horatia still in his arms. They surfaced spluttering, and she had to be lifted up again before she choked.

'Again!' she shouted.

'What if I throw you this time?'

'Yes, throw me!'

'She *is* like a fish,' said Emma. 'I wish Horatio could see her.'

She lowered herself and launched forward into the water, swimming slowly away from the beach. The sky was grey, and a few drops of rain were falling. A single white sail was visible close to the shore, though the day had fashioned little breeze. She found the sea-bed with her feet, and used them to help her turn. Somewhere on the beach a bell was rung, and one of the horses was led down to the water to be hitched to a machine.

'You're like a father to her,' she told George Matcham, as she drew close to him again.

He smiled, and looked up into the sky. 'Rain,' he said.

'Oh, not much. It won't do us any harm.'

'Someone's teeth are chattering.'

Horatia shook her head, too cold to speak. It was time to go in for dinner, anyway.

When they had eaten they went for donkey rides up and down the beach. The animals were bored and sullen. 'Kick,' said Frank Matcham. They were at the water's edge, on the sand.

Horatia hung onto the pommel for dear life. 'I want to gallop,' she said, 'all the way to the end.'

Frank was eleven, and angel-faced. 'Well, kick,' he said. 'For God's sake, Horatia, it won't go anywhere if you just sit there.'

They splashed along quietly in the long curves of shallow water as the sun went in and out behind the clouds, and a new breeze blew up off the sea. Gulls were lifted high above them, watching but indifferent. 'Don't you have any brothers or sisters?' said Frank.

'You know I don't.'

'Why?'

'I don't, Frank. I don't have a mother.'

'You must have one.'

The donkey smelled of old sacks, and flies buzzed round its ears. Horatia sighed. 'She's dead. Go faster.'

They managed a slow, uncomfortable trot, past dogs and children and a laid-up fishing-boat. The sand in front of them and behind was pocked with donkey tracks and small, round, scattered droppings.

'How did she die?'

No one had ever told her. She was ill, and then she died. Horatia, holding a fistful of short, dusty mane, did not answer the question. Then, above their own noise and the racket on

217

the beach, she heard her name being called. 'My lady!' she shouted, turning in the saddle. 'That way, Frank!'

She was up on the promenade, dressed in a gown of flimsy silk with short sleeves and a ribbon under her breast. Frank yanked the bridle, and turned the donkey up the beach.

'You were going so fast!' said Emma, as she struggled over the shingle towards them. 'You stayed on, though, didn't you? You'll be riding as well as me, one of these days. Frank, my darling, where did you leave your shoes and stockings?'

'In the bathing-machine.'

'Good boy. I thought you might have lost them.' Emma rubbed the nose of the donkey. 'Five more minutes,' she said. 'We're going to Lady Dudley's, and you've got to change. No fuss, please.'

'What about Frank?'

'Yes, Frank too.'

'But he hasn't had a ride.'

'Off you get, then, and let him ride back.'

When she was on her feet, Horatia took Emma's hand and they made their way back up towards the front.

'We have to put on our thinking caps,' said Emma. 'Lady Dudley may want you to sing. We'll have to think of something not too difficult. Something pretty.'

'You sing with me.'

'Well, all right. That might be arranged. And what do you call Lady Dudley?'

'My lady.'

'And Princess Charlotte, if she's there?'

'Your Highness.'

Emma smiled and nodded. 'You!' she cried, clutching Horatia to her. 'You're such a young lady, now. You're my pride and joy, aren't you?'

My beautiful lady, with her lovely voice and her lovely dress, and the gold chain round her neck. Horatia swung her hand, and leaped over a piece of driftwood. Then she stopped in her tracks, and leaned down, pulling Emma with her. 'Shell,' she said.

'Well, bring it, sweetheart. We'll put it with the others.'

Mary Cadogan watched her daughter and her granddaughter as they made their way up the last bit of road to the house. They looked hot. Did sea air really do anyone any good? She herself didn't feel any better. Her lungs felt as if someone had crushed a newspaper and stuffed it into her chest. They were smiling, she saw, as they drew closer, and chatting. Now Emma had stopped, put a hand to her breast. Was she in pain? No, she was singing a line of song. Horatia laughed, and the two sounds reached the window, the song and the laughter. Then small things scattered on the road at their feet, and they both got down to pick them up. Pebbles, shells. Mary Cadogan pressed a finger to a small point of pain between her eyes. Emma did look better, it was true. Perhaps it was the sea air, perhaps it was distraction. Being elsewhere, with nothing, if you looked in the right direction, but sea and the horizon.

She tried to move away from the window, and found that she could not. She could feel a press of secrets behind her, like the press of ghosts. She even wondered if she was going to die, here in Worthing, by a window. Her heart made a small leap at the thought, as if it were a welcome one. It reminded her that there were other things to do, but she had become stuck where she stood, not looking forward, but back, until it was not Worthing outside that she saw but the Wirral peninsula. From the upstairs windows of the cottage in Denhall you could see across the estuary to the northern coast of Wales. It was a flat and windy place, a squalid village of a few cottages and a coal pit. Was that my own life, she found herself thinking, or someone else's? There was no one left to tell her any more. Her husband, Henry, had shod pit ponies; today she could almost remember his face. When he died, six weeks after Emma was born, Mary had taken her across the estuary to Hawarden, to her own parents. To the cottage with the thatched roof and the red sandstone steps. She saw her own mother, small and formidable, standing in the open door, and Emma, making a pile of stones for people to trip over.

They looked, the two of them, as if they had found a tiny civilisation at the side of the street. They were crouched low, the sun on their heads.

In those days Emma had been Emily Lyon, a wild and thoughtless child, with a heart of gold and nothing to do but run untamed all day. When she was twelve, she had gone to work as under-nursemaid with the family of a local surgeon. Mary Cadogan could remember brown walls, and the smell of senna and spirits of wine. A few months later they went to London, where Emma worked for a family in Blackfriars for a year, until she was given the sack for staying out until dawn, singing ballads at Cocksheath Camp and sailing down the Thames in a wherry. She went to the Linleys in Norfolk Street, off the Strand. He was the musical director, with Ford and Sheridan, of the theatre at Drury Lane; she was mistress of the wardrobe, and managed the accounts. She was a dragon, Mrs Linley, for a balanced book. That had lasted four months, five.

Mrs Cadogan felt the skin pucker on her chin, as if a stitch there had been pulled tight. She could see, suddenly, all the different roofs that she herself had lived under at that time. Dark walls, beds without springs, kitchens leaping with damp. Men with money, but not much. She lifted her eyes beyond the road to the small stand of weathered pines on the bluff, a grey corner of sea. That's enough, she thought. That'll do. But it wasn't, it wouldn't.

After the Linleys, Emma had lived with Madame Kelly, at Arlington Street. Never mind what that meant, or that she was only fourteen: some of those girls were only twelve.

Money. We do what we can, we use what we have. And we keep what we do to ourselves.

The father of Emma's first child had been a rich, lazy man,

with a long head like a horse's. He had taken her away from Madame Kelly's and set her up in a cottage on his estate in Sussex. He taught her to ride like the devil, and she danced naked on his dinner table, but when he had found out she was going to have a baby, he dropped her like a stone. She came back to London, and slept with anyone who would give her money for food and lodging.

There were stitches, tighter ones, under her eyes. We do what we can, she thought. Where was I then? Elsewhere. In another room with a broken bed and sooty walls.

Then Charles Greville had taken them in. He found a house for them in the Edgware Road in London. He made Emma change her name from Lyon to Hart, give up all her former connections and live a retired life. Mary had changed her own name to Cadogan; it sounded better, and put a greater distance between the present and the past. Emma's child was born in secret, and sent to her grandmother in Hawarden, to the cottage with the red sandstone steps and the thatched roof. For a few months, they had brought her back to live with them at Edgware Road, a wild and funny child of two; blue-eyed, wilful and affectionate. Then Greville had sent her off to Manchester, and paid for her to be brought up there with a family called Blackburn; to be raised and educated, and taught to have no expectations further than a quiet life in the north of England. He removed all traces of her from the house, and Emma gave her up entirely. It was either that or give up Greville. There was no choice – without Greville, they would have nothing. And if they were to stay with him, the past must be swept under the carpet.

When Emma married Sir William, Greville handed the responsibility of the child's care to his uncle. Mrs Cadogan had been to Manchester twice to make sure that she was well cared for and needed nothing, but the girl had never dreamed that this old woman was her grandmother. She had remembered fragments from her early childhood – a beautiful woman's hands around her, the steps at Edgware Road, and the tiles on the floor of the hall. She remembered, and she had put it all away again, because Mrs Cadogan could never say to her: Yes, that was so, yes, this is who you are. The girl would never know who her father was, but that Emma was her mother had been on the one hand always understood, and on the other never acknowledged. To Mrs Cadogan's surprise, and to her relief, Emma Carew had borne the cross of her uncertain parentage with extraordinary poise and discretion.

At Edgware Road, Emma had learned thrift and economy, and how to write her accounts. Gloves, letters, coach, mangle. One and six, fourpence, a shilling. You wouldn't think it, to look at her now. Careful lists of wood and meat, muffins, magazines and eggs. She had adored Greville. She no longer paraded in Kensington Gardens, or rode in Madame Kelly's carriage; she did not wander St James's market wearing next to nothing. She put on dull, sober clothes and stayed at home. She did everything she could to please him, and came out in a rash when he was cross with her. She tried to be like him, to do the same things as he did, and slept with no one but him.

Now Emma was getting to her feet. She'd find that easier, thought Mrs Cadogan, if she lost a bit of weight. Horatia stood, too. Perhaps I will die soon, she thought. And what will they do without me? What will I do without them? It occurred to her that she would miss them both, very much, when she was gone. It was a stupid thought, but not without resonance.

Greville had liked the idea of settling down with a young and beautiful woman who was not his wife. And she was very beautiful. Perfect cheeks and big blue eyes, and chestnut hair that reached her waist. But perhaps more important than this, to him, was the idea he had had of making money out of Emma by commissioning from his friend George Romney a series of portraits that Greville would sell for a small fortune. She had been, in other words, an investment. Or not, in the end, as nothing ever came of it. Romney painted her fifty or a hundred times, but Greville had paid for only a few of the pictures, and most stayed in the artist's studio.

Then, after three years, Greville struck the deal with his uncle. He needed a rich wife, and thought he had found one. He asked for something in writing, to prove that Sir William intended to make him his heir; something to show to the father of his chosen bride. Poor Greville. His chosen bride had chosen someone else, in spite of the letter, and he had gone off to Edinburgh, with his tail between his legs, to study chemistry. But not before he had packed Emma off, with Mary Cadogan, to Naples. They had thought it was only for the summer holidays; they had believed he would join them there. But he had abandoned Emma and broken her heart, and it was months before she understood that he would never come to take her away, that he had no thoughts of having her back. Sir William loved her, and she was fond of him, but she loved Greville and stayed devoted only to him through those first hot months in Naples. There had been many long nights of tears before she allowed Sir William into her bed.

Today, Mrs Cadogan had money on her mind again. She left the window at last, as Emma came into the room. 'Please at least look at this,' she said, putting her ledger on the table in front of her.

'I can't believe you brought that with you. We're on holiday!'

'This column here. This is what we owe. This is the column for what we've paid, and this is cash in hand.'

'For God's sake, borrow! We both know I'm going to get money from the government one day.'

'Perhaps. I'm talking about today, though, and tomorrow.'

'We've been over this. Old Q's going leave me money. He's on his last legs, we can borrow against that.'

'There's nothing,' said Mary Cadogan, 'in that column or in this one.'

'The Prince said he would give me a pension. He said he considers it a solemn obligation.'

'When? How can he? He has no power to give you a pension.'

'Ma . . .'

'We've been living off other people's money all year.'

'I don't see how we can manage on any less.' Emma held her hands up in front of her. 'You're right. We've got to do something. We'll talk about it later. I'm hot, I'm going to change. Don't forget Lady Dudley.' She gave her mother a sweet but intractable smile and left the room.

FOUR

Emma was lying on the floor. The side of her face was crushed against the carpet, and she had soiled herself. Her lips were cobalt. 'Wake up,' said Horatia. 'Please.' The fire had burned down, and the room was cold. Horatia leaned over her, took an arm and pulled it, but it was a dead weight. It was like finding a tree across the road. She rang for Berthe. Nothing. She went to the top of the stairs and yelled her name. Somewhere in the house a door closed quietly. She ran half-way down the stairs and called again. There was no one there. Not Berthe, not Monsieur Damas.

She ran back up again. Emma had not moved. She got down on her knees and listened. Breathing: in and out, then in and out. A hard, dark smell of wine. Horatia stood. The smell, too, of shit. Every time she came into this room, she felt herself submit to something older than her, beyond her years. She found herself hardly daring to breathe in the fearful loneliness of doing something for which she had neither knowledge, experience nor skill. She would never be good at it the way Fatima had been good at it. She would never know, really, what to do. This woman, her guardian, her godmother, was far out somewhere in the territory of death, and the closer she came, the more she threw herself at it, drinking her way through bottle after bottle. It was Monsieur Damas who brought them up, and no one could stop him. If he didn't, someone else would. Horatia had no power to prevent it; she would bring them herself, if she had to. She was afraid, too, of

225

Emma's pain, and because she was afraid, she could not console her. It was a suffering that she could only meet with incomprehension and a sort of grim obedience.

'I'm here,' said Berthe. 'Oh, *merde*.'

By now Horatia was standing with her back against the wall. 'I thought we could move her, you and me, but we can't. She'll have to stay there. I can't find Monsieur Damas.'

'He's gone to Abbeville.'

Horatia nodded.

'It's cold,' said Berthe. She lifted her eyes, and dipped her head. 'No, you're right, we can't. I'll do the fire.'

'Berthe, she's . . .'

The girl turned. She, too, could smell it. 'Hot water,' she said.

They had to wash her there, on the floor. By lifting and pulling, they got the bed gown off, but it was impossible to put a clean one on her. The stools were the colour of clay, and smears had dried on her skin.

Horatia's sympathy stood waiting on the edges of her mind for an unobstructed moment. She could feel it, an awful soaring pity, held off by anger and revulsion, by the smell and the stupidity of drink. It was drink that made Emma cruel, then weak, then comatose, and yet drink was the only thing that gave her any relief, that stopped the pain in her head and her belly, the wind and storm in her mind of everything that was gone and lost.

There was nothing to be done. They could not stop her drinking any more than they could stop her being ill. They were, in many ways, the same thing.

'I don't know,' whispered Berthe. 'We can't leave her there.'

'I'm not going to leave her.'

'Do you want me to stay?'

She did, but she shook her head. 'I might need you later, when she wakes up.'

'Well, put another cover on her. Wrap her up. I'll stay for a minute, and do the bed.' She pulled off the quilt and passed it to Horatia, then straightened the sheets. Then she stayed for a while, anyway, sitting on the edge of the bed, swinging her feet.

As night came on, Emma stirred. Horatia helped her to sit, and then to stand. She got a clean gown on her over her head, then pulled back the sheet and helped her onto the bed. Then she covered her again, one blanket and then another.

2

' "4 September 1811. I, Emma Hamilton of No. 150 Bond Street London widow of the Right Honourable Sir William Hamilton formerly Minister at the Court of Naples being in sound mind and body do give to my dearly beloved Horatia Nelson daughter of the great and glorious Nelson all that I shall be possessed of at my death money jewels pictures wine furniture books wearing apparel silver gold-plated or silver-gilt utensils of every sort I may have in my house or houses or of any other person's houses at my death any marbles bronzes busts plaster of Paris or in short every thing that belonged to me I give to my best beloved Horatia Nelson all my table linen laces ornaments in short everything that I have I give to her any money either in the house or at my bankers all debts that may be owing to me I beg that she may have I give to Horatia Nelson all silver with inscription with Viscount Nelson's name on or his arms I give to her would to God it was more for her sake I do appoint George Matcham, Esq. of Ashfold Lodge in the County of Sussex and the Right Honourable George Rose of Old Palace Yard Westminster my executors and I leave them Guardians to my dear Horatia Nelson and I do most earnestly entreat of them to be the protectors and guardians and be fathers to the daughter of the great and glorious Nelson and it is my wish that H. R. Highness the Prince Regent or if before my death he shall become King that he will provide for the said Horatia in such a manner that she may live as becomes the daughter of such a man as her victorious father was . . ." '

Emma sat, as Horatia read, in an old armchair. She drank slowly, cheap brandy the colour of tea. 'You see,' she said. 'Everything is yours.'

Horatia laid the document on her lap. It was three years old; there was nothing left. Only the few things that had been taken or bought by friends and stored in London; what remained of her toys, and the coat Nelson had died in. She didn't know what to say. 'Thank you,' she murmured.

'The government will give you something. I've never had sixpence out of them, but when I'm dead they might see sense. One day, when there's an administration with any heart or feelings.'

Emma had petitioned them every year since the death of Sir William, and every year she had been ignored or told that there was nothing for her. 'You're not going to die,' said Horatia.

'Go on. Read the rest.'

' ". . . I do most earnestly recommend her on my knees blessing her and praying for her that she may be happy virtuous good and amiable and that she may remember all the kind instructions and good advice I have given her and may she be what her great and immortal father wished her to be brought up with virtue honour religion and rectitude amen amen amen . . ." '

Emma had begun to weep. The tears slid down her face, fat and unchecked. Her mouth hung open, as if a catch in her jaw had broken.

' ". . . I do absolutely give her all I have I still hope Mr Matcham and Mr Rose will see to the educating of Horatia and that she may live with Mrs Matcham's family till she is disposed to some worthy man in marriage I forgot to mention that I also give Horatia all my china glass crockery ware of every sort that I have. Signed sealed published and declared by Emma Hamilton as her last will and testament." '

Horatia put down the will, and stood. She took the glass from Emma's hand, and placed it out of reach.

'Please, Horatia . . .'

'You'll sleep. If you lie down now, you'll sleep.'

Emma nodded. 'Do you know what I wish?' she said. Her voice was so quiet, the words so clearly spoken, that it seemed they had been said by someone else. Horatia, suddenly, was terrified.

'Never mind,' said Emma. 'I want to tell you something.'

Horatia sat down again. Her whole face ached, like a bruise.

'Listen.' Emma leaned forward over her knees, and straightened again. She did not look at Horatia. 'I've left a letter with my solicitor. His name is William Haslewood. One of these days, you may decide you would like to know who your mother was. It's up to you. I made a promise a long time ago to tell no one while I was alive, but when I am dead, Mr Haslewood will give you a package, and in that package is a letter to you, from me, with her name. You can read it or not, it's your decision. If you don't, then never mind. Haslewood will keep it for as long as you like. Perhaps when you're older . . .'

Horatia looked at her with something too full of distrust to be astonishment, and too weary for anger. 'For God's sake . . .' she said, then shut her mouth again.

Emma opened her hands on her lap, as if to look at words that were written on them. She had slipped back into her own world again. 'The horror . . .' she said. She lifted reddened eyes to look at her daughter. 'The glory, Horatia, and then the horror . . .'

'Come and get into bed.'

Emma, as she took Horatia's hand and allowed herself to be led the few feet from the chair to the bed, looked like a monstrous child. 'Watch the rug,' said Horatia. 'Don't trip.'

Hour after hour, she stood at the window that looked out over the street. She watched women with baskets, men with hand-

229

carts and pipes. She listened to the rain as it funnelled over the roof and sluiced into the gutter beneath the window. They were the only things of any interest, the women, the men and the rain. Everything else had been drained, until the words in her books were exhausting, and her fingers would not move to sew. The same strange and creeping dreariness, hatched in crisis, blanketed everything in the two small rooms in the rue Française. It was a wide, dread space in which she stood and moved around. It made every outline indistinct, and caused her to stare, without really seeing, at familiar and ordinary things. At night, she looked out through open shutters, and ached to go into the streets, to hear the ghostly slap of washing on the lines, and see the moonlight on the sea. To hear the tug of ropes in the water, and look at the empty fishing-smacks moored to the harbour wall. It was a longing that held a sharp and attractive fear, of dark streets and sudden, muffled noises. Inside these two rooms, her fear was dull and open. She could not see what might happen in the still and early hours of dawn, or tomorrow or the next day, and it seemed to her that if she stayed still enough, dawn might not come, nor tomorrow. She breathed onto a window pane, and watched the cloud that formed. The town was quiet and dark, as if it had vanished and left only one house, in the rue Française, and a few lamps here and there. All the people had gone. They had fled from an advancing army, or the plague, and had forgotten to let her know. In the morning the streets would be deserted, the market empty, a few lost animals bleating on the quay. She waited for Emma to wake, to get out of bed and move from one room to the other, to speak and require an answer, to remember something and laugh. But when she did wake, her movements were full of effort, and all she wanted was something to drink.

She missed Fatima with all her heart. She missed Janot. She was marooned in loneliness with not a soul, except Berthe, to talk to. She wanted to break things. She wanted to pick something up and throw it against the wall. She wanted someone to see her, to come in and take hold of her and say, Heh, what's this, what's wrong? Emma would die, because she wished to die. She was walking the deck in her own last battle, and would not take off her coat. The last remaining disappointment was that she would die without glory, without, in her present state, even the memory of that.

She stood up and walked from one end of the room to the other for the sake of something to do. She spoke to people in her head, to people who had known her father, and who offered to look after her. *Let us worry about this*, they said. She stood by the window, and saw a young man turn in the street and stop. In an instant, as if because of something heard, he retraced his steps and stopped again, his eyes turned to the windows of the second floor. Then she heard the door downstairs, his feet on the stone floor of the hall. Steps on the stairs, fleet and urgent. She found herself turning, waiting for his knock.

It is not a young man at all. There is her father, opening the door a crack, because no one has answered his knock. *Is this where you are?* he says. His face is weathered, and there are storms and battles in his cheeks. She can feel his strength, and see it in the shape of his wrist. He takes her chin in his hand, and studies her face. *My darling child, whatever have we done?* He holds her to him, and she can feel again the weave of his coat, the print on her face of his stars and medals. *This needs a bit of sorting out.* He is still a hero, he has not been forgotten. His hair falls the way it always did, and his voice is solemn and low. *Get your things, we're going home.* He lifts them up from the rue Française and takes them away. How? Just like that, so that they are elsewhere. And when they are there, he listens without speaking as she tells him everything.

FIVE

The ferry at Richmond had been replaced by a stone bridge in 1774. Heron Court lay just below it on the riverbank. The house belonged to the Duke of Queensberry; he had rented it to Emma when she was forced, within a year of their visit to Worthing, to put Merton on the market.

'Isn't it lovely, darling?'

Horatia looked over the river to a small island, thick with willows. Swans sailed past them with glancing eyes and a haughty brightness. She did not know if she had come here to stay or to live, if she would ever see Merton again, or Cribb or the animals. She looked back at the mansion behind them, its empty windows, its unfamiliar and solemn charm. There had been whispers and shouting, slammed doors and closed rooms. There had been people coming and going with documents and condescending smiles. Lists, tensions, trunks and boxes. She closed her eyes and tried to remember, without looking, what she was wearing today.

'We're going to be very happy!' It was almost a shriek. Horatia opened her eyes, but she found that when she tried to smile, her lip only trembled.

Emma turned away from the water, and began to walk back to the house. 'You stay and play for a while,' she said. 'I'm going to lie down. You've got a lesson later, don't forget.'

Emma had bills of over eight thousand pounds. Charles Greville had died that year, and his death had delayed the payments of her quarterly allowance until the Hamilton estate was passed on to his brother, Fulke. Emma had begun a dangerous game, borrowing against the annuity several times over, in spite of receiving a letter from one of the trustees telling her not to spend any more until the estate was settled. Things were desperate. Mrs Cadogan could no longer see their future, only a great darkness punctuated by the lights of late nights and glittering dinners. Emma was still reckless. The parties had not stopped, and clothes and presents still found their way into the house. The previous Christmas, their last at Merton, she had invited three of the royal dukes to stay for several days. She had made Mrs Cadogan order venison, turkey, goose liver and fish; jellies, pastries, wines. Filling the Prince of Wales had been like emptying food into a bottomless pit. He was a monster, and drank like a fish. And a houseful of royal servants to feed, as well.

Now it was summer, and Mrs Cadogan knew that there would be no trip to Worthing or Ramsgate or Ashfold. They would have to make excuses. The family still had a wholly mistaken view of Emma's finances, and believed she could go where she wanted. No one had come forward to give any part of their government grant to Horatia – not for want of heart but because they believed Emma had money. From the way she lived, the extravagance of her life in London and at Merton, and from the confidence that, as the widow of an ambassador, she would have been left plenty to live on, they drew their own conclusions. And she had been left money. Sir William had provided for her, and so had Nelson, but no one had any idea that she was so incapable of living within her means. Why should they? The deeper she fell into debt, the more she had to hide it.

Emma heard the patter of steps in the passage. 'Horatia, darling, I asked you to get ready.'

The child stopped dead in the doorway.

'Go and find Fatima. Do your face and put on some clean clothes. Come on, you're in a dream.'

It was time for her French lesson. She had a new French governess, Mademoiselle Roulants. She was thin and spiky, with long teeth and a narrow mouth.

'*Monsieur Paul n'est pas ici,*' said Mademoiselle. '*Il est allé à Paris pour acheter une pipe.*'

Monsieur Paul est tombé dans la rivière with all his clothes on and drowned, thought Horatia. *Il était* washed down *jusqu' à Notre Dame*, and no one found him *pendant quelques jours. Très triste.*

Everything had changed. Everything was wrong. Her head hurt and she wanted to use the privy all the time. She wanted to use it now. She asked to leave the room, and ran upstairs to use the night-stool in Emma's room. The pain came in waves that made her feel sick. No one came up, and she leaned forward over her knees. Tears fell down her cheeks, as if everything inside her needed emptying. When she had finished, she crept into her own room, and stayed there cutting shapes out of paper.

Fatima was sent up to find her. She took her to the front parlour, where Emma was walking up and down in front of the empty fire. Mrs Cadogan was also there.

'Where have you been?' said Emma. 'Why did you run away from Mademoiselle?' She looked like a dragon. 'I'm waiting for an answer. You're supposed to be learning something. Why do you think I spend a fortune on your education?' She thrust out her chin. 'So that you can grow up with something to show for yourself and be a credit to your poor father and to me.'

Her face was the wrong colour. It was yellow, and there were grey bruises under her eyes. Horatia could not look at her. She looked at the floor and wished that Emma would not mention her father. He was dead and would never come back to see whether she had accomplishments or not.

'I won't have you throwing everything away! Do you hear? Look at me, you're not even listening. Have you completely forgotten how to behave? You can go upstairs and stay in your room. You won't have any dinner, and I'll decide later whether you can come down this evening.'

'Emma,' said Mrs Cadogan, quietly.

'I mean it! I won't have ingratitude.'

Mrs Cadogan dipped her head, like a bird, and looked at Horatia over her spectacles. 'I'm sure she'll go back and finish her lesson.'

'No!' Emma was boiling.

'You're getting worked up over nothing,' said Mrs Cadogan.

'Let me deal with this, Mama. I tell her what to do, not you.'

Mrs Cadogan looked as if a book had been slammed shut in front of her nose. 'I beg your pardon?' she said.

'Just leave this to me.'

'I think I know as well as you do what's good for her.'

'Ma, I'm warning you—'

But Mrs Cadogan would not let it go. She, too, was angry now. 'For God's sake, Emma. The amount of fuss you make over her, anyone would think she was your own daughter.'

'Perhaps she is my own daughter!'

Horatia felt as if all the windows in the room might crack, and become like spider webs. Mrs Cadogan and Emma never quarrelled, and now they were at each other's throats. Something really wrong had happened. They both looked at her, and she felt as if she was strung between them, like something hung out to dry. The room was suddenly so quiet that she could hear sounds from outside. Birds and a shout from the river, a spade in the garden, going down hard into the earth. *Scritch*.

'Emma,' said Mrs Cadogan, though her eyes were still on Horatia, 'you and I both know better than that. Let's not get carried away.'

Horatia felt the floor shift under her. She did not understand why they were talking like this. Emma was not her mother.

236

Her mother was ill, and then she died. Ill, ill, ill. Dead, dead, dead. 'I had a pain in my stomach,' she said. 'I asked to be excused.'

Emma looked suddenly tired. Her whole face was grey. 'Upstairs,' she said. 'You can come down for dinner. I'll send for you when it's ready.'

That was when Horatia threw up. It went everywhere, all over the carpet. Mrs Cadogan took her upstairs, washed her and put her to bed.

2

She was ill throughout that summer. It came and went, and no one knew what it was. Her head hurt and she couldn't eat. She had diarrhoea and vomited. They did not know what to do for her, except to make her warm in bed with tea and milk to drink. At night she woke suddenly and completely, drenched in sweat and terror.

In April, Merton was sold. The money went straight to creditors, and even then it wasn't enough. At the end of the year, they had to move again. They went to Albemarle Street in Piccadilly, to furnished rooms in a tall, narrow house. It was ugly, grey and cramped. The landlady stuck her nose into everything, and made them tea that tasted of straw.

Then the biggest disaster since the death of Nelson struck. In January 1810 Mary Cadogan died. The sounds of Emma's grief, as they struck the walls and windows of the house in Piccadilly, were dreadful. Wherever she went, doors were closed behind her, and Horatia was taken by kind hands to the kitchen, the scullery, the attic. The house, even when it was silent, shook with grief, and the child feared that everyone would die, Emma and Fatima, too, leaving her on her own in a strange place. In a room above her, or in a room below her, there was always either the sound or the silence of a woman who was inconsolable.

Emma herself was afraid. Her mother had been her rock; without her, she felt as if the lid had come off the world, and there was nothing between her and the sky. She had been there, with her, always, and now she was not. Never again would anyone love her the way her mother had loved her, and now that the sound of her calm, rational voice was gone, Emma felt all the more exposed and at risk. There was no one, any more, who knew who Emma Hamilton was. There was no one to look after the house, the money, the debts, or to work out what, each day, they would eat. She went to bed, and did not get up for weeks.

Then they moved again, this time to 76 Piccadilly. They were still near to the Duke of Queensberry, who lived at the Hyde Park end, but in December, he died, too. He left Emma five hundred a year, half the amount he had led her to expect. The bequest was contested and went to Chancery and she was told that, very likely, she would never see any of it. There was still no money from Fulke Greville, though he was supposed to send her two hundred pounds quarterly. She moved house again. In April she asked George Matcham to lend her a hundred pounds. He sent her the money, but only because by luck he had it to hand. Otherwise, everything he had was invested on behalf of his wife and children. Knowing nothing, still, about her real situation, and believing that she was in only temporary difficulties, he asked her to pay it back as soon as she could, and not to mention to anyone that he had lent it to her, as he did not want his trustees to hear about it.

Drawing room, dining room, bedroom. Glass and china, clothes and pictures. Ornaments, books and rugs. Emma heard someone on the landing, and turned. 'Hello, darling.'

'What are you doing?'

'Come and give me a kiss.' A fire had been lit, but the drawing room had not warmed up yet. Horatia had been out with Fatima for a walk.

'Not again!' said Horatia.

Emma gathered her in her arms. 'Lovely pretty cold cheeks,' she said. Outside, it was a bright day with sudden clouds and a bitter wind.

'What are all these boxes?'

'Today's the day!'

Horatia looked around her with dismay. She was ten and tall for her age. 'Where?' she asked, in a solemn voice. They were in lodgings in Dover Street. They had moved four times in three years.

'It's a lovely house in Bond Street,' said Emma. 'Don't look at me like that. We're going, and that's that.'

Their lives seemed made of crates and straw. Horatia didn't know any more what belonged to them and what did not. She stood by the fire and stared into it. They were alone now. Everywhere they went, their world became smaller and their friends went away. Her head ached, and her ears still burned with the cold.

'Come on, cheer up.' Emma sat down on a sofa, and patted the seat beside her. 'Jump up,' she said. 'Don't look so worried! We're not out on the street, you know. We'll have some breakfast, and you can help me. The men will do most of it, but I want to pack the small things, anything precious that might get broken.'

'But why do we have to go?'

Emma placed her hands on Horatia's cheeks. 'We can't stay here,' she said. 'Mrs Damier is robbing us blind. She sits up there in her awful little room adding charges to our bill for things I've never heard of. We'll be happy at Bond Street – it's only round the corner. We'll settle down and never have to move again. You'll have a lovely room and we can put all your things in it. I'll take you shopping tomorrow and we'll find you some cushions or something. Come on, take your coat off.'

While men in brown aprons packed the glass and silver in the dining room and began to lug crates into the hallway,

Horatia, Emma and Fatima packed the most delicate things upstairs in the drawing room.

'Look!' cried Emma. She held up a small ornament, a china figurine. 'I gave this to your father on his fortieth birthday. Do you remember, Fatima?'

Horatia sat back on her haunches. She was on the floor, surrounded by straw and strips of rag. 'Where?' she said.

'Where? In Naples. Lovely sunny Naples. He'd just come back from the Nile. Poor Nelson, he was worn out. I gave him asses' milk to drink, and he bathed in it, too!'

'In *milk*?' She had heard it before, but she could hear it a hundred times. 'Not true,' she said.

'Cross my heart and hope to die. They made him a baron. He should have been Duke Nelson, Marquess Nile, Earl Alexandria, Viscount Pyramid, Baron Crocodile, and Prince Victory—'

Horatia gaped, and slid down onto her backside. 'Baron Crocodile!'

'Why not?' Emma smiled, and then sighed. 'But the cabinet thought otherwise. Baron Nelson of the Nile and of Burnham Thorpe. Still, what a party we had for him! Eighty people to dinner, eight hundred for supper, and a thousand more again to dance at the ball. Can you imagine? Every button and ribbon had his initials on it, every plate was printed with the glorious date of his great battle, and there was a column in the middle of the ballroom with the names on it of all the captains who served under him then. There were songs and dancing all night. Fatima danced, didn't you?'

Fatima was wrapping a clock. 'No, I never. Not at that party.'

'You danced with a midshipman from the *Colossus*.' Emma leaned down to whisper to Horatia, 'She denies it, darling, because she broke his heart. Right there on the dance floor at the Palazzo Sessa!'

Fatima winked at Horatia. 'I was just come to Italy from

Alexandria,' she said. 'I was still shaking in my shoes to see all those bright lights of the ball. I hid away.'

'In any case, it was glorious.'

'Did the Queen come?' said Horatia.

'The Queen, King Ferdinand, the prince and princesses. All of Naples society.'

'That queen were a funny one,' said Fatima. 'She was not very beautiful, except with white skin and white hands. The people called her Mouthful of Rissoles, because of how she gobbled her words when she talked. She was very devout, and wrote short prayers and stuck them in her stays, and sometimes she swallowed them.' Fatima shrugged. 'If you want to know why, I don't know why. Maybe she think they will come true. Maybe it made her more holy, if she swallowed them. Me, I think it gave her the shits, if you want the truth.'

Horatia was watching her as if the words coming out of her mouth were small and fascinating creatures. 'Then what happened?'

There was a crash from downstairs. They waited. After a minute, a round face, furrowed with drink and worry, appeared in the door. 'Nothing broken, my lady.'

Emma gave Horatia a small Etruscan bowl to wrap. 'Make yourself useful. All hands on deck. What happened next? Well, we went to war.'

'*You* did?'

'She marched to Rome,' said Fatima, 'with the King and General Mack.'

'She did not!'

'Of course I didn't. But the Austrians were in the north, fighting against the French. Nelson and Sir William were very wise. They knew that the time was right for Naples to invade Rome and throw out the enemy – they knew that Italy could be cleared of those ragamuffins in a month. There was a grand muster of the troops and the Queen rode to inspect them in a blue riding habit with gold fleur-de-lis at the neck and a general's hat with a white plume.'

'But them soldiers,' said Fatima, 'was peasant boys and convicts, without any boots.'

'It's true, they had no boots. And General Mack spoke no Italian. They took Rome, though. Horatia, put it in the case, but make sure there's some straw underneath it. Big things at the bottom, small things at the top.'

'Did Lord Nelson march with them?'

Emma shook her head. 'He sailed to Leghorn with a squadron and five thousand infantry to cut off the French as they retreated. King Ferdinand marched into Rome, and the French left without a murmur. It was a great triumph, but not for long. We were betrayed.'

'Them Frenchies marched right back again,' said Fatima.

'They did. They took the artillery and tents, and ten thousand prisoners. I'm afraid to say, my little one, that victory turned to defeat. Not for ever, but for then. We had to flee Naples, me and Sir William and all the royal family. I'll tell you that story, too, but not till all this is done. We'll be here until midnight, otherwise.' Emma put the figurine, wrapped in linen, into the chest. She straightened, and looked around the room. 'We have some lovely things, don't we? And they'll all be yours, one day. Everything!'

'Where will we sleep tonight?'

Emma frowned. 'I'm not sure. We'll have to see.'

SIX

I

Then Nelson has gone again, and her mother is there, lifting an arm to take off her hat. She is young still, and slim, and wears a long grey coat. *Do you know what I would love?* she says. *A cup of tea.* She looks at each object in the room, taking in the weary furniture, the books, the sewing-box. She tells Horatia she has kept it very neat. She weeps, because it has come to this. *I thought that you were dead*, she says. Everything has been the result of a string of mistakes without blame. For a long time, it was true, she had been ill. Lord Nelson was told that she was dead, but she was not dead, only in Northamptonshire – Lincolnshire, Florence, Rome. She, in turn, was told that her daughter had perished after only months. Her heart was broken, she tells Horatia. She felt it go, like the break in a china dish. But never mind, all that is over and past and gone. Now they talk of a small house on Chertsey Mead, of chickens and the river. There are geese, yes, and a dog.

Horatia stands. She picks up a book and throws it into the fire. Sparks fly out into the room, and she picks the embers off the floor, burning her thumbs. She sits down again and leans forward over her knees, her face a foot from the floor, and weeps with her mouth wide open, as if she were being sick.

She dances. Back, side, together; back, side, together. The boards in the sitting room creak under her feet. She dances

slowly, humming to herself. Then she remembers her fear. She
keeps on dancing and the fear is like a dark shape on the end of
her bed. Left, side, together; right, side, together.

She remembers his coat, his medals. He is a shape, a low voice,
a wrist. He is a ghost she sat with under the table in the dining
room, in a boat on the lake. He is fixed in two or three places,
a look of concern on his face, or a smile. We should be able to
buy back the past, she thinks, just as, one day, she hopes to be
able to buy back from the *mont-de-piété* the things that he
gave to her.

She weeps for love. Every person should have love. Everyone
must have a hand laid from time to time on their back or a
cheek, that says you are mine and I love you.

'You're not going to die,' she says. 'Please don't die.' There is
no movement or sound from the shape in the bed, and for a
moment she thinks perhaps Emma is dead, and that she hasn't
noticed, she has missed it. She has become, in a moment of
inattention, completely alone. A tiny glitter, like the glitter of
fish scales, lies between the lids of Emma's eyes. 'Wake up,' she
says. Nothing. She leans forward and prods the shape with a
finger. 'Please.'

She sits by the bed and fixes her eyes on the shape beneath the
covers, and when she has been sitting and watching for a time
something strange begins to happen, and she finds that she can
see Emma's suffering as it is, as a pain that has embraced
Emma Hamilton and wrapped her up and taken her away, and
laid claim to a kind of privacy that nothing and no one can
breach. It is familiar with every part of her – her uncombed
hair, the ruby spot where she has slept on her hand, the yellow
skin on the soles of her feet. It will not relinquish her, and she
has already gone. It has made her more lonely than can be

understood. Horatia feels the dreadful waste of it, the pity and the ruin.

She begins to recognise the women who live in the street, although because it is winter they walk with their heads down, wearing scarves. The men go out before dawn, and from her bed in the alcove she hears doors closing up and down the rue Française. She knows every flaw in the window pane, where the glass has bubbled, where the colour is slightly different. She can see into the window of the house opposite, a dark and empty room, a bed, a crucifix. Then the shutters are closed, and she can't see any more. She wonders why she is who she is and not someone else. She regrets that she will never be this or that person, to live for a while another life instead of this one. She will never be a girl born in Calais, living out by the fort, or a boy, or from India, and she thinks about this with wonder. She will be who she is until she dies, whatever may happen to her in the meantime. She imagines that she is the daughter of a fishwife in the market. The air smells of fish guts and pipe-smoke, and underfoot it is a shallow lake of mud. Her hands are chapped from the cold and from handling salt, scales and blood. She is that girl, there below on the street, who knows it's going to rain again and has begun to hurry.

She was right, it is raining again. This time it's a downpour. In a matter of seconds the windowsill is wet with standing drops, as if they have landed there expecting to grow. They fall with a quiet thud on an open book, and the paper begins to swell. She closes the window and pushes up the bolt. She can see the surface of the street as it turns from grey to black. The rain falls quietly at first, then gathers strength until there's a sound like carriages on gravel, and suddenly it's coming down with such force that the gutter in the middle of the street is running like a stream. Litter appears from nowhere and is carried in eddies until it disappears or is stranded on the cobbles. The rain

245

bounces off the road so that she cannot tell if is coming down or up, and there is a mist of spray a foot off the ground. It sounds as if the whole town has slipped its moorings, and is being driven away from the mainland on a high sea. Then, impossibly, it comes down even harder. She thinks of someone who weeps at the news of a tragedy and then, in the act of weeping, realises it is even worse than that. She can no longer see people below her, only shapes, making a dash for it, then no one.

She stands by Emma's bed and shakes a finger in the air. Don't you speak to me like that, she says. I've been like a mother to you, and all you think of is yourself. She lifts an arm, and cups her elbow in her hand, as if she is addressing the Roman people. You've got no spine, you have to spoil everything. The shape on the bed moves, and she becomes as still as a statue. I don't know what's the matter with you, she whispers. Grow up.

Sometimes she believes that there is a letter waiting for her with the solicitor in London. Then she remembers all the other lies and manipulations, and does not know what to believe.

She wonders what it's like to be dead. What is the mole-catcher thinking now? His body is six feet under the ground in the graveyard at St Pierre. It will never move again, or feel. Though she believes he has gone to heaven, that is not where she sees him. She sees him wandering, confused by his inability, in fact, to wander. He misses his body with useless regret, and trudges without it between the hedges on either side of the lanes. The leaves have gone now. He can't understand, not yet, how he is supposed to go on. Sometimes he lingers by his own grave, as if waiting for a coach, not sure whether he is early for it, or late. He lies back down among his bones and he does wait. Surely there must be a sign from somewhere else; surely he does not have to guess what he must do next.

SEVEN

I

At the beginning of January 1813, Emma was arrested for debt and taken to the King's Bench prison. She was immediately made free of the rules, meaning that she could live outside the prison walls on parole, in a sponging-house belonging to one of the bailiffs. With Horatia and Fatima, she moved into 12 Temple Place, Great Surrey Street. It was one of a terrace of houses that bordered St George's Fields, meanly furnished and very cold. She was allowed to walk within an area of roughly two miles around the prison, but otherwise her movements were circumscribed. If she was found in any prohibited places, or outside the given area, she would be deemed to have escaped, and would be rearrested and thrown into a cell.

There was snow on the ground, and the fires drew badly. Horatia was still getting over whooping-cough.

'For God's sake, Horatia, this isn't my fault! I haven't hurt anyone.' Emma strode from one end of the small grim room to the other. 'I wish you'd take that look off your face and make yourself useful.'

It had been a long day and a hard one. 'I'm not living here.'

'None of us wants to.'

'We can't! Look at it.'

There was a bad smell, of damp walls and sour milk. The whole house seemed exhausted, waiting to die, and the walls leaned in on each other as if they were not only old but hard of hearing. The curtains were stiff with soot and age, and the rugs were lined with tracks of wear. Horatia turned on her heels, and started to make for the door. Emma pushed past her and blocked her way. 'Listen to me, Horatia, stop.'

'No!'

'You stand still and listen to me.' They heard the front door slam, and someone clattered down the kitchen steps a floor below them. 'I've done everything humanly possible for you. Don't let me down now by sulking.' Horatia's face was white. 'Listen, it's this or a prison cell. You choose. I'm going to write some letters. Fatima's finding us something for supper, and you can sit by the fire.'

Horatia felt her chin tremble. The room was freezing, the fire was a small, smoking glow, and the chairs were ancient. The only thing to eat or drink was the jug of porter on the table that Emma had sent out for. It was half empty already. 'Get us out of here,' she said. 'You got us here, you get us out.'

'Don't you speak to me like that! And you needn't stick your chin out, either. Pull yourself together.'

'You've been drinking. We've been here five minutes, and you're drunk.'

Emma picked up a plate and threw it against the wall, where it shattered with such force that the pieces flew back into the room. The house rang with broken silence, and they both stood still, as if waiting for pain or blood. Horatia looked at Emma, and then at the shards on the floor. Somewhere outside someone laughed. Then Emma stormed out and upstairs to her room. For a while there was no sound except for a trickle in the chimney, and the whine of damp coal. The uneven creak of Emma's footsteps on the floor above as she paced from one end of the room to the other and back again. Horatia perched on the edge of a chair, her face set in an empty gaze. After twenty minutes, Emma came back into the parlour and held up her hands. 'Not one word,' she said. 'We're not going to talk about this.'

'I'm sorry.'

'Don't, Horatia. I warn you, just don't.'

She sat down and wrote a letter to James Perry, editor of the *Morning Chronicle*. Perry had been a neighbour at Merton. He was a stooping man, with a darting glance and a fund of stories, who devoted himself at weekends to feeding hens and fattening pigs. He had helped her out before, and she appealed to him again. She wrote memorials to the King and to the Prince Regent, restating her claim for the reimbursement of the funds she had spent in the country's service in Naples. In her petition to the Prince, she declared that both George Rose and Lord Canning, the Navy Treasurer, had given their solemn word to Nelson, before he left England for the last time, that they would support Emma's claims to a pension. There was not a word of truth in this, but she wrote it anyway.

Letters came to the house, but not about that. Mrs Matcham wrote, begging her to send Horatia to Sussex. They would come and get her and take her home with them. Emma put away the letters as soon as they arrived.

'What's this?' said Horatia, finding one under a pile of stockings. She took it to the window and held it to the meagre light. It was a morning so grey that it was hard to see the words on the page. 'They want me to go to Ashfold! When did this come? "You know she's one of us . . . her uncle could come to get her in the coach, and she'd be here by dark . . ." You weren't going to show this to me.'

'If you look over the page, you'll see she also says that there's so much snow down there they can't get out of the house either in the carriage or on foot.'

'I could go there! Look, read it.'

Emma stood, and snatched the letter from her. 'Give that to me. You're not well enough to travel and I need you here.'

'No, you don't!'

'The subject's closed. If you've nothing else to do, go and help Fatima.'

'My uncle wants me to go. If I'm well enough to stay in this . . .' Her eyes travelled the room. It was godforsaken, a lost place. 'If I'm well enough to stay here, I'm well enough to go to Ashfold. Please.'

Emma shook her head. 'I've said no, and that's that.' If nothing else, Horatia was her only hope of getting anything out of the government.

Or perhaps not. The Home Secretary, Lord Sidmouth, wrote to tell her on behalf of the government that there was no possibility, ever, of her receiving anything from that quarter. They had other people on whom to spend their scanty means of relief and assistance, and that was that. He did not give any further reasons, but the fact was that Emma, by making such constant and extravagant claims – both true and false – had lost any vestige of support she might once have enjoyed. She had turned even George Rose against her. Worse than that, she had also lost the government's good will towards Horatia.

Emma threw a breakfast cup at the mantelpiece. It brought down a leaky china vase, which smashed on the brown tiles of the grate. She went to bed for a week and made no attempt to get up. The Matchams sent potatoes, and sometimes a turkey.

The river froze over. Between Blackfriars and London Bridge, people walked on the ice. Booths were set up, and watermen charged tolls of two or three pence for access. Horatia and Fatima walked to the top of Great Surrey Street to watch them, their fingers numb with cold.

2

Somehow, James Perry managed to get Emma bailed out in mid-February. She lived, for the next few months, a hunted life, hiding out with friends in and around London, but by July she was back in prison, and the contents of the house in Bond Street were being sold off to pay creditors.

Horatia was still not well. The doctor gave her medicine to take, and she slept. At times she could not tell what she had dreamed and what was real. She lay in bed and saw the hands of old women clutching the sheets. She saw dogs, low to the ground, sliding up and down the alleys behind Temple Place, or over the bare boards in her room. She spent hours looking at a picture in a book, until it lifted itself from the page and began to stalk the house. The rattle of a carriage outside turned itself into the sound of distant hills collapsing, a great rubble of rocks and stones leaping down Great Surrey Street to the river. The roll of a barrel on the pavement became a bear, as big as a house and swaying from side to side.

The bill for coals for one quarter was seven shillings and eightpence, for washing and general expenses one shilling. The outstanding item, on a separate sheet, was for breakages: thirteen pounds, four shillings and eleven pence. A hundred and eighteen separate items had been smashed in twelve weeks.

There was nothing to do but wait. Nothing to do but to plan another party. A month after she had been committed to prison again, Emma sent invitations to three or four friends to come and celebrate the anniversary of the battle of the Nile. They drank to Nelson's immortal memory well into the night, and stumbled out to find carriages, those who were free to, in the dark hours of the morning.

At Christmas there was another one. The rain was coming down in torrents. The Duke of Sussex came with his mistress, Lady Buggin. The Duke was the King's sixth son, an unintelligent and sickly man, with a long nose and a weak smile. James Perry was also there. Horatia watched them as they sat in the grim small room, barking with laughter and drinking mulled wine. They were too loud, too pink in the face. She held her hands in front of her and waited for the door to crash inwards, for someone to come in bearing a stick or a gun to tell them that they had no money to pay for this or freedom to enjoy it.

Emma raised her glass and demanded songs. A few sincere

and valuable friends, the distraction of wine and company: she looked, for the moment, transformed.

Join we great Nelson's name
First on the roll of fame,
  Him let us sing;
Spread we his fame around,
Honour of British ground
Who made Nile's shores resound
  God Save our King

Then they sat down to dinner. Fatima had made the table festive with candles, and with ivy pulled from the wall of the Magdalen Hospital chapel. A centipede crawled out of the greenery and wandered over the tablecloth. For the first course there was soup, trout with garlic and tomato sauce, stewed eel and anchovy toast.

'Good God,' said the Duke, at the sight of such a spread in a sponging-house.

'How lovely,' said Lady Buggin.

'Do you know,' said James Perry, in a low voice, leaning close to Horatia, 'what this eel was doing yesterday?'

'What? No.' There was a small frown between her eyes.

'Putney Bridge. Singing.'

She blew a short laugh through closed lips.

'True. It's noticeably colder down by Putney Bridge in December than in October or November, and they sing to keep themselves warm. In really filthy weather, when the river freezes, they make a truly awful racket. You can't hear them, of course, because of the ice. And because they have no chest cavity to speak of, no real volume. You have to make a hole and get down as close as you can. I've known strong men lose their ears to frostbite, listening to the eels in winter.'

Horatia was grinning. She lifted her eyebrows, and pushed her chin forward for more.

'What do they sing?' said Perry. 'Ballads. Love songs. They

go from door to door, and people give them a shilling to go away again. Not people, fishes. Sturgeon, whitebait, dace. Kipper salmon. "Take this and go away," they say. "Go to Fulham or Hammersmith, for God's sake, with your wretched noise." '

'Even the love songs?'

Perry shook his head. 'No. The love song of an eel is a sentimental and touching thing. A good love song by a Thames eel will sell out in a morning.'

Horatia laughed out loud.

'Oh, where are you going, my darling young eel
Deaf to my heartfelt and tender appeal?'

The Duke of Sussex, hearing Horatia's happy splutter, swivelled in his seat.

'Hear this lament I so somethingly drone
Next to the man sixth in line to the throne.'

'Me?' said the Duke. 'What?'

'This particular one,' said Perry, spearing the piece of eel on his plate, 'was one of the best at it. So much so that we ran his obituary in the *Chronicle* this morning.'

'No!' cried Horatia, pushing away her own plate.

' "Simon Arthur Jenkins Eel, of Jenkins's Steps in Putney . . ."'

The Duke dropped his fork, and pushed back his chair to retrieve it.

' ". . . was a slippery customer, but one whose short career on the back benches will be remembered by generations of parliamentary eels . . ." '

Next came roast turkey with prune sauce. Perry was asked to do the honours and carve the bird. It was a good size, but there was nothing to cut it with. Time passed, and no one came up with a knife. Fatima seemed to have disappeared, and there were no more clean knives on the table, far less a sharp one.

'You don't have to stand on ceremony here!' Emma shouted, seeing his dilemma at last.

He smiled and pushed up the sleeves of his coat. 'I didn't want to do anything I shouldn't in front of His Royal Highness, but since you say so, I'll use my fingers. Horatia, if I could have your plate . . .'

There was laughter as he took the roast to pieces with his bare hands. 'Now, this turkey—' he said to Horatia.

'No, please. I won't eat it if you tell me it could sing.'

Afterwards, Fatima brought up a dessert of apple fritters, piled high and dusted with sugar.

3

In April 1814 Napoleon abdicated. He was given a pension, and the tiny Mediterranean island of Elba, and there was peace in Europe at last. The whole of London, when it heard the news, was illuminated at night, and people went out to parties, receptions and balls. From Temple Place they could hear the guns and the fireworks, and they could see, across the bridge, the lights going up and down to Ludgate Hill, to Fleet Street and the Strand. The Surrey Theatre, on the other side of the street, had new plays, songs and choruses: *The Downfall of Tyranny*, *The Allies at Paris*; Mr Gilbert singing 'The Devil and Bonaparte'. They could see the boards on the front of the building, and the lights in its windows; they could see the people going in and coming out, waiting for carriages, standing on the steps half in one world and half, still, in another. The French King came to London after his years in exile, on his way to Dover and France. They read about it in the papers: the levee at Grillon's Hotel, the cavalcades and receptions, the banquets and reviews. King George had gone completely mad, and the Prince of Wales was now regent, playing the leading role in a hundred different dazzling uniforms, basking in reflected glory. It was the moment Emma had been waiting for for years, the moment when he would have the power to give her what he had promised: the official recognition of her claims to a pension.

Except for one thing. Ten days after the news of the abdication, a book of Nelson's letters was published anonymously, and there for all the world to see was proof of what had only been whispered about her connection to him. The editors claimed to have the originals in their possession, and they did. They were the letters that Nelson, years before, had begged her to burn, including those from Mr and Mrs Thompson. They were the letters she had shown to a man called Harrison when he was writing his biography. Emma had given him everything he needed; she had supported his family while he wrote the book, which had said everything nice about her, and everything bad about Fanny. More than likely it was James Harrison who was behind this new book, which cost a guinea, and was published in two octavo volumes.

It revealed, too, the truth of Nelson's feelings for the Prince of Wales. Jealous, hateful, murderous. From the moment of its publication her petitions, if there had been any hope for them at all, were doomed. She wrote to James Perry at the *Morning Chronicle*, denying that she knew anything about the letters: they were the invention of some vile and mercenary wretch, and Nelson had been too much attached to the Prince to think or say a bad word about him. But it was too late, the harm had been done.

She had no secrets any more, and her reputation, what was left of it, was crashing on the floors of every drawing room in London. She did not see the book, and would not allow it in the house. When the advertisements appeared in the papers, she hid them from Horatia and made Fatima burn them.

At the end of June, thanks to months of effort by James Perry, the demands of Emma's immediate creditors were met, and she was discharged from the King's Bench. She was not out of debt, though, and she could not lead a free life. There were so many other claims which could not be met that she had no choice but to leave the country.

'Come on, darling, get a move on. Why it is that every time I tell you to hurry up you do everything more slowly? We have to be at the wharf by ten.'

'Why can't we go from Dover?'

'Because that's where they'll expect us to go from. I'd just be arrested again. Fatima, what have you done with my shoes?'

Fatima was packing the last few things. She was not going with them, not now. She would join them later, when they were settled. James Perry would provide her travelling expenses. Until then, she was going to stay with Cribb and his wife in Wandsworth. 'You're wearing those ones, milady. The rest are packed – they're all at the bottom.'

When they boarded the *Little Tom* that night at London Bridge wharf, near the Tower, Emma had fifty pounds in her pocket. It was 2 July 1814. The passage to Calais took three days; there were storms off the coast, and they were both sick. As soon as they arrived they went to Dessein's hotel, where Emma took rooms for them both. It was the best hotel in town, and filled with English travellers on their way to Paris and further afield. It stood in the rue Royale, near the watch-tower, and was like a small château, with flowering shrubs and creeping vines.

'I feel better already!' Emma declared, throwing open a window and stepping on to the balcony. 'Everything's going to be different here. We're safe, and the weather's lovely. I told you we'd soon be able to forget, and now we can. Look! Come here and look.'

Below them, the women of Calais went to and fro in their wooden clogs, their short coloured petticoats and round white bonnets. Their baskets were filled with fat loaves, bewildered chickens, fresh fish, bottles of wine. People in fine clothes walked up and down between the walls of the old town, and carts brought trunks to and from the quays. Horatia stood motionless, though the floor was shifting under her feet with the roll of the sea still fixed in her limbs.

'You're tired, darling. Never mind, you can sleep. You can do whatever you want. You have a sleep while I unpack. Tomorrow we'll find a maid. It'll be like the old days. Already it reminds me of Naples. We can swim! We'll make friends and you'll go to school.'

'*Nous sommes en France.*'

'*Oui!*' Emma clapped her hands. '*Nous avons de la bonne chance.*'

Horatia smiled at the rhyme, and lifted her eyes to the sky. Perhaps they were lucky. Perhaps now they really could leave prison and loss and misery behind them. Perhaps here they could be nice to each other again. 'How long will we stay here?' she said.

'As long as we like!'

'Can we afford it?' She looked back over her shoulder into the large room.

'Don't you worry about what we can afford. We're here. Later we're going to have a lovely dinner and a long walk by the sea. Oh, God, Horatia, I do love the sea. We'll make a little world here all for ourselves.'

No one knew where they were. Not the Matchams, not the Boltons, no one; perhaps three people that Horatia could think of. Otherwise, they might have vanished from the face of the earth. Yet here they were, with all the bustle of the seaport around them, the quiet hum of expectation and fatigue, of change and promise; the strange beauty of bad smells and a foreign language. They were here and yet they were adrift; they were adrift and yet they were on solid ground, cast up in this strange place with the conversation of fellow guests, deep carpets, the hush of dining rooms. Porters with gold braid on their caps, servants in green aprons. Beyond the walls of the hotel, Calais was a town with small mean streets haunted by beggars, with water-sellers crying up and down the boule-vards, with men and women yelling names and greetings through blackened teeth. Boats and carriages came and went, rooms were taken and left, trunks were opened and packed again, but underneath all that was the steady purpose of short people living ordinary lives.

'Truffled veal sausage,' said Emma, when they sat down to dinner. 'That's for me, I think. *Matelote au vin de Bordeaux*. Either that or the salmon. *Rond de veau* with artichoke hearts and a salad. What about you? Have the rabbit. Or stuffed partridges. They do them on pieces of fried bread, with lots of juice. We need to feed you up. Oh, look, kirsch soufflé. Leave some room for that.'

Horatia made a face.

'Well, for God's sake, darling, you don't know until you've tried it. Don't say you don't like something until you've eaten it. Come on, have a sip of wine.'

At the next table, an English general and his wife were struggling with the menu. Within mintues Emma had made them her bosom friends, and was telling them what to eat. 'Horatia turns up her nose at everything,' she told them.

Horatia smiled. 'I do not.'

'Well, what have you decided on?'

'*Potage de poissons à la russe. Filet de volaille à la maré-chal.*'

The general's wife clapped a hand to her bosom, releasing a scent of bergamot. 'Listen to that,' she cried. 'How clever! Her accent's very good.'

'She speaks French like a French girl,' said Emma. 'And Italian, German – English, of course.'

The general's wife, though pale, had a kind smile on her soft, round lips. She was off her food and she wanted, she said, only a little *consommé*. 'It's a fine thing,' she said to Emma, 'to have a daughter one can be proud of.'

'Oh, she's not mine! She's my *protégée*. I've brought her up, that's all, but even so, you're right – I am proud of her.'

The world had turned the right way up. They had slid across its surface a little, and they had landed in a place they did not know, but there was no one outside the doors of the hotel, waiting with bills or warrants for arrest.

At eight o'clock every morning, Emma took Horatia to a day school run by an English woman, and at one in the afternoon she fetched her again. She learned languages, the harp, the piano. The weather was fine, with long warm days and a soft wind off the sea.

By August, they were all but penniless. They left the hotel and moved to the farmhouse in the Commune de St Pierre. A week later, Fatima took the Dover packet, and joined them there. During they day they could hear the cackling of geese from a neighbouring farm, and at night, sometimes, they heard wolves.

EIGHT

Horatia sat in the chair by the bed. Downstairs, a door closed quietly. Monsieur Damas, coming in or going out. The shutters were closed and the room was dark. Outside, the streets were filled with freezing fog. She heard the cry of a rooftop gull, the distant thud of a cask being dropped. 'Wake up,' she said.

She sat where she was for a long time after Emma had stopped breathing. Then she got to her feet. She went to one of the windows and opened it. The shutter clicked in the latch on the outside wall. The fog was white and still over the town, as if the sky had come down to look for something lost. Below her, a woman was walking on the rue Française; she looked up at the window, and down again. It was one o'clock. Horatia could feel small points of exhaustion in her cheeks. She turned back into the room. A pair of shoes lay on the floor by the washstand, as if they had not yet understood. A cloth hanging over the bowl was still damp. She stood motionless, her eyes on the chair, a folded shawl, the mirror. She whispered a prayer. Our Father, which art in heaven. Amen, amen, amen.

Monsieur Damas contacted the English consul. By coincidence his name was Henry Cadogan. He came immediately to the rue Française with his wife. Mrs Cadogan introduced herself, and for a moment Horatia was bewildered by her name. Mrs Cadogan was dead. She was old, and then she died. Then her mind let go, and dropped it. The knowledge of death wandered in her head as if deciding where to place things in a new home.

Elizabeth Cadogan smiled. Her hair was pulled back from a quiet, intelligent face. Though pinched by the cold, her skin was supple and clear.

'We'll look after everything,' said her husband. 'All you need is a coat.'

She turned to look at the door, now closed, to Emma's room. Dead, she thought. She waited for something inside her to lift up its hands in awe and sorrow. Nothing did. It only occurred to her how strange it was that when death comes we do not vanish, everything and all of us. The clothes we died in, the pins in our hair.

'If there are any papers . . .' said Mr Cadogan.

Horatia nodded. Papers. The room that she stood in remained ordinary and bleak. The papers were where they always lived, in the writing-case on the table. Her life from this moment had changed, in ways inconceivable yet to her, but there was no sign in the objects that surrounded her, the few things she still possessed, that anything was any different.

The consulate was spacious, freshly painted and clean. She was given a room that looked out over trees. She wept solidly for a day, and did not know whether it was grief she felt or something else. It felt, as far as she knew, like something else.

Cadogan wrote to her uncle, George Matcham. 'I dread to think,' he said to his wife, 'what she's been through these last few months. She's as white as a sheet. Is she all right?'

'She's young,' said Mrs Cadogan.

'I know, that's what I mean.'

He saw, going through Emma's papers, that she had wished to be buried in England, and arranged to have her body embalmed, though in the end there simply wasn't the money to send her remains across the Channel. She was buried on 21 January, after a funeral mass had been read over her by the priest from the Église de St Pierre. Henry Cadogan, as well as all the captains and masters of the English ships in the harbour at the time, followed her bier to the burial ground near the rue Richelieu. Horatia did not go. The town was ringing with frost, and all the sounds in it were like the sound of bells. Between them, the consul and his wife paid the undertaker's account for the coffin, church expenses, priest and candles.

They also paid off the wine merchant – nearly eighty pounds – and the pawnbroker. Horatia's possessions were returned to her: her watch, the shawl, the pictures and bits of jewellery. There were still people who were owed money, though, and they weren't put off by the consul's promises of payment from England. Horatia was still not free to come and go. They were waiting for her in the street. Some of them she knew by sight, though their faces now seemed lean and almost feral. Butcher, chemist; even Francine Caillois, from St Pierre. Emma's death had brought them out again and they were circling, aggressive with the fear of being dodged. Until instructions came from George Matcham, she was still a prisoner. It was a week before they could be persuaded to let her leave, and even then she had to cross the Channel, under the escort of Mr Cadogan, dressed as a boy.

'It's only for a few hours,' said Mrs Cadogan, 'and at least you'll be warm.'

At times, gratitude threatened to overwhelm her, so that she could hardly distinguish it from grief. But each time she turned towards a door, each time she felt the sense of expectation that surfaces, briefly, in loss, it was Fatima she hoped to see, not Emma returned from the dead.

'It's a good thing you've got short hair,' said Elizabeth Cadogan. 'The coat's big on you, but that's good, too – you can keep it buttoned up. No one will see what you've got on underneath. It'll hide that bit of bosom, as well.'

She came down with them to the boat. Horatia wore nankeen ankle-length trousers, and shoes with buckles. She wore a neckcloth, and a blue overcoat. The wharf was crowded with men and women, with carriages and porters, children and dogs. Packages, bags, a side of beef. A sailor stepped back without looking, and caught her elbow with his arm. '*Pardon, M'sieur*,' he said. Henry Cadogan took her arm and led her onto the boat. She stood on deck until they had pulled away from shore and navigated the narrow entrance to the harbour, until the town began to vanish, its face white and blinking in the early light. The larger sails were being set, catching, as they rose against the sky, a breeze. Then, because it was cold, she went below.

EPILOGUE

Horatia left France on 28 January 1815, on the eve of her (real) fourteenth birthday, and only weeks before Napoleon's escape from Elba. Her uncle, George Matcham, met her off the ferry and took her to Ashfold. Matcham was a handsome man, with charm and energy, money, and an inventive mind. He adored his family, and thought of little else. After everything that had happened to her, Horatia was worn out, but she found herself at the centre of a warm-hearted and cheerful household, where the relationship between parents and children was loving and civilised. Later that same year, after the battle of Waterloo, Matcham saw the opportunity he had been waiting for to take his family abroad. Horatia went with them to Lisbon, where they stayed for five months and where she caught the eye of more than one of the young British officers stationed there. In short, she blossomed. Remarkably, she seems to have carried few scars and little anger with her through the rest of her life, and though she never pretended to have loved Lady Hamilton, she usually spoke of her with compassion. She also made the point that the four thousand pounds Nelson had left her in his will, although Emma had had control of it, remained intact; only the interest had been used, and, until the last few months, only for Horatia's education and welfare.

In February 1817 she went to Norfolk to live with her Bolton relations, who were as kind to her as the Matchams had been. When she was twenty-one she married Philip Ward, a young clergyman, also handsome, also generous, though he never had much money. They had ten children, eight of whom survived childhood. In 1830 William Nelson, as Canon of Canterbury, gave Philip the living of Tenterden in Kent, where the family lived for nearly thirty years. In January 1859 Philip died, aged sixty-four. Horatia moved to Pinner where she lived for the rest of her life. She died on 6 March 1881.

There was no letter waiting for Horatia in 1815 with the solicitor, William Haslewood. She made great efforts to find out the truth about her mother, although she always refused to believe it was Emma. She hoped to prove that Nelson had been infatuated while serving in the Mediterranean, and that this passing affair had resulted in her birth. The letters published in James Harrison's book of 1814, in which the truth was plain to see, she dismissed as fakes. She had seen a side of Emma's character, never revealed to Nelson's family, that had caused her great pain, and it has been suggested that she was too appalled by the thought of being Emma's daughter to give it any credibility.